the magical world of
MADAME MÉTIER

the magical world of

MADAME MÉTIER

a novel

DAPHNE ROSE KINGMA

Skyhorse Publishing

For Suntah

celestial light
forever love

Skyhorse Publishing books may be purchased in bulk at special discounts for sales promotion, corporate gifts, fund-raising, or educational purposes. Special editions can also be created to specifications. For details, contact the Special Sales Department, Skyhorse Publishing, 307 West 36th Street, 11th Floor, New York, NY 10018 or info@ skyhorsepublishing.com.

Skyhorse® and Skyhorse Publishing® are registered trademarks of Skyhorse Publishing, Inc.®, a Delaware corporation.

Visit our website at www.skyhorsepublishing.com.

10 9 8 7 6 5 4 3 2 1

Library of Congress Cataloging-in-Publication Data is available on file.

Cover design by Erin Seaward-Hiatt

Print ISBN: 978-1-5107-1926-2
Ebook ISBN: 978-1-5107-1927-9

Printed in the United States of America

Time: Then.
Maybe fifty years ago.

Place: Here and There.
Ici and *La bas*.

PART I

CHAPTER I

Madame Métier, Mademoiselle Objet, and Monsieur Sorbonne

Madame Métier

Madame Métier was a middle-aged widow. Her husband, a doctor, had died untimely, leaving her with no insurance, when they had been married fourteen years. They had had a daughter, who had also died. She was born still, with no breath, a tiny pink rosebud that would never unfurl. Madame Métier liked to think of her now as the prettiest pink rose in heaven.

Madame Métier had many talents. They lay in botanical realms. When she was young she had used them, inventing medicinal cremes, but during her marriage, she had misplaced them, or rather, her husband had served to estrange her from them. It wasn't suitable, he said, for a woman of her social position to be carrying on with botanical cremes. She was a doctor's wife after all, destined for much better things. And so, at his insistence, she had given up her inventions and devoted herself to being a wife.

Wifing was always an effort for her, for although she had much to bring to the task—she was beautiful, she had a sweet mellifluous voice that was charming at parties—in a far, small corner of her heart, she was distressed. She thought there should be more to a life than just making a good appearance.

Mademoiselle Objet

Mademoiselle Objet had grown up in a madhouse. Everyone around her was constantly losing their marbles. Tearing their hair out. Screaming. Throwing pans. Her father, a *sous* chef, was an alcoholic and could be found on most summer evenings asleep with his head in his plate.

Mademoiselle Objet found solace in moving things around, putting her pencils in line, making sure that each strand of her hair was perfectly arranged, dividing her time into blocks that she wrote down in squares on white calendar paper, filling the blocks in with words that stood for various activities. Which, depending upon the degree of her upsetness when the time came, she either did or did not do.

Monsieur Sorbonne

Monsieur Sorbonne was very handsome. He had been given away by his mother and father when he was a very small boy, to his wealthy uncle and aunt. His real mother and father had been strange and interesting. They wanted a strange and interesting life—travel, art, music, parties—and it soon became clear that they could never have such a life if they also had to look after a child.

Monsieur Sorbonne, therefore, had been raised by his uncle and aunt, who were rich but not the least bit interesting. They did, however, buy him very expensive toys, and it was these with which he played. As a child, he played with children's toys. As a young man, he played with boats and planes and hang-gliding wings. He had microscopes and telescopes and hockey sticks and skis. He loved the stars. He read about astronomy. He had a fine mind, a gifted eye, and a prodigious curiosity.

~

CHAPTER 2

Madame Métier and Her Work as a Young Woman

Madame Métier had come to the profession of making cremes, their concoction and various uses, through her father, who had been a botanist. By walking with him through his gardens when she was a little girl and listening to him as he recited the names of the plants and discussed their particular properties, she had learned many things. It was this knowledge that she applied to the manufacture of her cremes. She began this work when, as a girl of sixteen, overdogged by her mother about her untidiness habits, she ran away from home.

After leaving her parents' house, she had lived for several years in a sizeable mansion owned by a landlord who let out rooms of various sizes. The only room she could afford was small, but it had an alcove balcony window with a deep windowsill, upon which she set out the pots of the various plants she was growing. It was there that she began her work, experimenting with fronds and pollens and seeds, distilling the myriad essences from which, in combination with natural oils and emulsions, she first created her cremes.

All this delighted her. She loved to handle the flowers. She loved their fragrances. She loved the oils and emulsions from which she developed her cremes. She loved the bottles and jars in which, eventually, she packaged them.

As regarded her work, she had only a single problem: it was that in her mesmerized excitement, she was often unable to keep track of time. She could become so engrossed in the invention of a creme that hour after hour would fly softly by. She would work all afternoon and then look up at the windows to see that dark night had fallen and the stars were shining in. It was then, in the dark, it seemed, that her work became most magnetized. Transfixed, she would work until three in the morning, smelling, mixing, and stirring until the new compound was perfected. When at last it had attained perfection—often just before dawn—she would retire to her bed, allowing her petals and crumpled leaves, her stalks and pollens and seeds (to say nothing of the dozens of opened jars of essences and liquids), to sit on her table exactly where she had left them.

This sometimes troubled her, for no matter how often she promised herself, she had never been able, in spite of her numerous resolutions, to learn—as her mother had always instructed—how to "pick up after herself." She would often state her intention to be tidy, but then, instead of allowing time to clean up, she would find herself inventing another creme. She would go to her bed exhausted, and late the following morning (for that was when she would ordinarily wake up), she would return to her table with a new idea for another creme. Before even thinking of clearing up the previous night's disaster, she would set in to work with new fronds and petals and stems until, once again, she had only elaborated upon the mess that was already there.

This had gone on for several years. Because of her enthusiasm, she had already invented—and let out into the world—a great many cremes. In a small little way, she was beginning to be known. The more she was known, the more they (the "they" who establish an inventor's reputation) requested her cremes, and the messier her workroom became.

∾

CHAPTER 3

Madame Métier Meets the Doctor

It was in this small apartment workroom that her husband, the doctor, first encountered her. Tall and verging on handsome, he had a beard, which camouflaged, she guessed, a weak chin. He had learned of her from one of his patients who claimed that one of her cremes had healed a hideous surgical scar. The doctor therefore had come to her for some "youthifying" cremes. "To make me look young," he explained, when she looked at him, puzzled. "My cremes," she graciously informed him, "are for ailments, wounds, and pains, and not for vanity."

The doctor was most disappointed to hear this, and although he was somewhat put off by the chaos of her workroom (it needed major surgery, in his opinion), he was quite stricken by her beauty. In spite of the odd unusualness of her work and her unwillingness to help him, he decided to romantically pursue her.

In spite of her initial somewhat negative reaction (a vain man was somehow even more disturbing than a vanity-clogged woman), Madame Métier found as time went on that she was surprisingly susceptible to him. He brought her flowers, for one thing (which of course delighted her—she could use the wilted petals in her cremes). He admired her for being entrepreneurially successful (which made her believe that she could go on with her cremes). He admired her beauty (which pleased her as a woman). Twice he took her dancing (which, deliriously, she liked). Several times he brought her home to his fine big house, which had, on its second floor, a very large sunroom with windows that looked out on an apricot tree and the vacant bowls of a long-abandoned rose garden.

The size of his house intrigued her. Perhaps if she had a large room to work in, things wouldn't get, as her mother had always said, "so terribly out of hand." She had lived alone and been self-employed for many years; she had stayed up alone numerous nights until three in the morning; her father had died long ago and her mother had used up his funds before dying herself; it had been years and years since she had been provided for by anyone but herself—because of all this, when finally, the doctor proposed, she decided to marry him.

~

Chapter 4

Madame Métier's Work After Her Marriage

When Madame Métier was married, her husband the doctor was able, quite handsomely, to provide for her, and this he quite preferred to do. He didn't want her to have a profession or money of her own. He wanted her to belong to him (he had after all, acquired her), to be in a sense his possession, to serve as a fine reflection of him and his undertakings. He wanted her beauty as his asset. He wanted her as an object he could be proud of. He also wanted her to make him feel important, to brag about him to all her friends. He wanted also to impress her with his medical expertise, his long Rx prescriptions, his many terminal patients, his expensive surgeries.

Although he was a doctor, he really believed in neither healing nor death. He believed in what he called "medical corrections." He didn't believe that diseases could be cured. Malignant organs could be cut out, removed, or chemically repealed. Pills could be given also, in order to take away the pain, but once a disease had staked its claim on any particular organ, it was destined to take over. His mission as a doctor was to monitor, with scientific accuracy, its progress through the body.

Just the same, in the early days of their marriage, he allowed Madame Métier to carry on with her cremes. A doctor's wife should have a hobby, he opined. It made her look legitimate, an amusing society column item. And so, with his blessing, she moved her botanical items into the sunroom.

In the morning, when he left for work, she would shut herself up in her room and happily make up her cremes. For the doctor she had completely changed her schedule, doing her work in the mornings now, and the early afternoons, so she could cook his dinner every evening.

In the late afternoons on Tuesdays and Thursdays she would go out and distribute her cremes. Her old cremes, "familiar cremes" as she called them, she would deliver to health stores and herb pharmacies, while her new cremes she would give out to strangers and friends who were suffering this ailment or that. And although she still thought of them all as merely experimental, her friends would often report astonishing improvements.

News of this came to the doctor and it made him nervous. In fact, he was greatly disturbed. As time went on, it was becoming apparent, even to him, that her cremes indeed had healing properties. And it was when more and more people—total strangers now, no longer mere friends—began requesting her cremes, claiming they had medicinal powers, that he began to put a stop to her.

He started by criticizing what she did, mocking what he called her "frivolous pursuit." "Witch hazel here, columbine there, what difference does it make?" he would stride into the sunroom and say. "How can a twig cure anything?"

Furthermore, it wasn't appropriate, he said, "this poppycock about cremes," for a doctor's respectable wife. He wanted her to behave like a wife—not have a life of her own. He had married her, after all; that was all the identity she needed. Besides, she didn't have to work; he gave her everything she wanted, didn't he?

Eventually he insisted. It wasn't good for his reputation, he finally said, point blank; and so would she now please put all her plant things away, attend a charity ball or two, or put on a rummage sale?

Because he had been generous with her—he *had* given her the sunroom, after all—(which now of course she couldn't use) and because she believed what everyone told her, that she was lucky to be married to a doctor, after grieving for seven days, she packed up all her petals and fronds in a green striped hatbox, put it up high on a shelf in the closet, and quietly gave up her work.

From then on, as he asked, she attended bazaars. She had her hair, as he insisted, washed twice a week and curled professionally. She took up tatting and knitting, at which, because of her manual dexterity, she was extraordinarily proficient. Still, a certain small part of her felt sad—what would she do with all her father's botanical knowledge, and what would become of the strangers and friends who had benefited from her botanical inventions?

~

Chapter 5

A Change Comes to Madame Métier's Life

In her own way, Madame Métier had loved her husband very much. And so she was saddened one day to learn that he had died in a high-speed accident. Madame Métier was still in her young middle years when he died, and she was still quite beautiful. She had actually been beautiful all her life, but knowing this had escaped her. Her parents, both understated Europeans, had never thought to tell her. They were of the school that believed that children, complimented, might get an inflated view of themselves, and so they were very conscientious in relieving her of this possible burden.

In all her life, they never uttered a single beauty-praising word. This made her a perfect candidate for the doctor's attentions, who wanted, for his own reasons, to keep her somewhat subdued. This he had done by providing her with various criticisms. He often compared her (unfavorably, of course) to current movie stars, and proved to her time and again (by holding her face in the mirror next to magazine photos of ingénue starlets) that she couldn't hold a candle to them. He also insisted, when they had been married a year, that she give up all her lipsticks and rouges. They gave her face an unnatural look, he insisted, and so she should get rid of them.

Madame Métier had wanted to love her husband, and although this too seemed to make her life less fun, with only the littlest sigh, she set all her make-ups aside. Sadly, from time to time, she remembered her former faintly glamorous days. She lost the lilt in her step, and when she looked in the mirror, her face seemed to be not so bright as it had always been in the past.

When Madame Métier's husband died, she was at first quite shocked by the news. He had driven his low black sports car too fast and scrambled himself, like an egg, all over the road.

When they had gathered up his pieces from the asphalt and arranged them all in a more or less human form on the slab in the morgue, Madame Métier was called in. Although his body was now quite beyond recognition, because of his beard, she was able, quite quickly, to identify him.

She had his remains boxed up and buried. She stood alone in the rain as they lowered his casket down and wondered if she would toss a flower in the grave or if, (since, it occurred to her now, he had really been quite unkind), she should simply let bygones be bygones.

～

Chapter 6

Mademoiselle Objet and Her Husband

Mademoiselle Objet had not always been Mademoiselle Objet. She too had been married. She had married, in a time of financial desperation (when her father's alcohol-drunkenness had all but expired the family funds), a TV and furniture salesman who was a genius at setting up lifetime credit card payment plans and had, as an ancillary talent, a quite remarkable proclivity for cooking dinners and dusting.

Mr. TV, as Mademoiselle Objet preferred to refer to her husband, had turned out to be supremely boring. When he had finished with work each day, made good with all his accounts, and done the dishes and dusting, he would plant himself down in front of the television tube on his brown Barking Lounger chair (two items with which he had made his small fortune) and sit there pasted like an octopus to the glass side of an aquarium until sleep would, nightly, overtake him.

Night after night she sat, as it were, at home alone. In order to escape from the sound of Mr. TV's TV, she went to another room in the house, a pink room, from which, amazed, she contemplated him. There she read poems and organized and reorganized the objects of her desk (the pencils and pens, the tablets with lists, the bills, old letters, and old Valentines) all like the endlessly rotating contents of a fine kaleidoscope, in hopes that finally—if only she could arrange them right—she would find peace.

This, however, did not occur. For the more she heard his TV, the more deeply she perceived his octopus-like boringness, and the more she perceived his boringness, the more fiercely she became upset. When she became upset, her hands developed a rash, which she presumed had been caused by so often handling the various sharp edges of her objects. This drove her to tears, which, when she cried them into her hands, caused her rash to redden and her to scratch it miserably until it began to bleed.

One night, sitting alone in her pink poems room, she realized that the rash had perhaps not so much to do with all the sharp edges of her objects as with the nonstop irritating sound of Mr. TV's TV. She decided that if only she could find a way to have him watch his TV in silence (so that the endless repetitive commercial syllables—*Buy this! Buy that! Make this white! Make that clean! Make that pain go away!*—would no longer assault her ears and cause her to attack her hands), perhaps then she would have a chance to read her poems books in peace.

Since she knew that objects could often provide a solution, she decided to find an object with which she could silence Mr. TV's TV.

~

CHAPTER 7

Monsieur Sorbonne and His Wife

Because his wealthy aunt and uncle adopted him, Monsieur Sorbonne had never learned to work. He was given, instead, to curiosity, to endlessly observing things—objects, architecture, weather, tools, and machines— and learning what made them go fast or slow, why they were the colors they were, the way they behaved in combination with other objects and items, the consequences they had, the questions they raised, the answers they could give. Monsieur Sorbonne loved learning. The stuff of life was his school, and he was its finest pupil.

When Monsieur Sorbonne arrived at that sorry state of adulthood in which most people give up their curiosity and go to work, he realized he had a serious problem. Work in itself could not be interesting, he thought. Work was just work. Unlike learning, it held no fascination for him.

When it became clear to him that he had no inclination to work, he decided to solve his problem in some other fashion. *If you don't know how to work yourself, perhaps you could learn by example*, he thought. As a thing to be learned, work held an odd sort of interest for him. *Or if you can't work yourself,* he further considered, *perhaps you could marry someone who can.* This was a viable theory in general, of course, and in particular, it held promise because Monsieur Sorbonne was quite handsome.

Having thus set aside his problem for the moment, Monsieur Sorbonne decided to continue his life as a student of all things. One day, while he was out having new business cards printed—

MONSIEUR SORBONNE
Considerer of All Things

—he made the acquaintance of a Miss Gutz.

Miss Gutz worked in a print shop where, daily, wearing an unspectacular oilcloth apron, she aligned the type and inked the press. She was not particularly pretty but she had, as Monsieur Sorbonne observed, considerable fortitude, a fortitude which for quite a few years now, had enabled her to be gainfully employed.

Since she, apparently, knew how to work, he started talking to her, and it became apparent before too long that they had a number of things in common—an interest in typefaces, for one. (Monsieur Sorbonne preferred above all the Egyptian Extended, while Miss Gutz, quite more conservative by nature, preferred Palatino and Times Roman.) In order to continue their conversation—Monsieur Sorbonne thought he might learn even more about the various inks, fonts, and colophons—he invited Miss Gutz to a fishstick lunch. This was not to his ordinary taste, but as Miss Gutz had a mere half-hour for her noonday repast, she removed her inky apron and suggested they mosey across the street to the Fishstick Restaurant.

It was there that Monsieur Sorbonne disclosed to her one of his lifelong dreams, which was to sail around the world in a boat. "It would be wonderful," he said, "to learn about the sea from being in its midst." Miss Gutz allowed as to how she also, from time to time, had had a similar dream. She had quite a sum of money in her savings account from having worked so diligently hard and for so long, and offered, with it, to supply him with a boat if, just for the ride, she might come along.

Although this was enticing, it seemed somehow inappropriate to Monsieur Sorbonne, who, although he had been endlessly supported by his uncle and his aunt, had never been supported by a woman. He was indeed obsessively curious, but he was not an opportunist, and so in exchange for the boat she would provide, he offered gamely to marry her.

They were married later that day, when, after removing her inky print apron and asking permission from her boss, she got off early. Within weeks she liquidated her funds and he purchased the boat, which he furnished according to his unusually excellent taste. Then with almost no further ado, they set out to sea.

Unfortunately, once at sea, Monsieur Sorbonne was once again bored. He wasn't learning one-tenth as much as he'd hoped—about waves, fish, work, the night configuration of the stars, or even cooking at sea. And Miss Gutz—she never did take his name (fortitude, in her opinion, was worthy, while learning was mere frivolousness)—while sublimely proficient at manning the sails, was not, as it turned out, such very interesting company.

When they had finished their longish discourse on printing—inks, typefaces, colophons, and paper cuts—Miss Gutz had really little else to say. She exercised her muscle at the mast, while Monsieur Sorbonne, below deck, read again and again the few books on astronomy that he had brought along. It was thus that, not so happily, they passed two years.

~~

CHAPTER 8

Mademoiselle Objet Stumbles Upon
Monsieur Sorbonne

Monsieur Sorbonne and Mademoiselle Objet met at the International Exposition of All Objects, which was being held, uncharacteristically, in their city, on this particular year. Monsieur Sorbonne was attending the Exposition because having at sea discovered the intellectual limits of the fortitudinous Miss Gutz, he now, more than ever, wanted to learn some new things.

Mademoiselle Objet was there in search of a pair of glamorous earmuffs to block out the sound of Mr. TV's TV. These, it turned out, were not available. No one, it seemed, had thought of such a thing.

Mademoiselle Objet was pondering the foolishness of this—why it was that, given the millions and millions of TVs which could not be not-heard by the millions and millions of spouses of persons like Mr. TV, no one had yet invented an object that could block out this sound and still be attractive—when she encountered Monsieur Sorbonne.

Monsieur Sorbonne was studying an instrument that was capable of measuring the underwater mean circumference of stalagmites and stalactites, and had, on a whim, considered buying it. To be sure, it was of no immediate use, but his life had been so boring the last two years that it occurred to him that one day, if not soon, he might want to take up spelunking. And in that case, he might need just such an instrument.

Mademoiselle Objet, frustrated, was, if the truth be told, on the verge of hysteria because of being unable to locate the TV earmuffs she had so desperately had in mind. Her relationship with Mr. TV, she was beginning to think, was about to "go down the tubes" (as they were accustomed to saying in her neighborhood). She had started to feel that, even from another room, she could hardly bear to listen to one more unmuffled hour of TV. It was thus that, heartbroken and emotionally frayed, she bumped into Monsieur Sorbonne. She was about to depart the Exposition when, in her haste, she swerved precipitously around a corner, disrupting Monsieur Sorbonne's hold on the stalagmite instrument and causing it to ricochet off the display table and clatter onto the floor.

This was the absolute last straw, she thought, the fact that she had come to the International Exposition of All Objects and no one in the entire world had invented the single object which could save her life, or, to be more specific, her sanity. Now, bereft of all hope, she had bumped into a total stranger, causing a pathological and public disarrangement of objects, a spectacle of disorganization. She was overwhelmed. She burst into tears.

Monsieur Sorbonne was thus awakened from his reverie. He removed the red silk handkerchief from the inside pocket of his dark blue blazer and very tenderly wiped her cheeks. "There, there," he said kindly. He was pleased, in fact, in an odd sort of way, to have come across such a brittle, collapsible woman. Her obvious fragility was, he noted to himself, somewhat refreshing, standing as it did in marked contrast to the fortitude of the sturdy Miss Gutz. Besides, she had lovely green eyes, which reminded him of the sea. And her tears left perfect circles on his red silk handkerchief.

He wrapped his arm around her and without so much as a fare-thee-well to the stunned stalagmite-measurer vendors, he whisked her out of the Exposition Hall and into a tearoom down the street.

〜

CHAPTER 9

Monsieur Sorbonne and Mademoiselle Objet Have a Tête-à-Tête

Monsieur Sorbonne and Mademoiselle Objet sat in the tearoom staring at one another and at everything. Mademoiselle Objet was staring at all the objects—the beveled gilded mirrors with their planes and curlicues, the spoons, the napkins twisted in knots on the tables, the rows of oysters bedded in ice, the pyramids of fruit, the beautiful menus (Palatino Light, Monsieur Sorbonne observed to himself, thinking momentarily, and fondly, of Miss Gutz), the tufted leather seats, the lilting chandeliers.

For once, thought Mademoiselle Objet, *everything is perfect. I don't need to rearrange a thing. Everything is exactly where it belongs.* She heaved a soft little sigh and settled back into her tufted leather seat.

Monsieur Sorbonne was looking at her—at her lovely green eyes, which had taken in all the objects in the room; at her hair, which was long and shiny and clean and shimmered like a wave in the drifting light of the sparkling chandelier; at her hands, which were pale and white, their little nails polished like tiny pink shells from the sea. She was breathtaking! Except for wanting to know *her*, she had dispelled him of all curiosity.

Monsieur Sorbonne then ordered a bottle of very expensive wine. Having come back from the sea, he was given again to the practice of his wealthy expensive tastes. Mademoiselle Objet was impressed. She liked the looks of the bottle, the way it stood, like an obelisk, between their two glasses on the table. She lifted her glass and he clinked it. For a moment she felt like she was falling in love.

She ordered a salad with shallots and mushrooms, and a grilled breast of chicken. He ordered a salad with crayfish (he liked their orangey color, the little jet beads of their eyes), a tureen of dried eggplant soup, and a large plate of lamb. Mademoiselle Objet, who had quelled an anxious pang at the arrival of the crayfish, was feeling quite soft and intrigued. A man who eats crayfish with eyes couldn't possibly watch a TV, she opined.

It was late in the day. They had finished their dinner. Monsieur Sorbonne and Mademoiselle Objet, without saying a word, walked slowly down the avenue and when, shortly, they came to a small hotel, without hesitation, they walked in.

Because she had aroused his curiosity, he wanted now to know her as a person. Because he had brought her to a restaurant—and now a hotel—where there was no TV and everything was perfectly arranged, she followed him up to the room. She adjusted the ashtrays on the table. Monsieur Sorbonne pulled back the sheets on the bed which, immediately, she rearranged in a perfect triangle, and then, very inquisitively, he made love to her.

∾

CHAPTER 10

When Mademoiselle Objet Got Home

When Mademoiselle Objet got home it was well after midnight. Mr. TV was asleep in front of the TV. He had dusted and washed half the dishes. Her dishes, awaiting her dinner of boiled potatoes and fried ground meat (which she promptly flushed down the toilet) were still set out on a placemat on the table. She quietly washed them and put them away, and then she awakened Mr. TV.

"Come to bed now,"—or some such thing, she said.

"Did you just get home?"—or some such thing, he said.

She told him that, no, she had been home for hours, that earlier she had been gone. Had he forgotten, she had gone out to the Objects Exposition? She had come home early. He had been sleeping already, in front of the TV. She had been sitting for hours in her room, arranging her objects and reading her poems.

Mr. TV nodded, and, in a sleepwalking daze, made his way to the bedroom. It's bad luck to use truth for a lie, said Mademoiselle Objet to herself. Then putting all her pencils in line, she followed him into the bedroom and turned out the light.

∼

CHAPTER II

When Monsieur Sorbonne Got Home

When Monsieur Sorbonne got home, his life was out in the street. His telescope, his stuffed parakeet (he had forgotten all about that!), his hockey shoes, his hang-gliding wings, his drafting tools, his maps, his clothes, his books on flying and sailing and astronomy, his Dopp kit with its pig-bristle shaving brush (the only possession he owned which had once belonged to his real father)—had all been crammed in a pair of plastic garbage bags with twistee-lockems twisted tight around their necks.

Surprised, but not entirely alarmed, Monsieur Sorbonne approached the front door. "It's all over, you fool," said Miss Gutz in her sturdy but unpoetic way and slammed the door in his face.

≈

Chapter 12

Monsieur Sorbonne After His Wife

Monsieur Sorbonne picked up his things and put them into his car. He had an Oblong Purple Credit Card—a gift from his wealthy uncle and aunt, which gave him access to special funds.

He dialed up the bank with his card and withdrew $200,000 on the special after-hours bank account.

He took all his objects out of the two despicable green plastic bags and arranged them very lovingly on a blanket in the back seat of his car. (These were the things, after all, that had whetted his mind and assuaged his curiosity. They were his school! His friends!)

He drove downtown, and with the memory of the curiously anxious Mademoiselle Objet still fastened in his mind, went back to the hotel and asked for the room they had just occupied.

He opened the door to find the ashtrays and curtains all still pleasingly arranged as Mademoiselle Objet had arranged them. But alas, the linens had been changed, and there was not so much as a single one of her shining hairs detained upon the sheets.

∾

CHAPTER 13

Madame Métier After Her Husband

Following her husband's death, Madame Métier had to regroup herself. Since she had been left with no money, she decided, in the manner of most widows, to put her house up for sale. However, when the first comers—a man, his wife who chewed gum, and two children with music-producing electronic earmuffs wired to their ears—strewed their way up the walk, Madame Métier thought better of the idea. She told them the house had been sold and forthwith removed the sign from the curb. She would have to think of something else.

Shocked by the prospect of actually having to leave the house in which, when she had worked, she had worked very well, she decided to scrape it down for all possible saleable items.

First of all, there was her husband's Medicines Chest. After several days of searching, she was able to locate its key wrapped in cotton-wool batting and stuffed in the toe of his left green lizard slipper. This she removed, and after locking all the doors and pulling all the blinds in case she should uncover anything untoward, she went upstairs to the Medicines Chest and immediately opened it up. Inside were various items: his gold-plated toothbrush, a small flask of whiskey, some toothpicks, some red cough medicine and aspirins, stocks of various prescription items (these he had been known to generously dispense), and, in a rusted quite sizeable tin in the far righthand corner, a large quantity of white powder in a tightly rolled up plastic bag. This, when she put her finger to it and licked it, tasted quite strange. Fearing it was something deadly—or, contrarily, that it was something of great medicinal value—she sealed up the box and decided to think things through.

She went to her bed, hoping a good night's sleep would clarify some things—whether to sell her house or her husband's possessions—but unfortunately, she was unable to sleep. Her mind was a maelstrom. It was, she noticed, quite distinctly agitated. Perhaps seeing her husband's things was more upsetting than she had imagined. Perhaps she had loved him more than she guessed. In any case, she lay vividly awake all night, fretting about her precarious future.

When at last the sun came up she realized that, in fact, she had been briefly asleep. This gave her hope. As soon as it was reasonable, she called up her husband's best friend, one Monsieur Morte, the mortician (his work took up where her husband's left off), in hopes that perhaps he would buy, or give her advice about how she might sell, her husband's medicines.

Monsieur Morte's main undertaking in life was to store up as many gold bricks as he could in his downtown security vault. These, he supposed, would forestall (at best) or embellish (at worst) his own inevitable demise. For, although he commerced in death, he himself was afraid of it.

Monsieur Morte arrived around noon, wearing a pork pie moustache, a tall fur hat, and black gloves. He did not smile when she opened the door, nor extend her any further condolence—he had done that already, she supposed, when he gave her a bargain burial—but proceeded directly behind her up the stairs to look at the Medicines Chest.

She opened the door to the chest and he looked at the various items: the toothbrush, the red cough syrup, the quantity of stock prescription items. He seemed disgruntled, as if to say, *how rude of you to ask me to look at all this when I could be back at my office, profitably embalming someone.* But then, with a flicker of interest, he opened the rusted tin box. An unusual, somewhat enthusiastic expression passed through his eyes and was then at once dispelled. He closed up the tin, passed his glance once again across all the various items and suggested that, if this were acceptable to her, he would give her $5,000—for the lot. The white powder, he explained, was a rare but somewhat valuable bulk medicinal substance and perhaps he could sell it to some of his colleagues and friends. Some medicines, of course, were worth more than others. There were some virtually useless over-the-counter items here, but, nevertheless—he repeated himself—he could give her $5,000 for the lot if she could settle it now and if she would make a point in the future of failing to mention what, precisely, had transpired between them.

Almost before she could make up her mind he had withdrawn the black glove from his thick left hand, pulled out the fifty one-hundred dollar bills that were rolled up in his pocket like a plump croissant, and handed them to her.

Madame Métier was amazed. "I'll get you a bag, then," she said. She went down to the kitchen to fetch him a sack for his things—the bottles of pills and the curious tin—but by the time she returned he had already packed them in a large manila envelope, which he had handily stored in his inside coat pocket. Overwhelmed by the five thousand dollar croissant in her hand, she offered also to give him the Medicines Chest, but this he refused. Perhaps she could find some use for it herself, he said.

In a fluster—she was scarcely able to comprehend what had just occurred—Madame Métier showed Monsieur Morte downstairs to the door. It was now well past noon. The sun was up and the roses were singing in the garden. The strange agitation that had made her so wakeful the whole night before seemed now to have passed. She breathed in the sweet summer air, closed the door, took the handful of bills, and folded them into her lingerie drawer. Then she drew off her clothes, and with the cool summer air floating in through the windows, she lay down on her bed and fell into a deep, restful sleep.

~

CHAPTER 14

Madame Métier After Selling the Medicines Chest

Now that Madame Métier's financial worries were temporarily over and she had something to go on—she wouldn't have to sell the house; she could start up with her cremes again—she decided to fabricate a life.

She went through the house and stripped it of all the dead doctor's items—his oxblood loafers, his books on death and disease, his dirty socks, his suits and ties, his brandies and vodkas and gins, his sports car magazines.

She was happy. She had the soft tinkling feeling that something new was about to occur. She felt, as she watched the trash man pull out of the driveway, hauling the last batch of her husband's things away, that a strange, immemorial load had been lifted from her. She felt joyful. She felt a strange sense of magic. She felt young. She walked through the house, which was perfumed now with the scent of fresh roses, with the lilt of a dance in her step.

She went to her lingerie drawer and peeled off three of the fifty one-hundred dollar bills and decided to go shopping.

～

CHAPTER 15

Madame Métier Goes Shopping

It had been some time since Madame Métier had been out shopping on her own. Since her husband, the doctor, had always had strict ideas about what she should wear, he had always picked out her clothes.

Thus now it was a treat indeed to go shopping for herself. She bought a new dress (Prussian blue), new stockings (camellia white), and shoes (silver pumps), and, passing a summer vacation display in an avant-garde boutique, she went in, and on impulse bought herself a new red bathing suit.

It was somewhat daring, perhaps even outrageous, the suit, with bold geometric cut-outs in its field of red—an oval here, a triangle there— revealing planes and curves of her body that she hadn't seen for years.

Having thus indulged herself, she decided also to buy some flow- ers. She wanted to make a bouquet to celebrate her repossession of the house. Walking gaily with her bags down the street, she headed toward the Flower Vendor's Stand, whiffing the roses and chrysanthemums, the dahlias and baby's breath. She wanted to make a huge bouquet, but of what, precisely, she couldn't yet guess. But as she was looking over the flo- rist's vases of long-stemmed roses, delphiniums and gladiolas, her father's face, illumined and faintly smiling, appeared for a moment, intaglioed on the back wall of the Flower Vendor's Stand. She paused, blinked, disbe- lieving; but when she opened her eyes again, it was still there—distinct and unmistakable, an image of her father's face.

It was strange, she thought, how the unexpected could quite unex- pectedly occur—first her weirdly subsidized shopping spree, and now, out of the blue, this vision of her father. A few tears came into her eyes. Did things mean things, she wondered? Or were such odd occurrences, as her mother had always said, "just her imagination gone wild"? Did the occult—as perhaps it might be called—appearance of her father's face mean something now? A blessing perhaps? A sign that she should return to her cremes? Or did it mean nothing at all? She looked again at the wall where his face had just appeared, but the image was already fading, pixel by pixel disappearing from the wall.

In a few more minutes she had dismissed it, wondered in fact if she had seen it at all, and yet when it had entirely vanished, she found herself choosing not armloads of irises and lilies to make up her celebration bouquet, but ruined lavenders and roses, fading poppies, wilted saxifrages—the plants whose healing properties her father had always talked about. In fact, it was really quite strange, but all the fresh flowers had suddenly lost their appeal.

Having emptied all the flower urns of their worn-out and shabby editions, she gathered them up and paid the flower vendor for them. He looked at her strangely, as if she were somewhat deranged. Feeling his judgment as she waited for him to hand her the change, she averted her eyes, and, as she did, she noticed a sad but lovely young woman at the opposite end of the flower stand. She was selecting pink rosebuds and daisies and little blue forget-me-nots and arranging pretty nosegays.

This gave her pause. For a moment she reached back in her mind to the old sweet time just minutes ago when flowers had still been flowers and not what she now perceived them to be—the raw material for cremes. She felt a thin veil of sadness whispering across her eyes like curtains in a summer breeze. A few tears striped her eyes, and when she blinked them away, she saw once again the image of her father's face—now strongly smiling—and she knew somehow that forever, everything had changed.

∼

CHAPTER 16

Monsieur Sorbonne After His Marriage

After some days at the downtown hotel, Monsieur Sorbonne decided to check out his situation in life. Perhaps after her "it's-all-over" tizzy, the fortitudinous Miss Gutz had come to her senses and would now let him come back home.

This thought in mind, he drove to the print shop, where it was reported to him that Miss Gutz was off on a two-hour lunch with a farmer. Something strange had happened to her, a print shop cohort said. Two days ago she had lost all verve for her work. Her moods had veered from melancholia to rage, and she was threatening to change professions. She was tired of working so hard, she said, tired of slaving for her useless husband. She had sat around on a boat with him for two years, while he sailed by the stars and read his astronomy books (so the cohort reported) and now—she had stamped her foot—she wanted more, something better. She wanted to be cared for and paid for, to be treated like a wife.

A farmer had shown up two days ago needing some stationery printed for his hog farm. He had then somewhat courted Miss Gutz, telling her tales of farmhouse sunrises. It was he who had taken her to lunch.

This didn't bode well, thought Monsieur Sorbonne. He thanked the informative cohort, got in his car, and drove on. As he approached his house, he wondered what might be the point of trying to reinsert himself into his life with Miss Gutz. They had had a brief, curious marriage. They had had a good trip in the boat—speaking in general, that is. They hadn't turned upside-down and both drowned or come down with scurvy. But they had also had no romance, no heartfelt conversations beneath the moon, no tenderness, no passion. It had been for them both an effort, an exercise in fortitude.

Perhaps his indiscretion with Mademoiselle Objet—impulsive at the time—represented an unpremeditated but much needed scintilla of joy in his drab daily life. It was, in fact, perhaps a clue that his marriage was over and he should move on. He regretted, for Miss Gutz's sake, the awkwardness of it all. He hadn't, in truth, ever wanted to hurt her; and now, he supposed, he should apologize, at least express his regrets, or leave her a note at the door. But when he arrived at the house, the front door was barred with two black, creosote railroad ties, along with a sign in big block letters— Times Roman, 1000 point, he noted to himself—which said, "KEEP OUT, and this means YOU!!"

It really was over, Monsieur Sorbonne surmised, supposing the YOU referred to himself. Slightly stunned by the odd finality of it all, he backed his car out of the driveway and headed back to the hotel.

∼

CHAPTER 17

Mademoiselle Objet After Her Marriage

Feeling guilty and somewhat disarranged the morning after her unexpected *soirée* with Monsieur Sorbonne (it was one thing to misplace your objects, but quite another to misplace yourself in your own life), Mademoiselle Objet had a momentary inclination to confess her indiscretion. Speaking the truth—perhaps this could be the beginning of something real between herself and Mr. TV. But Mr. TV had already gone off to work, and so, alas, he was not available to hear her confession.

This was most unfortunate, since (despite her behavior of the night before) Mademoiselle Objet was a young woman of the highest moral character, and knew she would have to do penance for her sweet self-indulgence of the night before. The minute she had organized this thought, a prickly pain overflooded her heart, and a rash appeared on her hands.

Since she couldn't, it appeared, confess, perhaps she could work out her guilt in some other way. She could make Mr. TV a TV dinner, but it would be cold by the time he got home. She could scrub and mop the kitchen floor, but that had, even as a penance, exactly no appeal. She could bring wheeling meals to the infirm and old, or—Aha, Ah, yes!—this did have some appeal—she could bring flowers to the children at the Orphans' Hospital.

She got dressed, thinking irrepressibly of Monsieur Sorbonne—his blue jacket and red handkerchief, the aplomb with which he had ordered the wine and turned down the sheets and made love to her—and so thinking, she drove into town.

At the Flower Vendor's Stand she noticed a quite unusual woman. She was tall and slender and had white-blonde hair. She was beautiful in a strange, extraordinary way, and had a quite melodically lovely voice—Mademoiselle Objet could hear it, even from where she was standing at the far end of the stall. But the strangely beautiful woman seemed to have an odd way with flowers. She seemed to prefer all the wilted ones, the already bowed-over roses, the drooping poppies and shriveled lilies. All this intrigued Mademoiselle Objet, who, with her exquisite hands, was busy arranging half a dozen nosegays (one for each hour of her happy indiscretion) to bring to the joy-forsaken children at the Orphans' Hospital.

When she had finished—when she had every petal of forget-me-not in place—she looked up to see that the quite unusual woman who had been there only moments ago had now started walking—huge bundles of wilted flowers in her arms—quite gracefully down the street. There was an aura of something—though Mademoiselle Objet couldn't tell quite what—that was so strangely captivating about this wilted-flower woman, that it occurred to her for a moment to leave her nosegays behind and run down the street to try and meet her. But when she considered it further, it seemed such an odd thing to do that she just stood there and watched as the rather unusual woman, holding two elegant shopping bags in one hand and piles of wilted flowers in the crook of her other arm, turned the corner and disappeared.

∼

CHAPTER 18

Mademoiselle Objet Goes Home

When Mademoiselle Objet returned home that night, Mr. TV said that tonight, before he watched his TV, he had a thing or two to say to her. Hearing this, Mademoiselle Objet was inclined once again to confess her indiscretion, but before she could so much as mutter an "I'm so sorry," Mr. TV announced that he had been offered a job in The Very Big City selling sofa recliners. This job represented not just a promotion, he said, but also a sizeable raise. He would, as a result, be able to buy them a big color TV. He would have to begin there next week, though—the previous salesman had died. From a heart attack. At a movie. While eating a jumbo, double-buttered popcorn, so Mr. TV was needed at once and he had already agreed to go.

She should start packing, he told her—those poems books would take a long time to pack—and on Tuesday they would leave.

Hearing all this, Mademoiselle Objet felt suddenly as if her confession was now obsolete. She thought quickly, which it was uncharacteristic for her to do and said that, if it was all the same to him, she would just as soon have this be the end of their marriage. She wouldn't, she thought, be happy in The Very Big City (not to mention two minutes longer with Mr. TV). Besides, she couldn't pack her poems books in time. She wondered, therefore, if, instead of buying the new TV to share with her in The City, he would be willing to give her half the price of the color TV in cash.

Mr. TV was enraged—though not by the thought that this was the end of their marriage—"you do have a point there," or some such thing, he said—but by her claim on the still-unpurchased big screen TV. "What makes you think you deserve half the price of a brand-new big-screen color TV?" he said. "Before I've even bought it? You've got your nerve!"

"I don't know," or some such thing, said Mademoiselle Objet, who was by then quite jittery and shaken. The rash of the morning, which had subsided whil she was visiting the Orphans' Hospital, had now started crawling in itchy red blotches up both her arms. "Forget it," she said. "It was just an idea." And although she no longer felt guilty, she started to cry.

Here Mr. TV momentarily (and uncharacteristically) took a small pity on her. He would not, he asserted, give her the sum of half of the price of a new large TV, not in cash anyway; but he would leave behind the old black–and–white, his Barking Lounger chair, and all the kitchen items. That way, he said, she could watch TV sitting down and, if she wanted, could also heat up some TV dinners to dine on. In addition, he would pay her rent for one month.

With regret—what would she do with an old TV, a pitiful six-teen-inch black and white, a Barking Lounger chair, and some used pots and pans? She didn't quite know. She thanked Mr. TV for his kindness, gave him a peck on the cheek and, while he stayed up late in the living room watching TV (from his still-his Barking Lounger chair), she curled up alone in her bed wondering where, if ever, she would see Monsieur Sorbonne again.

∿

CHAPTER 19

Monsieur Sorbonne After His Foray Back Home

Having faced the music—his marriage was over, his house was barred, his wife was on her way to a hog farm (where, it occurred to him now, she might prefer to be)—Monsieur Sorbonne went back to the hotel, which made him think sadly of Mademoiselle Objet.

Although he was inclined to think endlessly of her (into what social void had she disappeared? From what social matrix had she first emerged?), he decided that no matter what, she had been a real gift. She had appeared, with her tears and her exquisite hands, at precisely the right moment to excise him from his marriage. That in itself was a small-time miracle—and now? Why, now he must go on.

He *must* go on—that was quite clear, whether or not Mademoiselle Objet would ever again emerge from the vapors. To that end, he must make some decisions. First of all, what must he do? How could he support himself when the $200,000 from the Oblong Credit Card ran out? If he gave up his lifelong career of appeasing his curiosity, what new career could he or should he now undertake?

He contemplated many options: race car driver, pilot, inventor, bibliographer, antiquarian. These all appealed to his prodigious curiosity, and offered a chance to learn more facts about more things; but as he considered them all, a deeper thought took hold of him. He no longer wanted simply to learn—to acquire the facts, parameters and uses, the characteristics and quirks of various things; he wanted to apprehend, to see into and truly know the mysteries of the world about him. The notion of knowing things in their essence intrigued him greatly. But how could he do this? He had already learned so much, from books and from his own observation. And yet there seemed to be much more to know, more than he, with even his great curiosity, had learned. How, then (or rather, how now) could he learn more? By looking? By paying attention? By carefully observing? By using his mind? By thinking? Perhaps he could see things more deeply by making an image of them, by drawing their pictures with charcoal or pens, by photographing their image, translating it through a lens. The thought of photography—this pleased him greatly.

The thought of seeing things differently, through a second, wise eye, with light falling this way and that way, the thought of trapping an image, of trapping a moment, an essence, and making it last—the more he thought about it all, the more photography intrigued him. Perhaps captured in time, held still, suspended, an object might gradually give up its secrets and show its quintessence to him.

This last thought returned him sadly to Mademoiselle Objet. Thinking of her almost brought tears to his eyes. He turned down the blankets and sheets, wishing emphatically and sadly that he had made an image of her small, exquisite fingers turning down the sheets. He got into bed and turned out the light and, closing his eyes hard to block her image from his mind's eye, he decided that in the morning he would buy a camera at the Flea Fair.

∼

CHAPTER 20

Mademoiselle Objet as Time Went On

When Mademoiselle Objet woke up the next morning, the reality of Mr. TV's imminent departure suddenly hit her. She had been living, she realized, in a kind of fairyland, having Mr. TV pay the bills, going her way as she wished, thinking her thoughts, arranging her pencils, reading her poems books in her pink room.

Now all that was over. An elephantine shudder ran up and down and sideways along her spine, and her rash reappeared. She had one month's grace, a few horrible items with which to raise some revenue, and a wide-open life—that gaped like the loose trouser leg of a war-wrecked amputee—in front of her.

What would she do? The Barking Lounger chair, the TV, and all that pot and pan nonsense, even if she *could* sell it, would probably meet her expenses for scarcely a week. She scratched her rash fiercely, at last drawing blood. Then suddenly it occurred to her that if only she could stop scratching and weeping, she might have here not a problem, but an opportunity.

For had not a single, albeit magical, indiscretion provoked the demise of her life with Mr. TV? And was this not what in her secret heart she had always, albeit unconsciously, desired? She hadn't the courage to straight-out desire it, but now that it had been given to her, it felt oddly correct.

She had to take her life by the horns now, which meant she had to get a job. Perhaps she could work at the Orphans' Hospital, be an Aide Nurse and talk to the little sick children. No, that would be uncomfortable. That would be sad. That would upset her and make her even more tearful. Her rash would come out all the more. But perhaps she could arrange the pencils and papers or schedule appointments for the doctors. Perhaps she could do some straightening work in the Office of the Administrative Experts.

Mademoiselle Objet got up from the dining room table where she had been sitting while contemplating all this. It was ironic, she thought, as she passed now through the living room, that her future should be set up—that is to say, financed—by Mr. TV's TV (and Barcalounger chair). Life was certainly strange.

As she walked to the bedroom and dressed to go out and look for a job, she thought wistfully of Monsieur Sorbonne. She thought of his wine and his soup tureen, and his crayfish dinner, his stunning blue jacket and his red silk handkerchief; and she was poignantly sad.

∼

Chapter 21

Mademoiselle Objet Is Employed

Mademoiselle Objet had been employed already three weeks at the Orphans' Hospital (sitting at the Reception Desk, tidying up the pencils, directing—albeit a very minute—stream of visitors to the orphan children's sick rooms) when, on a particularly rainy Thursday afternoon, she noticed, in one of the long medicinal-smelling corridors, the very interesting woman she had seen some weeks before at the Flower Vendor's Stand.

Asking the phone girl, her accomplice in the Reception Cubicle, if she might take an early break for tea, she excused herself and started down the hall.

As she tiptoed along, the sights she saw were all quite nearly unbearable to her delicate eyes. Behind the thin plastic curtains (printed with bears and cactus plants and blocks of ABCs) that shrouded each bed lay the small sick orphan children recovering from whooping coughs and tonsillectomies.

In one room, she saw a small tousle-haired boy sitting up alone in his bed. With small, disturbed hands he was fingering the air, then flailing his arms out desperately forward as if reaching for an imaginary mother.

Mademoiselle Objet was so overtaken by this sight that her own hands at once reconstituted their rash. She hated seeing him like that, and started backing out of the door. It was there, on the threshold, that, unexpectedly, she collided with the very interesting woman.

"Pardon me," said Mademoiselle Objet.

"Excuse me," said the woman. She paused in the doorway a moment, then passing her hands in sort of a whispering way across Mademoiselle Objet's left hand, let herself into the room. Then she set a large silver bag on the floor and sat down on the bed beside the boy.

Mademoiselle Objet stood in the hallway watching as the woman took the little boy's wandering hands into hers and for a moment quietly held them. Then—and this Mademoiselle Objet could scarcely observe through the crack in the long plastic curtains—she removed a few small bottles and jars from the silver satchel on the floor. One of these she carefully opened and then applied its contents to the boy's meandering hands, while speaking some soft-sounding words. Because of the absorption factor of the curtains, Mademoiselle Objet couldn't hear, exactly, the words she was saying, but the woman seemed to be singing almost, as she gathered the little boy's hands into hers. Gradually, his hands stopped flailing and clawing at the air. He looked at the woman and smiled. At that very moment Mademoiselle Objet took pause to look at her watch and noticed, to her astonished amazement, that she had been gone on her tea break for almost an hour.

Returning to the Reception Desk she apologized to the telephone girl, explaining about the unusual woman she had just encountered in the hall.

"That's Madame Métier," said the telephone girl. "She always comes here on Thursdays. To amuse the children with her cremes."

"To amuse the children?"

"Yes," said the telephone girl with catty abruptness. (She had, after all, endured by herself the almost hour-long tea break.)

To amuse the children? To Mademoiselle Objet it had seemed something more—although she couldn't tell quite what. But when she left the hospital that night, she was distinctly aware that on her left hand, where the very unusual woman had passed her hands across it, the hateful rash had disappeared.

~

CHAPTER 22

Mademoiselle Objet Makes a Decision

Although she was working by day, Mademoiselle Objet, at night, was becoming quite sad. She sat in her house, *sans* Mr. TV, reading her poems book aloud to the empty Barking Lounger chair on the far side of the room, and wondered what, besides work, her life might one day contain.

Pondering this, her reptilian rash reappeared, and, pondering it, an emotion bordering on despair took hold of her. At times, scratching fiercely, she desperately wished for some objects to rearrange; but in her own house, alas, she had already arranged and arranged things to the Nth degree.

Perhaps if she made a *big* change—moved downtown, for example, took up watercolor painting, or wrote a few poems herself—her outlook would improve. She contemplated various things, and then one night, in a stroke of genius, it occurred to her that she was depressed because she was living with a Barking Lounger chair as her only nighttime companion. What might she think and what might occur if the hideous lounge chair were no longer here?

It was thus that, after charming the maintenance men at the Orphans' Hospital (she brought them Mr. TV's last box of TV enchilada dinners from her freezer), she arranged to have them deliver it the Flea Fair, where she would sell it for who knows how much, thus finally putting herself both feet into the future.

～

CHAPTER 23

Monsieur Sorbonne at the Flea Fair

Monsieur Sorbonne was a man of great luck, and when he arrived at the Flea Fair, he came, almost at once, upon an ancient, but perfectly preserved, View Camera. This, he knew, was a rare and out-of-date item, a camera whose square wooden box and oversized negatives allowed it to capture, in large, the exact existential aspects of something.

It was being sold by a garage mechanic as an antique box. It was something he'd found, he said, in his eccentric art professor uncle's garage. It had been lying—at time time of his uncle's death—under a large black shroud, and, although all but obscured by a layer of thick gray dust, it had seemed valuable. Along with a dozen tubes of his artist-uncle's rolled-up watercolor paints he would sell it for, say, seventeen dollars so he could buy some new gaskets for his truck.

Although Monsieur Sorbonne *did* know exactly what kind of camera it was (he had read at length on esoteric everythings), he wasn't sure it contained all its necessary lenses and parts. Hesitating uncharacteristically over the seventeen dollars—he'd spent more than that on yesterday's lunch—he was about to move on when the garage mechanic produced a small maroon velvet bag containing several large lenses, a few rolls for film, and at its bottom, curiously, a small gold chain with a pale-blue crystal heart suspended from it.

"I'll throw this in for another fifteen dollars," the garage mechanic said. He'd meant to throw it in for free, but was suddenly reminded of his long-term longing to buy a new a rear-view mirror for his truck.

Monsieur Sorbonne agreed at once, for, in spite of the camera's curious antiquity and possible uselessness (he couldn't be sure if the lenses in the bag were the lenses for this camera), he had now become enchanted by the pale-blue crystal heart.

He peeled off some bills and handed them to the garage mechanic, who handed him his things: the camera box in its black cloth shroud, the maroon velvet pouch with the two big lenses and the small blue heart, and also, at his insistence, the dozen tubes of rolled-up watercolor paints in a ragged gray Belgian linen bag.

～

CHAPTER 24

Monsieur Sorbonne Has an Incident
at the Flea Market

With the view camera, the maroon velvet pouch, and the Belgian linen bag in hand, Monsieur Sorbonne was making his way past the flying-saucer-shaped concession stand and out toward his car when he was almost run down by a middle-aged couple, Mister and Missus Midd L. Klasz, who were awkwardly carrying, sideways and upside down, a brown authentic vinyl Barking Lounger chair.

As Monsieur Sorbonne tried gamely to avoid them, Mister Klasz, skidding on the irregular parking lot gravel, lunged inadvertently at Monsieur Sorbonne, causing him in turn to hit Missus Klasz in the upper right thigh with the formidable View Camera. She let out a pained dog-like howl, and let go of her hold on the upper section of the Barking Lounger chair, causing it to drop indignantly down, while in the background, a finer, more flute-like scream rose up from the sales booth at which, apparently, the lounge chair had been purchased.

Being momentarily distracted by this sweet but quite distressed cry, Monsieur Sorbonne did, nevertheless, help dust off Missus Klasz, set upright the lounge chair, and offer to assist Mister Klasz with its further removal. Mister Klasz, meanwhile, suggested that Missus Klasz remain behind, go back to the booth where they had just purchased the chair (Number 32, he reminded her—and not too far away), have a Soda Diet Drink and collect herself until they both returned.

Reluctantly, Monsieur Sorbonne gave in to her temporary keeping the new View Camera ("I'll watch it like a dog," she said) and beneath the gray non-sun of noonday, assisted Mister Klasz across the parking lot and helped him install the chair in the back of his ranch roving wagon.

When Monsieur Sorbonne and Mister Klasz returned, Missus Klasz, distraught, was anxiously approaching them. Her favorite daytime TV soap story, *The Nights of Our Days*, was about to begin. She had had two Soda Diet Drinks and was feeling better. Her upper thigh was fine, and she wanted to get home pronto to try out the new Barcalounger chair while watching her TV show.

That wooden box (the camera), that foolish pouch, and that scratchy linen bag, she had left, she said, with the woman at Booth 32. Thanking Monsieur Sorbonne for his efforts (by giving him two coupons for imitation sausage flavored pizza). Mister Klasz took his wife by the arm, and relieved to be finished with this effort, Monsieur Sorbonne headed to Booth 32 to retrieve his View Camera.

⁓

CHAPTER 25

Monsieur Sorbonne Retrieves His Camera

As he approached Booth 32, Monsieur Sorbonne was amazed to see there—in the shadows of its awning, in the angular light of its parallelogram front opening, in the spangled gray mist of the no-sun day noon, could it possibly be?—the long falling hair, the inviting sweet lips, and exquisite hands of Mademoiselle Objet.

Shyly, she stepped out from behind the counter on which there now remained nothing—except Monsieur Sorbonne's View Camera, the maroon velvet pouch, and a scratchy gray linen bag. Gingerly, as if he were an apparition and might disintegrate at any moment, she walked toward him. As she did, he reached his right out hand invitingly toward her, and then with his left encircling her neck, he embraced her and gave her a long and delicious kiss.

In the aftermath, they stood there together transfixed, staring into each other's glad eyes. Little tears rolled down out of Mademoiselle Objet's eyes, causing Monsieur Sorbonne to retrieve from his linen pants pocket a white handkerchief with which he wiped them away.

Remembering the blue crystal locket in the maroon velvet pouch, Monsieur Sorbonne now unwound himself from her embrace, walked over to the stall counter, and, slithering his hand past the two large lenses in the pouch, retrieved the little treasure. Then, kissing her once again, he fastened it about her neck.

When they returned to their senses after this little event, Mademoiselle Objet picked up her purse; Monsieur Sorbonne picked up the View

Camera, the maroon velvet pouch, and the Belgian linen bag, and arm in arm, swingingly, they walked out through the parking lot, leaving the Flea Fair behind.

∼

CHAPTER 26

Monsieur Sorbonne and Mademoiselle Objet
Have a Reunion

Two hours later—Mademoiselle Objet had returned to her house and changed her clothes (she put on a seal gray dress with a lace-etched portrait neckline); Monsieur Sorbonne had bought some square fine film for his new camera, returned to the hotel, unearthed his blue blazer and his red silk handkerchief—they were once again poised across the table in the hotel restaurant.

Monsieur Sorbonne had ordered the wine—and various other things. Mademoiselle Objet had ordered a salad, and now, like a lovely lily, was leaning across the table toward him.

Eyes upon eyes, they spoke of many things—their marriages, their respective present conditions, the miracle of the Flea Fair, the magic of their first meeting. Light shined in her eyes, and in the several chambers of his heart, Monsieur Sorbonne could feel a rushing flood of emotion, like the shimmering passage of stars. She was so very lovely. He was such a fortunate man.

In the half-light of the restaurant, the crystal glasses glistening, casting bright shadows, Monsieur Sorbonne reached over to the thick upholstered seat beside him, and retrieving one of the large glass lenses from the maroon velvet pouch, attached it with surreptitious aplomb to the camera box, in order to take her photograph.

While she was spooning red raspberries into her mouth, Monsieur Sorbonne captured her image—the delicate fingers, the small silver spoon, the blue crystal locket in the portrait neckline of her dress. And then afterward, after the coffee and cream, when the last berry was gone, he spirited her, like a treasure, quietly up to his room.

～

CHAPTER 27

The Next Morning

The next morning the sun was shining. The fine square hand with which, yesterday, Monsieur Sorbonne had managed the camera, was now resting handsomely on the pillow; and Mademoiselle Objet's hair, that dark avalanche, was falling over her cheek like a curtain.

It was late—how late they couldn't tell. Mademoiselle Objet was due at work. Monsieur Sorbonne had an appointment in town to renew his Oblong Credit Card, but, alas, in the room, there was no alarm clock.

In order to find out the time, Monsieur Sorbonne got up from the bed and—Mademoiselle Objet could scarcely believe this—turned on the TV!

On the screen—and this too she could scarcely believe—was the woman who, only a few days ago, she had seen with the boy at the Orphans' Hospital. She was talking in a soft, mellifluous voice about the medicinal properties of plants and of how, if applied in the form of tinctures and cremes, they could promote not only true physical healing but also console the mind.

"What a fine woman," said Monsieur Sorbonne, retreating again to the lace-edged white sheets where, against the propped-up pillows, he situated himself at Mademoiselle Objet's side. He had forgotten entirely why, in the first place, he had turned on the TV. Beneath the covers he reached for her hand and held it, as together, transfixed, they watched while in her benedictus voice and with her strange and elegant gestures, mesmerically, Madame Métier talked on.

～

CHAPTER 28

Mademoiselle Objet Is Late to Work

Mademoiselle Objet was twenty-nine minutes late to work and this resulted in a reprimand (and subsequent threat of disemployment). One reprimand per month was all any employee was allowed, and so she'd betterwatch her step. This was a hospital after all—and besides, there had already been that incident with the tea break just two weeks ago. Make no mistake, her management said, it had all been annotated on her record.

Mademoiselle Objet felt somewhat put out because of all this. It was an unfit aftermath to her happy reunion with Monsieur Sorbonne, whose elegant ways enchanted her, to say nothing of the fact that it crimped her joy at having been given at last an extended miraculous glimpse of this Madame Métier, whose words, via the hotel TV, had utterly intrigued her.

Feeling thus upset, her rash reappeared. Between setting up the pencils and pens she scratched it viciously until it bled. When teatime came, she bolted her administrative cubicle, lifted up by wild hopes and a prayer that this perhaps was the day that this strange Madame Métier would be frequenting the hospital and might give her some assistance.

~

CHAPTER 29

Monsieur Sorbonne Is Late for His Appointment

Monsieur Sorbonne, in the meantime, had arrived too late for his appointment regarding the Oblong Credit Card. So much so (according to the Credit Guard who had been holding his re-application form for the requisite fifty minutes), that not only had he missed his appointment, he had missed entirely his chance to re-apply.

Fifty minutes was the waiting limit, the Credit Guard announced. Anything important could be done in fifty minutes. Why, even psychoanalysis, engaged in for the rearrangement of a person's personality, could readily be accomplished in a fifty-minute hour. Besides—and furthermore—anyone who couldn't arrive within the requisite fifty minutes was obviously artistic, unreliable, scatterbrained, and definitely unworthy of an Oblong Credit Card.

However had he got one in the first place? snapped the Credit Guard. It was unthinkable, he said, (and here he studiously studied Monsieur Sorbonne's black striped Italian suit and red silk handkerchief) that anyone who wore real silk and wool should be permitted to have credit on this kind of credit card. They absolutely could not be counted upon. Persons who wore polyester, on the other hand, his research showed—now that was another matter entirely. Their owing records were impeccable; they owed and owed and owed.

Monsieur Sorbonne was not entirely dejected by the news, for it had been subterraneanly occurring to him that, as a man, he should have real work, a life's calling—employment at least—as his *raison d'etre*. And it was now time—or long past time—that he should find his.

Without waiting for further verbal flagellation from the salty Credit Guard, Monsieur Sorbonne, in a state of terror and sweet anticipation, returned to the hotel where, once again, he had agreed to consort with the lovely Mademoiselle Objet.

～

CHAPTER 30

Monsieur Sorbonne, at the Hotel, Contemplates His Condition

Monsieur Sorbonne, sitting in a red velvet chair and through the hotel window perusing the leaf-shadow patterns on the boulevard below, was awaiting Mademoiselle Objet. He was in a rather sorry state. Now that he was home, that is to say, ensconced once again at the hotel, he felt frankly afraid about the future.

Who would he be and what would he do without his Oblong Credit Card? He did, of course, have his new (old) camera, but how could the taking of photographs beome a life's gainful work?

There were, of course, thousands of things that one could take photographs of. There was the retouched family photograph sent out on family Christmas cards, the graduation yearbook shot, the engagement photo glamor pose. There were scenes, buildings, products, or, if a photographer for news, traffic jams, disasters, and catastrophes. But what could they all add up to in terms of paying one's bills? Besides, there were already a thousand-and-one photographers plying their trade in the world.

Thinking of them all out clacking their shutters for money, he wondered what he had done all these years. The shadows of the leaves were becoming slightly elongated now on the sidewalk on the boulevard, and it occurred to him for a moment, with uncharacteristic self-compassion, that for his entire life really, he had been in search of something—that his curiosity itself had been a search of the deepest, most inordinate kind. He had been looking—without quite knowing he was looking—for something that would give his life meaning. He had imagined that meaning would come through indulgence, through having and then more having.

It had never occurred to him until precisely this minute—that meaning might arrive through finding his true vocation.

As he composed himself around this insight, a feeling of peace descended upon him. He looked out the window. The shadows of the leaves were now virtually indistinguishable from the sidewalk below, so gray and still had the light become. He had the sense, deep and true, that in time, in a way that still eluded him, he would indeed discover his true life's work.

He rose to light a lamp on the far side of the room, and as he did he heard what he knew was the knocking of Mademoiselle Objet's hand at the door.

~

CHAPTER 31

Mademoiselle Objet Returns to the Hotel

When Mademoiselle Objet appeared in the hotel room, she was in a down-hearted stew. She had been unable to locate Madame Métier in the hospital corridors and her search (conducted with her all the while scratching at the hateful rash) had been undertaken at such length, that when she returned from her elongated tea break she was informed by the management that, this being in a single month her second violation, tardy-wise, her employment at the Orphans' Hospital had just been terminated.

Before she could tell him any of this, she fell on Monsieur Sorbonne's neck, embroidering the shoulder of his fine blue coat with tears. "What will we do? Ruin is upon us! Life isn't fair," she was practically shrieking.

"Don't worry," said Monsieur Sorbonne, soothingly. "We're together now. We'll figure it out."

"We're together!" wailed Mademoiselle Objet, "as if that in itself means anything!" It was wonderful, his saying that they were together, but it was awful, too. No employment and a rag-and-bone pile of a future— and by the way, how had it gone, she wondered, with the Oblong Credit Card? But before he could answer, she guessed. They hadn't renewed it, had they? Just as she thought! This was just like at home with her father the drinker—life falling apart at the seams: unemployment, tragedy, disruption—and all these spontaneous ugly ailments on her hands. She felt like jumping out the window, she said, or blowing out her brains.

Monsieur Sorbonne was stunned by this outburst. He had never before observed Mademoiselle Objet in such an emotional tenor; but then, as he reminded himself, he hadn't known her that long either. Besides, he trivially observed to himself, life was full of surprises.

He sat her down on a tufted red chair and dabbed at her eyes with his red silk handkerchief. It was remarkable, he observed to himself, how her outplay of hysteria had calmed his own existential tremors.

"Don't worry," he said, a little shaken. "We're together now, and a way will appear." And with that he rang up Service-for-the-Rooms and ordered—although it was now nearly dark and many hours after tea-time—a small pot of tea and a tray of cucumber sandwiches.

The moment he hung up the phone, Mademoiselle Objet was smiling.

What a mercurial temperament, he thought. *One minute suicidal, the next as bright as a star.*

"I'm so happy," she said. "I'm overjoyed. I can't believe it—what you just said. You said '*we!*' You said '*we're*' together! You said '*we'll*' solve everything. Does that mean that we are an *us?* Or that we could be? Or that maybe we already are?" She started jumping almost, up and down.

Monsieur Sorbonne was shocked by her sudden enthusiasm. He was, if the truth be told, somewhat put off by the wildly gyrating emotions of Mademoiselle Objet, and was trying to incorporate these current explosions into his earlier softer impressions of her.

The shy young Mademoiselle with the tears and the sweet little hands had become . . . a what? He wasn't sure, but indeed she had seemed for a moment to be an out-and-out hysteric.

Just then the Service-for-the-Rooms man knocked at the door and rolled in with a white-clothed table of cucumber sandwiches and tea. Mademoiselle Objet sat demure and lovely, waiting in grace while Monsieur Sorbonne signed the check and poured out the tea. "I'm so sorry for my outburst," she said, as he handed her a cup. "It's just that when things get out of control, so do I." She sipped at her tea, trying to recompose herself. "I guess you didn't know that about me," she said. "Or did you?"

"As a matter of fact, I didn't," said Monsiur Sorbonne. "But it doesn't really matter. Because I love you anyway."

He was surprised to hear himself say this, surprised even more to notice that it felt true. Feeling the truth of it made him feel, suddenly, two other things. He felt happy. And responsible. She needed peace, this agitatable Mademoiselle Objet, and he seemed—just with his words—to be able to calm her. Perhaps, in a way that he had never had been able to before—he had made his mother and father unhappy simply by being born; he had made his uncle and aunt unhappy by never settling down—he could bring joy to another human being.

Having poured his own tea, he sat down, once again, in his chair. He could no longer see the leaf shadows on the boulevard because the deep darkness had fallen, but in it he could see some things.

"I think we should find a small house and make a life together," he said.

"You do? We should!? We can! That makes me so happy!" said Mademoiselle Objet. "Just hearing you say that makes me feel calm."

"Yes, I do," said Monsieur Sorbonne. "We should. We can. And we will. But now, let's sleep. We'll work it all out in the morning."

∼

CHAPTER 32

Mademoiselle Objet and Monsieur Sorbonne Make Some Plans

In the beautiful morning—*the soleil was* shining, the birds were twitting in the trees—Monsieur Sorbonne and Mademoiselle Objet agreed that she would go out and look for a house. She was the Mademoiselle of All Objects after all, and a house, in a sense, was an object, although an exceptionally big one. She would know just what it should look like and just where it could be found. Meanwhile, he would go out and look for a job, attempt to acquire gainful employment.

Since he was a man, he thought once again, as he soaped his head in the shower with *vetiver* shampoo, he *had* to find a job. A man's job was having a job, after all. To only the gifted and predestined few fell the privilege of having not just a job, but that most rarefied form of gainful employment, a meaningful life's work, a *métier*.

With the one-hundred-dollar check that Monsieur Sorbonne had drawn against the dwindling balance of the Oblong Credit Card, Mademoiselle Objet set out on her quest. She was tiptoey happy because she knew she could accomplish it. Never had there been an object, no matter its size or purpose, whose whereabouts had eluded her (except for the TV-silencing earmuffs, which had occasioned her meeting with Monsieur Sorbonne). She was happy because she liked the idea of starting a new life with him. She liked his blue blazer and his red silk handkerchief. She liked the way he commandeered the Service for the Rooms. She liked the way his words could deliver her to calm.

Monsieur Sorbonne—and this he managed to conceal—was not quite so happy, however. He was, in fact, quietly mourning the loss of his Oblong Credit Card, a friend, as it were, which had brought much joy to his life (fine tureens of soup, fresh crayfish, astronomy equipment)—and woefully contemplating what he could only construe to be the ignominy of having to go out and look for a job.

Nevertheless, he put on his fine blue blazer, fastened the red silk handkerchief in its pocket and, having kissed Mademoiselle Objet good-bye, went out to seek his fortune.

∾

CHAPTER 33

Mademoiselle Objet Goes Out to Look for a House

When Mademoiselle Objet went down to the streets, she went at once to the Newspaper Vendor's corner. It was only 10 a.m. but she knew—because she knew these things—that at 10:18 or thereabouts, the new newspapers for the day would be delivered to the corner.

She also knew that anyone having a house to rent or share or sell or trade would have placed an ad in the paper, and that anyone wanting to rent or share or borrow or buy a house would look at the paper long before five o'clock when the papers would be hand-delivered to all the local subscribers.

She smiled. She was tap-tapping her toes at the Paper Vendor's Stand. Such things as this—lying in wait like a bandit for the papers to be delivered—brought forward another, as-yet-unknown to Monsieur Sorbonne, somewhat barracuda-like aspect of Mademoiselle Objet's personality. For when it came to objects, and in particular to objects that had or would come to have a purpose, Mademoiselle Objet was a wizard of one-pointed focus.

She could smell, feel, think, or blink her way into the presence of the desired item, obtain it with dispatch, and put it to use on the day, in exactly the way that would make her life (or anyone else's) resoundingly improved.

"Doing objects," as she called it, seemed to be her purpose in life. Even arranging the pencils in the hospital had been a source of delight. It was people, who seemed to turn everything upways and sidewards, that gave her the problems. People—with rules and ways and ideas and notions particular to themselves. Unlike objects, people could change on a whim, be perfectly kind and nice one day and then, on another, be some way entirely different. It was this, she supposed, the changing emotional tides all around her, that brought on her terrible rash. As well as from time to time, she had to admit, her own emotional monsoons. People, alas, were *trés compliqué*. Unlike objects, she never could get them quite exactly in line.

But how and for whom would she arrange things now that she was no longer straightening pencils in the Orphan Children's Hospital? Monsieur Sorbonne, to be sure, had various things to arrange—his clothes, the camera, a telescope, some naval instruments—but he seemed to know how to arrange things for himself. His things were already carefully stacked in the hotel broom closet (as they must have been on his boat), with no need, it seemed, for her intervention.

She was thus engaged in twirling her mind when the newspapers truck arrived and a man, unseen, slung out a strung-up bundle to the papers-vending man, who speedily untied them.

Mademoiselle Objet took out her monies at once and no sooner had she exchanged them for a paper than she was off to a park bench she knew of (park benches, too, were objects she adored). Minutes later she sat with her pen poised over the Ads-for-Houses section. She marked three and numbered them 3, 2, 1, then headed, pronto, for a phone booth, where, in order, she called them all and made a trio of appointments.

House #3 was a converted greenhouse under an aging citronella tree. It had four rooms, the largest of which was a bathroom the size of a volleyball court. This, with plumbing, had apparently been the original greenhouse, and the three other rooms, lean-tos with closets, had been added on. She thanked the owner, but no thank you, and moved hastily on to #2 which, according to #2's owner, had just been rented to someone whom he had supposed was Mademoiselle Objet. (A young woman had come within minutes of Mademoiselle Object's conversation with him, and so he had assumed that she was Mademoiselle Objet— with whom he had just been talking.

"Well, you could have just asked her, point blank," said Mademoiselle Objet—"if she was me—or herself."

"Some people don't know the difference," snapped the owner, and stomped off in a huff.

People again, thought Mademoiselle Objet, *just turning things—without any warning at all—so totally sideways up.* As she had this thought, her rash began, ferociously, to itch, and once again she scratched it, drawing blood.

The third house, which was in fact #1 on her list, was distinctly hard to find. It was on a road that loop-zig-zagged around, then went up a small hill. If her object-senses hadn't been so thoroughly developed, Mademoiselle Objet would never have found it at all, for it was not on the streetline proper, but under a high wrought-iron arch suspended between two pillars on a narrow private lane.

Outside the little house and leaning up against its front wall was a slightly scary-looking man. He was wearing mirrored blue sunglasses and a black leather jacket with oversized zippers edging its wide lapels. With his four-fingered right hand—its pointer digit was missing (and, as Mademoiselle Objet observed, had been quite raggedly cut off)—he was smoking a long, brown cigarette.

Put off, somewhat, by his appearance, Mademoiselle Objet was about to turn around and depart, when, in the nicest of voices, he said, "Aren't you the young woman who just phoned about the house?" *People again*, she was thinking. You just never could tell. You simply couldn't expect them to be the way they appeared, how you thought they were or wanted them to be. *How troubling*, she thought. *How truly unnerving and odd.*

"I am," she said, turning away and once again attempting to leave, but the scary-looking man went on:

"Don't go away! I know my finger looks awful. People are always upset when they see it. I'm a carpenter—I shredded it on a chainsaw. A miracle really—my trigger finger—it kept me from going to war."

"I see," said Mademoiselle Objet, yet again trying to get away.

"Wouldn't you like to see the house? I know that's what you came for. Come," he said, and graciously opened the door.

The minute she stepped inside, Mademoiselle Objet was enchanted. The little house, which had once been a caretaker's quarters, consisted of four quite small but utterly exquisite rooms, the largest of which was the blue high-ceilinged living room. It had tall narrow windows with floating half-moons at their tops through which she could see the tall waving fronds of some huge extraordinary plants. The kitchen was tiny, but nicely arranged with cupboards and shelves of interesting sizes and shapes. The bedroom was small, but it too was lit by two narrow windows which also had floating half-moons at their tops, and the bathroom wasn't a squash court; it was the size of a bathroom.

"Do you like it?" asked the scary-looking man. "If you do, then I hope you'll take it right now. My little girl's sick. I've been up with her almost all night and I'm worried half to death. I'd like you to have it—you and the man that you mentioned. You'd be good neighbors, I can tell. Just give me a little deposit, a hundred dollars or so, and you can move in tomorrow."

How had it happened so fast? For a minute Mademoiselle Objet was worried—what kind of a landlord would he be? But then he smiled and handed her the key and showed her how to turn the lock. Then with his raggedy-fingered hand he shook her exquisite hand and said that, if she didn't mind, he'd like to go back inside now. "I need to get back to my baby," he said. "She's in there alone and she's scared—I can feel it. And soon she'll be crying."

∼

CHAPTER 34

Monsieur Sorbonne Looks for a Job

Monsieur Sorbonne was depressed. He was himself, in fact, teetering on the brink of hysteria. He simply could not, although he had promised, look for a job, however one did it, whatever it took.

That settled, he headed for the Artifacts Museum. It was in a magnificent old building, the ancient elegiac dimensions of which sublimely affected his eyes. As he entered the huge glass doors laid over with exquisite wrought iron work, peace descended upon him. He walked up the old marble staircase and instantly he felt at home. He went to Gallery 13, where, for a month a collection of Gaelic razor blades (and other wrought iron personal items) were on display. He was transfixed by them all, by their ancientness, the ingenuity of their design, the fact that forever in time, human beings for no reason whatsoever and for every reason had been creating beautiful things.

Monsieur Sorbonne moved on from gallery to gallery, like a dancer lost in an ever-so-intricate choreography until, amazed, he looked at his watch and discovered that it was already four-thirty in the afternoon.

What would he tell Mademoiselle Objet? And what, eventually, or tomorrow, *would* he do about a job?

With these somewhat unsettling thoughts infesting his mind, he stepped down the stairs. At the bottom, like a jackal in the jungle, the Curator-in-Chief of the museum, wearing a charcoal gray, boiled woolen suit with a brass falcon badge in its right lapel, and looking uncomfortably like a policeman (or so it seemed to Monsieur Sorbonne) was sitting behind a long table, lying in wait for him.

"Are you the same man who entered the museum at 9:32 a.m.?" asked the Curator-in-Chief.

"I am," said Monsieur Sorbonne, feeling the small little hairs rise up on the back of his neck.

"I have been watching and following you," said the Curator-Chief, "as you have conducted your sojourn through the museum, and I have made note of the considerable passion and curiosity with which you perceived every object. It was truly remarkable," said the curator, "unusual, the high degree of your interest, a pity that you are a visitor merely, since the qualities you possess would be so perfect in a Museum Sub-Curator . . . one of which," he continued, "we are desperately in need of."

Monsieur Sorbonne was so beset with thoughts of how he would discuss his failure to get a job with Mademoiselle Objet that he only one-third heard the words that the Curator-Chief had uttered. He had, in fact, been about to excuse himself to get back to the hotel, to tell Mademoiselle Objet God-only-knows-what, when the Curator-Chief continued. "Is there any possibility," he asked, "any miniscule chance whatsoever that a person of your perceptual ilk, your aesthetics-appreciating character might possibly be available—for a salary, of course—for such a Sub-Curator position?"

He paused for a moment, as if waiting for his hopes to crumble like an ancient artifact, but then he went on, "One is needed immediately in the Gallery of Etruscan Artifacts; and you, I can tell, would be perfect. Could you, or would you, consider . . . such a position? Or is my enthusiasm—excuse me, and I beg your pardon—tragically misplaced?"

Monsieur Sorbonne was by now at least beginning to hear the words that the Curator-in-Chief was saying, and he was overjoyed and amazed by them. Composing himself in the midst of his shock, he replied that he would be pleased indeed to become the Sub-Curator of Etruscan Artifacts. Should it please the Curator-in-Chief, he said, he would appear at 9 o'clock—salary to be discussed—the following Monday morning.

The Curator-Chief shook his hand, and, opening the high bronze door in the vaulted basement corridor, directed Monsieur Sorbonne up a flight of white marble steps that led out into the velvety night, where, already, the sky was alive with stars.

∼

CHAPTER 35

Monsieur Sorbonne and Mademoiselle Objet Convene Again at the Hotel

It was late and dark when Monsieur Sorbonne returned to the hotel. Mademoiselle Objet had ordered his favorite repast from Service-for-the-Rooms (tea, fumed salmon, toast points, horseradish and capers, lemons, mayonnaise, and grated egg yolks) to celebrate the finding of the house; but she was now becoming nervous because of Monsieur Sorbonne's extensive tardiness.

Sitting on one of the velvet red chairs, feeling a mixture of excitement (about the new house) and distress (about Monsieur Sorbonne's elongated absence), Mademoiselle Objet had once again started to scratch at her hands, and was now hovering at the brink of starting to cry.

Why was it, she wondered, that everything so utterly affected her? One minute she was happy, on top of the world—Monsieur Sorbonne loved her, they were going to move in together, she had found them a wonderful house—but now his lateness had left her feeling homeless, hopeless, and abandoned, as if all the good things she'd felt just a minute ago were a figment or a phantom.

She hated her temperament. It was so temperamental, so endlessly exhausting, and the rash it caused would, sooner or later she knew, be the ruin of her hands.

The rash had started years ago, in the early days with Mr. TV. He had given her a Teflon frying pan one Christmas. She hadn't known what to say—she was so upset—she'd wanted a bottle of lily perfume, and after he said, "It'll be great, don't you think, for grilled cheese sandwiches?" and she had said, "Yes, yes, I think it will," the rash had suddenly appeared. She had scratched it all winter until finally one day in spring, when Mr. TV had gone out of town for a croquet tournament, she put some old white gloves on her hands, taped them both shut at the wrists, and, instead of scratching her hands for five nights, she had cried herself to sleep.

She was thinking of all this when Monsieur Sorbonne turned the key in the door. He handed her a little pink box, which was tied with a braided gold ribbon. He kissed her, and sat down beside her in front of the table brought in by the Service-for-the-Rooms.

"I'm so very sorry I'm late," he said. "I've had a most interesting day. I got a new job." He paused. "Well, to be more truthful and specific, I got my *first* job, and, to celebrate, on my way home I stopped to buy you a gift, a bottle—I do hope you'll like it—of lily perfume."

～

CHAPTER 36

Madame Métier Returns to Her Cremes

Madame Métier was starting again to work with her cremes. In the fresh air and freedom of her now-extinct husband's absence, she was exploring again the medicinal possibilities of plants.

To that end, she often frequented the local flower stands, particularly on the days when she knew the flowers were wilting and she could feel, as her father had always called it, the "cell-magnetic power" in them. There was a certain spring of energy, he had often told her, which, if captured before it exhausted itself in a plant's final breath, could be condensed and suspended in various medicinal emulsions.

Buying the plants, drying them upside down in her sunroom, dividing the dried leaves and petals in the proper proportions for the recipes (some remembered, some newly invented), storing them in various boxes and bottles and jars, submerging them in a variety of solutions, reminded her of her father, whom she realized now, belatedly, she had adored.

It had taken her quite some time to realize how deeply she had loved him. He had died when she was in her young twenties. She had been occupied at the time with her husband and with the loss of her daughter. It was only as time went on and she met and talked with a great many people with whom, for one reason or another, she seemed to be unable to converse (they seemed to like to talk only about the things they wanted to buy or to get) that she realized that her father had been a most remarkable man, and that, in a very deep way, he had shaped her

He had spoken to her about many things: the rotation of the planets, the perfectly symmetrical pattern of the molting of feathers on birds' wings, the elevation of Mount Popocatépetl, the folly of politics (and, in particular, the words of politicians), the importance of doing in life what you love—whether or not there seem to be positions open in the field—(or fat remunerations for doing it), the fragile balance between every leaf and tree and bird and animal on earth.

Once, briefly, she had entertained the disturbing notion that it was perhaps only because he had died that now she so admired him. Perhaps like her husband, whom now, in his absence, she could quietly appreciate, her father, too, simply by virtue of being no longer alive might have become, belatedly, an object of her adoration. But entertaining this thought on a day when she was shredding blue thistles, she suddenly sneezed, and deeply inhaling their vapors (which gave her clarity of mind), she realized that, of course, this couldn't be the case.

Her father had had an irregular life (and thereby had made her an heir to one). Unable to please his wife, who wanted only to keep things in order, unhappy with the various professions which as a youth his parents had insisted upon him (he had become a lawyer for his father, a banker for his mother), he found himself repeatedly bored and insulted by the straight-line thinking which these esteemed professions seemed always to require. As a result, he found himself surreptitiously studying plants, which endlessly fascinated him; and in his fifty-fourth year, after both of his parents had died, he became a certified botanist.

Unlike the law or banking, botanical riddles charmed him. What—or who—had made all the plants the way they were, with their frivolous, gorgeous (possibly pointless), but endlessly colorful variations? What, for example, was the botanical lineage of the plant called Lamb's Ears, and how could you account for the fact that when you touched its leaves, their silvery furs, like the nap of a velvet, insisted on going in only a single direction? For what purpose did roses have thorns, or holly have pricks, or persimmon no leaves while showering their fruit? Or, as he noticed much later, why was it that tea infused with the leaves of blue thistle should have the effect of creating mental clarity? (This he had discovered quite by accident one night while making himself a cup of tea. A bouquet of blue thistles he was drying collapsed from its thread on the kitchen ceiling and crumbled into his open pan of boiling water, and he had noticed, after he drank it, that he was able to think more clearly.)

Madame Métier had often walked with her father (who walked to escape the orderliness of his wife) on Sunday afternoons. It was then that, passing through meadows or alongside moss-covered creek banks, or walking up and down the rows of the experimental garden plot he rented from the city, he had taught her the names and properties of many plants. It was then that, in passing, he had told her how to take note of even the subtlest differences in the tenor of their fragrance, the various oils that they contained, and when and how to harvest them for optimum results.

As she started now with plants of her own, his spirit at times seemed to haunt her, to speak to her from the midst of the slowly dehydrating petals and fronds, such a deep sense of peace did she feel each day as she gathered and dried them. When she felt his presence thus, at times a great sadness would overtake her, for she wished that while he had still been alive, she had talked with him more about life itself and the meaning of things.

One day, a few years after she had married the doctor, the city, by the right of eminent domain, bought up her father's experimental garden plot for the purpose of building an outskirts-of-the-city public parking lot. He was too old then, to begin another garden, or to transplant his esoteric specimens, and it was because of this (along with his wife's "now maybe you can settle down, stop fussing with all those fern fiddleheads and just read books or play canasta like everyone else"), that finally he invited death in.

So he had told Madame Métier on his death bed, anyway. "I knew he was coming eventually. I was tired, and so instead of resisting, I just opened the door and invited him in."

It was the young Madame Métier who sat with him at his deathbed, while, day after day, through the hospital windows, he watched the clouds mysteriously circling. One evening, together, they watched the rain and the sky, which was ribboned with rainbows. "You know," he said to her then, "when you think of it, life is just a little postage stamp, a colored bit

of paper that gets canceled when the letter finally gets sent to its permanent destination."

Between waves of pain he spoke to her of many things—of life, of
death ("it's just a new beginning," he told her)—and also, because at
times she wept to see him in such anguish, of suffering. "Don't worry,
Darling," he said, "this is just my cup of the suffering. Suffering always
asks you to change, to build your soul large. And because in one way or
another we all have to suffer, it's how we share in the human condition.
Don't be afraid of it, Darling. Suffering opens the doors to compassion."

One night, toward the end, when his feet had turned blue, Madame
Métier returned to her house. And while the doctor was at a Diseases
of the Heart Convention, she ground up some petals and leaves she had
saved in the green striped hatbox up in her closet. Then, working away in
the sunroom all night, she prepared her first edition of a creme.

The next morning at the hospital, after the nurses had bathed her
father and wrapped him again in white sheets, she sat down at the foot of
his bed and, humming softly, applied the creme to his feet.

From the top of the bed, with his eyes looking down to his toes and
his voice like a dry white wind, he said, "Thank you, Darling. That's
wonderful. My feet are ready to fly now. I'm going home."

Then, as she sat there, still holding his feet in her hands, she felt a
great rush of energy as if a million silver electric molecules had poured
into her palms. And when she looked up to the top of the bed, his eyes
had gone blank and his soul had flown away with the wind.

～

CHAPTER 37

Monsieur Sorbonne and Mademoiselle Objet Move into Their New House

Having finished their salmon and toast points, Monsieur Sorbonne and Mademoiselle Objet talked for what seemed like hours before they went to sleep. Monsieur Sorbonne told Mademoiselle Objet about his past life, and Mademoiselle Objet told him all about her parents—about her mother, who had worked sixty-plus hours a week at a clothes-cleaning shop as an ironing clerk, and her father, who was descended from princes but had been forced from his country by a sudden revolution, and who, in changing countries, had become a nothing. In becoming a nothing he had drunk without end while her mother worked all day and night at the laundering store. Mademoiselle Objet had tried to make her father happy (by throwing away all his bottles) and her mother happy (by arranging all the objects—the spoons and forks, the piles of mail, the clothes, the magazines), while her mother was away at work. None of this had brought peace to the household, however; and so, having met Mr. TV at an after-hours café where she had gone late one night to pick up a sandwich for her exhausted, over-worked mother, she had married him and gotten away from her parents.

Which had been, more or less, a good thing.

They had told each other their stories and then they had slept, and, in the morning, after a breakfast of coffee and tea cakes, they went off together to see the new house.

Monsieur Sorbonne, no longer wearing his blue Italian suit with the red silk handkerchief, was now wearing blue jeans and a well-pressed shirt. Mademoiselle Objet, using her arms grown strong from endlessly arranging things, gathered up all their objects—hers from Mr. TV's ex-house, and Monsieur Sorbonne's from the splendid hotel, and box after box, they installed themselves into their little new home.

"This is just the beginning, isn't it?" said Mademoiselle Objet, when finally having arranged all the things in the order from which tomorrow and thereafter she would re- and rearrange them, she lay down in the freshly made bed beside Monsieur Sorbonne.

"Yes it is," said Monsieur Sorbonne. "This is the beginning of every-thing," and with that he kissed her and turned out the light.

∾

PART II

CHAPTER I

Madame Métier Goes Cloud-Watching

Madame Métier had been somewhat pensive since her husband's death—not that she missed him in particular, but that in the void created by his absence, there was room for so much. She often wondered quietly to herself just what she was meant to do, now that she had been granted the unmentionable good fortune of being delivered from her husband and into a life of her own.

She was glad indeed to have sold off all the doctor's things, and in particular the white powder for $5,000, with which she had bought the large supply of flowers she was now drying in the sunroom, to say nothing of her new red bathing suit.

The doctor hadn't liked the beach—*it got sand in your crackers*, he always said—and since he himself hadn't liked it, he insisted that Madame Métier also avoid it like the plague. Now, though, with the whiff of fresh air provided by his demise, whatever spare time she had left after work, she would carefree spend at the beach.

At noon especially, she would put on her red bathing suit and a broad-brimmed straw hat and pack herself a lunch: a T-fish sandwich (*sans* sand), a pouch of rose-potato crisps, a pickle, and a bottle of sparkling spring water with half a teaspoon of cassis syrup stirred in, and head out for the beach. There she would sit with her snow-fluffy towel propped up against any rock that would serve as a chair, eat her lunch, and look down and down the long stretch of beach, past the curve of the cove that cradled the city, and on and on to the wild beach beyond. She wanted to see how the air was, how the birds were, how the grass bent in the wind. Each day when she had finished her lunch and packed up the crumbs, she would lie flat-out on her towel, looking up at the blue *ciel*, and doze and dream and watch the clouds.

Mesmerized, she would watch their sylphlike shifting shapes, their tantalizing dance. At times they appeared to be animals, playing after each other, at other times spirits conversing, their attitudes endlessly changing, at other times jewel-like, catching this or that aspect of light. Enchanted, she watched them for hours, until the clouds themselves became invisible, swam into the sea of blue sky and were softly consumed.

Cloud-watching thus, Madame Métier spent many a peaceful afternoon. The more she observed the clouds, the more she was transfixed by them, until cloud-watching in itself became for her a kind of sub-vocation. For, in time, it was not just the clouds that she saw, but in their endless mysterious movement—the way they would begin and end and then begin again, the way they appeared and disappeared and reappeared, the way they were always different and always the same—a reference to the endlessly changing sameness of things.

Indeed, at times, staring up at the clouds, she felt as if she had become them, as if she herself had been carried up and been somehow melted into them, so that now as a cloud she looked down at herself—a woman on a towel on a beach, wearing a red bathing suit.

Sometimes she would feel like the clouds, at other times like the woman, but whenever she looked up at the clouds, if she stared long enough, the boundaries would slowly dissolve between herself and them. It was then that she knew she had come from the clouds, from the light which so infused them. She knew the clouds were a part of her and that she was part of them. And she knew that in time it would be the clouds to which she would return.

～

CHAPTER 2

Madame Métier Begins Again With Her Cremes

Between her outings at the beach, Madame Métier was now working very hard on her cremes. She had taken the green striped hatbox down from the closet, made an inventory of all her assorted dried items and set up shop in the sunroom.

She bought a huge library table and on it she set out in piles the myriad leaves and petals and fronds that she had already preserved as well as the new ones that she had started collecting. She bought two tin file boxes and several packets of different colored filing cards on which gradually, as she experimented, she wrote down her new recipes. She ordered fluids and oils to serve as suspensions and emulsions for her cremes, and these in their various bottles and jars she stacked in the corner of her room. She bought cases of little containers, of porcelain, silver, and copper; of blue glass and white glass and clear glass, in which to serve up her various cremes, aware that the cremes themselves would perform one final alchemical change when they came into contact with the substance of their packaging.

She got up early each morning and, after having her tea, went into the sunroom, checked all the plants that were drying, sampled the various emulsions, and then set to work, admixing various tinctures, extracts, liquids, herbs and flower essences.

As she combined and mixed, evaluating each texture and fragrance, she waited, poised, for the mysterious moment when something, an unpremeditated alchemical event, would finally occur and the creme would achieve its optimum consistency, give off its beautiful fragrance and assume its permanent color. Then she would hear, as if spoken by a voice in her ears, the words announcing the ailment for which it was the remedy. Then and only then, would she write down the new recipe.

Her method was somewhat haphazard. She was never quite sure which afflictions she was attempting to cure, that is to say, whether she should seek to attain a particular creme for a particular malady, or whether a creme in its seemingly unique combination of fragrance, texture, and packaging—total essence—would reveal the purpose for which it had been invented. So far it had been true that each time a creme had achieved its essence, The Voice, as she called it to herself, had whispered in her ear and told her what it was to be used for.

So it was that at times she felt quite confident that simply by her experiments, she would arrive at exactly where she was meant to be going. At other times she doubted this, felt she should state her intention for a creme, develop a rigid, no-nonsense, specific, concrete, and orderly plan—and then steadfastly adhere to it.

One week, after a siege of many failures, she was feeling particularly desperate. One recipe, for no reason, exploded in its cruet, spattering the sunroom with shards of broken glass. Another, overnight, grew a frightening purplish mold. A third had curdled mysteriously and turned rock hard by morning.

Her table was a nightmare, a veritable Vesuvius of seeds and fronds, of scraps of paper and recipe cards, to say nothing of all the pots and jars of failed and/or perfected cremes that cluttered every spare surface of the workroom. She had certainly tried to clean up, and once or twice she had actually succeeded. She had taken her workroom down to the bone, filed all the wandering recipe cards, stacked all the jars of finished cremes, and cleared off the surface of her table. Each time she did this, she believed— for a few days at least—that she had finally learned to live by her mother's directive to always clean up as she went along. But then once again she would be inspired, and the process would start all over again. It seemed, in fact, as if only from chaos could she create. Tidiness had itself as an end, but chaos, it seemed, was the *sine qua non* of all her creations.

Perhaps she was mad. Perhaps this business with cremes was a folly— *poppycock* as her husband had said. What did the world need cremes for anyway? She wished she could have talked to her father, asked him for some advice. What would he have said, for example, about these particular recipes? Did he think she was wise or foolish, for carrying on with her cremes? It was true, that with all these disasters that she hadn't heard the voice that ordinarily announced the purpose for each creme. She hadn't been told the ailment for which each one had been invented. Had wished she could have talked to her father. From where he was now, in a world beyond worlds, he would certainly know if this was her calling.

She thought of the room, 5244, in which he had died, and she wondered if—as with the plants when they themselves were no longer alive— some whiff of their essence remained, some molecules of her father's might still linger in his hospital room. In her wave of despair, she decided to go to the hospital, to the room where her father had died, to see if, by sitting where she had last felt his essence, some remnant of his being might offer up a message.

～

CHAPTER 3

Madam Métier Goes to the Hospital

When Madame Métier arrived at the hospital, she was distressed to see that her father's room, 5244, was occupied. The door stood open, and in the room, on a bed tilted slightly upward, lay a young man, probably in his twenties, fast asleep. He was wired up to an octopus-like configuration of machines and corrugated tubes. These were attached to a metal box on the back wall of the room, which displayed a series of lit-up colored lines that moved endlessly across it, as if across a TV screen.

He had needles in his arms and a hole in his throat, which had a gurgling fluid-filled tube inserted into it. A huge metal hand, the extension of yet another machine, lay over his chest and was pressing air in and out of his lungs. In spite of how strangely scaffolded he was, Madame Métier felt strangely drawn to him.

She stepped back to read his name on the door but, oddly, there was none. Then she walked down the hall to the nurses' station and, saying that she had been a close friend of his family's, asked if she might visit awhile with the young man in the room.

"Since you're sure you're a friend," said the nurse, suspiciously eyeing her, "I suppose you can go in. Stay as long as you like. They're pulling out the plugs any day now anyway."

Madame Métier was shocked, and this must have showed on her face because then the nurse added, "He's been unconscious for five weeks. His brain is gone. His parents just haven't decided when to pull out the plugs. Excuse me," she said, and disappeared down the hall.

Madame Métier walked back to the room where the young man lay still, very still on the bed. She pulled the door half closed behind her, and pulling up a chrome and orange plastic chair, sat down next to him. She watched as mindless, he breathed in and out, his chest rising and falling like the tides of the ocean, beneath the great metal hand, while his hands, like two beached fish except for occasional twitches, lay motionless beside him.

She sat there transfixed by him. His dark hair lay around him in shining bright ringlets on the pillow, and his eyelids, great lidded arcs with dark lashes, were closed. There was a mysterious peacefulness about him, and she wondered who he was and how he had come to be this way, suspended here as he was between life and its aftermath.

As Madame Métier sat there beside him, she felt her own breathing ever so slightly begin to change, until she realized that the two of them were breathing—in and out, in and out, in and out—in unison. As she sat with him there in the silence, she suddenly wished very much that whether he could feel it or not, she could apply a creme to his head, that just as she had for her father as he lay dying in this room, she could now do something for him.

But unfortunately in all her distress about her profession, she had left her house without any cremes, and so she had nothing with which to soothe him. Just the same, as she sat there, a curious thing began to happen. Her hands started ever so slightly to tingle, to seem to want to move in the direction of his head. And so she allowed them to move until finally, softly, she laid her hands on his forehead, which was cool and damp like a rain-washed stone. She could feel somehow through her hands—or rather she could see, almost, through the tips of her fingers— that his skull was cool and dark inside, like an empty cave.

Then, as she sat there, quietly resting her hands on his head, she began to "see" that the faintest thin threads and flickerings of white lights—like strings of carnival lights reflected at nighttime on water—had begun to inhabit the cave of his head, and as she continued to rest her hands on his forehead, these threads of light began, one by one, ever so slightly to brighten.

Beside her, the young man lay motionless in the bed. The room was still, no sound in it except the minuscule buzz of the octopus-like machine that monitored his every breath. Madame Métier continued to sit at his side, with her hands on his head a little while longer.

It had grown dark outside. The first stars had just pricked their way through the velvet blue umbrella of the high night sky. Madame Métier stirred, came back to herself, and realized that she had been sitting there in a sort of half-sleeping state for quite a long time.

The young man lay still as a stone, but he was breathing more easily now and through her fingertips she could see—or was this just her imagination?—that the faint, thin flickerings of light in his head were now noticeable strands, veins almost, of white light that moved through the hemispheres of his brain in a distinctive undulating pattern. She removed her hands from his head and brushed back his beautiful hair. Then she stood up, and before she could think, she leaned over and planted a kiss on his forehead.

When she came out into the street, a dark night had fallen. There was almost no moon, and as she walked outside, receiving the crackling crunch of the fallen chestnut leaves through the bottoms of her shoes, she felt strange. She had learned not a thing about her cremes. Her father had sent her no message. She had spent the whole afternoon with her hands on the head of a young man whose life-sustaining machines would soon be turned off because, according to medical science, he was already dead.

～

CHAPTER 4

Madam Métier Is Discouraged

Having thus discovered nothing, Madame Métier decided the following day that the least she could do was clean up her workroom.

Because of the previous day's explosion, the sunroom was now a full-blown disaster. Leaves and seeds were everywhere. In fact, it was in such a shambles that when she returned, she actually thought for a minute that vandals had come in while she was gone, and, in a mad search for money, had topsy-turvied everything.

She stared at her table, trying to sort out the recipe cards, of which she had six colors, but she couldn't find the box for them, and, besides, should she sort them by color, by the primary content of the recipe, or by the ailment for which it was a remedy? She couldn't tell. And so, without deciding or arranging anything, she moved on to the piles of petals and leaves she had stripped from the plants she was drying. Should she put them all in white medicine boxes, or small round tins?—she couldn't tell. And what about her fluids and oils—now that they had been opened? Where, and how, and in what should she store them? She couldn't decide that either.

She was surrounded by chaos, and the more she tried to correct it, the more impossible it seemed. She realized, in fact, that she had no idea at all of how to even begin to get it organized. Discouraged almost to the point of crying, she got up from her table, closed the door to her workroom, put on her new red bathing suit, and headed for the beach.

❧

CHAPTER 5

Madame Métier Returns to the Beach

The air was shiny and blue with high fluffy white clouds as Madame Métier propped herself up on a rock. In her hurry to get away from her mess, she had taken no time to pack herself a lunch, so on the way she had stopped at the corner Waters Store to buy herself a cranberry soda.

She was idly sipping her soda as, once again, she watched the clouds go rolling by. She wanted to think of nothing, certainly not of her room and her inability to clean, and certainly not of the silent young man in the hospital room.

The clouds, which had started out mushroomy, cottony, and fluffy when she first sat down, seemed to be becoming, as she watched them, gradually more vaporous, diaphanous, and gauzy, until they dissolved altogether into a fine white mist which totally obscured the sun.

Having now finished her soda, she watched in delighted mindlessness as the veil of clouds descended, became a fog, then moved ever so slightly, like a thin white curtain teased into motion by a summer breeze, until it had bathed the entire landscape in a silvery soft film. Trees melted in it. The line of the shore appeared and disappeared like a landscape in a dream, and although she was getting chilly because of the absence of the sun, she sat there mesmerized. Her mind was suspended in some gauzy in-between place, and the thoughts that had troubled her only minutes before, all seemed now to have been quite magically erased.

As she sat there thus, her mind unleashed from its gears, she noticed a man walking toward her. First a dot, then a form, then the form of a man emerging through the haze. She was surprised to see him. She had been there so often alone and the beach had always been so deserted that she had begun to think of it as a place inhabited by no one but herself. She was therefore all the more surprised when, with long loping elegant strides like the graceful movements of some ancient dance, the man emerged from the haze and seemed to be very intentionally approaching her.

He was tall and strong and had white-blonde hair, long arms, and large, beautifully formed hands in which he seemed to be holding something. He folded his legs and sat down beside her. He had round blue eyes, with which, intently, he studied her. For a time he said nothing, just sat there quietly in her presence. Then finally he said, "You're sad today. You're upset. Nothing is working. I'm sorry. Here," he said, "I've brought you a present."

He handed her a large white shell, which had a deep pink bowl inside and rolling white scallops along its edges. They curved upward and downward and upward again like the movement of the waves in the ocean. She took the shell in her hands and smiled, and, as she did, he stood up. Then, lowering his eyes to hers, he looked at her for a moment and added, "You might want to put an ad in the paper—to get yourself some help. You need it." Then he turned, and walking away through the veil of mist, he disappeared down the beach.

When Madame Métier got home, she opened the door to her workroom, which for some reason now no longer appeared so chaotic. The pale gray light of the late afternoon slanted in through the windows, falling in shimmering lattices across all her medicine boxes and tins.

She had brought the shell in with her and she cleared a space for it now on the middle of her table. Then, thinking reverently of the rather unusual manner in which she had acquired it, she lit a small candle, which, with a smile, she placed in front of it. There. Somehow everything felt better. She sat down at her table and started composing an ad for the paper:

Organizer of objects, chaoses, and mélanges.
Office magician needed. Desperately. And at once.

She sealed it in an envelope, put on a coat, and walked it out to the Post Box on the corner.

~

CHAPTER 6

Monsieur Sorbonne Is Happy With His Work

Having organized everything in the house—the herbs and teas and beans and peas in jars on the shelf in the kitchen, the sheets and towels and wrapping papers and quilts (down-filled for winter, pale-colored cottons for summer) in their closet in the hall, the papers in her desk, her make-up box, her hairpins and clips and ribbon bows, her poems books on the library shelf, Monsieur Sorbonne's socks in his drawer, his shirts (in order of design), on a high rod in the bedroom closet, his myriad pairs of cufflinks, his telescope and binoculars, his skiing and parachute gear, his cutting and sawing tools (these all she put away in the shed), his camera and its several lenses, the tattered Belgian linen bag with the rolled-up tubes of paint, and the maroon velvet pouch which, when she encountered it once again, reminded her that Monsieur Sorbonne had never developed the pictures of her that he had taken that first night. She found the disengaged film in a small metal canister and this she set aside to bring to Monsieur Sorbonne's attention. Having done all this, the lovely Mademoiselle now found, much deeply to her distress, that the hideous horrible rash had once again appeared on her hands.

She had had such a wonderful time here, sorting things out, putting them up and then relishing their put-upness, that she had scarcely noticed that Monsieur Sorbonne, the delight of her life, had been so constantly gone.

He had taken to the work of being a Sub-Curator at the Artifacts Museum like a drake to a pond. His first assignment was sorting out pot shards from an ancient Etruscan excavation site. There were 6,043 of them. Once having determined which set of shards formed which pot,

Monsieur Sorbonne was to supervise their gluing together, and, subsequently (when the shattered pots were all re-formed), to oversee the construction of the cabinets and backgrounds for their eventual exhibition.

The sorting had not, in particular, been Monsieur Sorbonne's cup of tea. After hours, on twelve occasions at least, he had whisked Mademoiselle Objet into his curator's cell to assist him. This, of course, had given her pleasure, for in even the organization of objects so esoteric as pot shards, she was a master. She felt a great satisfaction. But now Phase I of the EPP (Etruscan Pots Project) had been completed. The various bowls and vessels and urns had all been perfectly reconstructed from the pot shards, and Mademoiselle Objet had completed her brief after-hours tour of duty at the Artifacts Museum.

Monsieur Sorbonne, however, had not. He was now hard at work imagining and designing the backgrounds and foregrounds for their exhibition and this also kept him out late many nights at the museum.

Despite this lengthy over-work, Monsieur Sorbonne felt quite happy. For he had found, if not his life's work, for the moment at least, a quite engaging position.

∿

CHAPTER 7

Mademoiselle Objet Is Not So Happy

One day when Monsieur Sorbonne came home uncharacteristically early from work—he had finished a portion of his exhibition plan and designs and decided to come home in time to take Mademoiselle Objet out to dinner—he found her, hands scratched raw and herself in a puddle of tears, sitting on a chair in the kitchen. So distraught was she that neither his coming home, his hello, nor his coming-home kisses seemed to be able to brighten her spirits.

"What's wrong?" he asked. But she didn't answer. She just scratched her hands.

"You've got to do something," he said, finally. "You can't just keep scratching yourself to the bone."

"But there's nothing to do. It's all done!" she said, pouting. She was a crank—he could see it. She was using her two scratched-up hands like two combs, running them fretfully back and forth through her hair. "You think that I can just sit here for hours while you're at that ridiculous museum deciding whether to put sackcloth or velvet behind your stupid Etruscan ruins!"

"No, I don't. Not at all," said Monsieur Sorbonne, trying somewhat haphazardly to console her. But Mademoiselle Objet, still scratching, and now even more in a state, went on.

"You're off fiddling with pot shards while I just sit here all day alone, no more pot shards to sort, no things to arrange, no items whatsoever any more to organize. You don't understand! You're busy, but I'm here with NOTHING . . ."—and here her voice hit a high-pitched range the likes of which Monsieur Sorbonne's ears had never before entertained—"TO

DO! Of course I'm scratching my hands! There is NOTHING! NOTH-ING! NOTHING left for me to do!"

And here she let out a howl that was so high-pitched and piercing that Monsieur Sorbonne was frankly terrified. She had really gone round the bend, he was thinking, and he wondered what, if anything, he could do for her and if—or how—he could survive himself.

"And FURTHERMORE!" she screamed—she was a race car now, careening out of control down a hairpin curve on a mountain road, about to go over the edge—"YOU haven't done a thing around here! You haven't even taken that film with all those photographs you took of me a thousand weeks ago to be developed!" And with that she picked up the little metal film canister that she had placed in a prominent location on the kitchen counter and hurled it in his direction. Then, grabbing a sweater and her purse, she stormed out of the kitchen, slamming the door behind her.

～

CHAPTER 8

Monsieur Sorbonne Is in Shock

Monsieur Sorbonne was in shock. This all reminded him of something. The feeling he was having, that just being himself could be all wrong for somebody else, reminded him of being somehow too wrong to be kept by his mother and father, and of being, as a consequence, shipped off to live with his uncle and aunt.

He felt once again not good enough—to belong anywhere, to be chosen, or kept or loved just as himself by anyone at all. He felt wrong somehow now for working, just as in the past when he was a child, he had felt wrong simply for being born.

Tears fell from his eyes. He was sad, heartbroken, really. He loved Mademoiselle Objet, but her outburst had terrified him. He felt helpless, devastated in the face of it, and wondered how or if he could win back her heart or bring her to peace.

Quaking like a sycamore leaf in the wind, he picked up the small metal canister, tucked it in his left jacket pocket next to his red silk handkerchief, and went out to get the photographs, belatedly, developed.

∾

CHAPTER 9

Mademoiselle Objet Is in Shock

Mademoiselle Objet was in her own kind of shock when, desperate, she hit the streets. She had done it again, the terrible thing. The words had come flooding into her brain like a venom, and like an artillery of poison darts, she had just hurled them. Having done so, she now felt a kind of relief. The pent-up everything had been released and she had regained a kind of equilibrium; but what, oh what, she wondered, had her outburst done to Monsieur Sorbonne?

As if that weren't enough, her hands were driving her wild. Her outburst had brought on another onslaught of the rash, and, after slamming the door, she had started to scratch as if there would be no tomorrow.

What could she do?! If only there was a cure, an object with which she could quiet her brain, so that no matter how distraught she became, she wouldn't explode. If only she could somehow desist the ruinous scratching of her hands.

Thinking this, she suddenly thought of Madame Métier, the woman she had seen first at the Flower Vendor's Stand and then with Monsieur Sorbonne on their hotel room TV. Perhaps *she* could help, with those cremes she'd been talking about. Believing some good would come of it, Mademoiselle Objet determined to somehow find her.

~

CHAPTER 10

Madame Métier Hears a Knock at the Door

Madame Métier was already in her dressing gown (a white silk robe printed over with lovely red roses) when she heard a knock at the door. She had tried all day to make some sense of her room, and, in spite of the benefi-cent presence of the shell, the pink bowl of which she had filled with the petals of various roses, she had accomplished almost nothing.

There had been several phone calls, orders for cremes from persons who had seen her on TV. These she had somehow managed to fill: calen-dula/saxifrage creme for the deeply-burned hand of a three-year-old who, enchanted by the flickering flames, had put her hand in the fire; lemon/aster creme for a mother whose temper flared at dinner time; lily/ violet creme for a girl whose heart had been broken when her fiancé had jilted her.

To each of these, she had added a note. She had found some old tis-sue paper and wrapped all the jars, then crumpled outdated newspapers and new magazines and put each creme with its letter into one of the cardboard boxes she had ordered for this purpose.

She was about to seal up the boxes and mail them all off when she discovered that she could find neither her packing tape nor her scissors. She looked at length, rustling through frond and leaf and petal piles, but the scissors and tape were both exactly nowhere to be found.

Defeated, she had decided to make herself a tea. She had just settled into the white wicker chair by the window to read a fashion magazine and had started perusing the new lingerie, when, most unexpectedly, she heard a knock at the door.

With a red silk rope, she sashed up her robe and started down the stairs.

～

CHAPTER 11

Mademoiselle Objet Is Impatient

Thinking that no one was home and that, once again, her worst fears were about to come true, Mademoiselle Objet pounded fiercely one final time on Madame Metier's door. Which instantly opened.

"How can I help you?" asked Madame Métier. Her voice was steady, a pillar of calm in contrast to the imperious staccato of Mademoiselle Objet's somewhat desperate door-pounding. In person and at close range, she was much taller than Mademoiselle Objet had imagined, a woman of stature, queen-like, who had white-blonde hair and very blue eyes. There was a shining about her that made her seem young, but where she had smiled many times she had lines on her face revealing more age.

"Have you come about the ad?" asked Madame Métier, reaching her hands across the little distance that separated them, and taking Mademoiselle Objet's really quite ruined hands very gently into her own. "Oh, but of course not,"—she suddenly remembered it had been only last night that she had posted the envelope—the ad could not have already appeared. "It isn't the ad, then," she concluded. "So why are you here? How did you find me, and how can I help you?"

Mademoiselle Objet was instantly calmed by these simplest of questions. "Find you?—I went to the Orphans' Hospital first because once I saw you there, but no one on the night shift had heard of you or knew your name. So then I went to the flower vendor man, where I also saw you one day, and he told me your name. Then I called the Phone Informations and asked for your address. I hope you don't mind." She withdrew her hands from Madame Métier's and held them up in the porch light. "I was desperate," she said. "It's this horrible, awful, endless, deadly ugly rash."

Madame Métier observed them, and taking her by the hand, invited her in. Then pointing the way, she proceeded to guide her up the long flight of stairs to her workroom. "You'll have to pardon the mess," she said, as she situated Mademoiselle Objet on the couch, "but it's out of my control."

Mademoiselle Objet could scarcely believe her eyes. This room was an outright disaster, or, depending on how you looked at it, a veritable feast. Never once in her entire life of setting things straight had she ever beheld such a maelstrom of things out of place. These items all were interesting and difficult and strange—a world-class challenge, she thought, getting those petals and fronds boxed up, controlling those strewn-around cardboards and boxes for packing. Her hands were itching, as it were, to get to work.

"So let's have a look at these hands," said Madame Métier, and, taking the young woman's hands very tenderly into her own, she half-closed her eyes as if with some far inner vision the more clearly to perceive them, and thus ascertain what exactly was causing the problem. She lifted each one of them, smoothing them both, top sides and palms with her palms. Then she paused, held them both still for a moment, and looked out the window.

"You have such pretty hands," she said to Mademoiselle Objet finally. "But you're mean to them. And you're mean to yourself in some other ways. And I think," she said, pausing and now even more slowly rubbing Mademoiselle Objet's hands as if like a genie in a bottle they might offer up a message, "you were mean today to somebody else."

"I was," said Mademoiselle Objet, who now, across from Madame Métier was quietly sobbing. "You're right, I was terribly mean, and now of course I regret it. I screamed and yelled at the one I most love. About something—right now I can't even remember what. But I was terrible. I screamed and I even threw something at him, and then I slammed the door and ran out. And now I'm so sorry. I'm horrified, but I don't know what I can do—how I can fix it. Which of course I want to."

Beside her, Madame Métier was in a sort of half-trance. Like a reader of the Tarot, she was turning Mademoiselle Objet's hands over and over like the backs and fronts of fortune cards, studying them one at a time, topside and under, palms and tops, nail petal surfaces, smooth tips of fingers underneath.

"Your hands aren't happy right now, with what you're giving them to do. They like intricate work, and you've insulted them. They feel ignored, degraded, and forgotten. But I will give you some cremes to make them feel better—and help them remember the wonderful tasks they would so much prefer to do."

So saying, she let go of Mademoiselle Objet's hands, and passing her own hands very softly across them one final time, she stood up and went to her table and picked out two small jars of cremes. "This one is for healing your hands," she said, offering Mademoiselle Objet a small white glass jar, "and this one," —she handed her a small translucent blue glass jar—"is for the man—the one you most love. Tonight, before he goes to sleep, have him rub just a little under his eyes, so in the morning he can see you differently."

With that she stood up and started down the stairs. Mesmerized, Mademoiselle Objet followed her. "How much do I owe you?" she asked, when she reached the bottom of the stairs.

"Nothing," said Madame Métier. "Today's consultation is free. These are still experimental cremes. But someday," she laughed, a tinkling and delightful laugh, "you can help me clean up my room."

∼

CHAPTER 12

Monsieur Sorbonne Contemplates Certain Things

Monsieur Sorbonne left the house and, after dropping the film tin off at the Films Development Store, went out for a walk. He wanted to think things over; he needed to recompose himself.

Mademoiselle Objet's high decibel performances were very troublesome indeed. They scared him half to death. He wondered if they would improve or worsen over time. Had the enchanting Ms. Hyde become a Mademoiselle Jekyll overnight, and would she go on forever changing back and forth? That was the question, and yet, in spite of the question, she did have a point. He *had* been gone long hours at the Artifacts Museum; she *had* run out of things at home to arrange and rearrange, and her rash *was* truly irksome. Thinking about it now he realized in fact that it was more than merely irksome. It was frightening. Scratching it as she did, she was ruining her pretty hands.

And what about him? Why *did* he stay so long afterhours at the Artifacts Museum? Did he love it, sorting out pot shards? No. Did he love it, designing backdrops for *plus*-ancient things? Not particularly.

He realized, as he contemplated it now, that he stayed so long at his work because he hoped that by staying so late, his work would start to have meaning. It hadn't, though, come to have any meaning. It had just taken up time and saddened and frightened Mademoiselle Objet with his absence. It was paying the bills, that was all. It did nothing for his spirit. Was it possible, he wondered, ever to have a work that had meaning, that nourished your spirit, that gave you the sense that your life had a purpose? Or would work always be only work—the thing you did to pay the rent, to buy the clothes, the food, and all the distractions from work that enabled you to go on working?

Contemplating all this got Monsieur Sorbonne somewhat riled up, and, stopping at a Coffee Restaurant, he sat down at a small corner table and ordered a large cafe creme and a chocolate charlotte.

On the table next to him lay the first edition of the evening news. Fingering through it while waiting for his mini-repast to be served, he stumbled upon an ad:

> *Organizer of objects, chaoses, and mélanges.*
> *Office magician needed. Desperately. And at once.*

It was odd, the ad, he thought, but it seemed perfect for Mademoiselle Objet, and after he picked up the film, he would carry it home.

∽

CHAPTER 13

Mademoiselle Objet Is Penitent

When Mademoiselle Objet got home she was very penitent indeed. She was glad beyond words that she had found Madame Métier and that she had obtained the medicinal cremes, for although it was only minutes ago that she had administered the premier application of the creme, her hands seemed already to have somewhat improved.

Just the same, she was still feeling bad about how she had treated Monsieur Sorbonne. Her explosions frightened her. They seemed to come up out of nowhere and she always wondered if this time she had gone too far. When would she cross the small invisible line in his heart, the point from which he couldn't recover, and what could she possibly do to recompense him for her tirades? Worrying thus, she heard the turn of his key in the lock.

She was so overjoyed to hear it, that at once she raced to the door and threw her arms around him. "I'm so sorry, sorry, sorry" she said, "for everything! You know how I am—I get to a point and then I just go over the bend. I'm so sorry!" she said once again, but before he could get a word in edgewise, she pressed on . . . "But I did go and find that Métier woman. I got us both some medicine. Mine's already working and yours . . ."

"Settle down," said Monsieur Sorbonne. Her apologetic hysteria was almost (but not quite) as hard to take as all her violent volcanoes of anger. "That's enough," he said, and he sat her down on a chair. "Let's start all over. I'm glad you're sorry. Thank you. I *do* hate the way you carry on—frankly, it scares me to death. But I also need to apologize. I *have* been gone too much and you *do* need some things to arrange. So here," he said. "Look at this," and, kissing her on the forehead, he handed her the newspaper with the curious ad.

∾

CHAPTER 14

Mademoiselle Objet Speaks with Madame Métier

Mademoiselle Objet slept peacefully next to Monsieur Sorbonne, who also slept peacefully after dabbing the special creme under his eyes. In the morning they had a nice breakfast of teacakes and tea, and afterward, when Monsieur Sorbonne had departed for the Artifacts Museum, Mademoiselle Objet rang up the number in the ad.

"How can I help you?" asked Madame Métier on the other end of the line.

"No, you don't understand," said Mademoiselle Objet, who was astonished to discover that it was Madame Métier who had answered the phone. "I'm calling to help *you*. I'm answering your ad. For an organizer of objects, an arranger of items. It's me, Mademoiselle Objet. I was there with you with my scratched-up hands just yesterday."

"How wonderful and odd," said Madame Métier. "How amusing and delightful, and how fortunate it's you. Then you certainly don't need me to explain. You've already seen it. You saw it all yesterday." She laughed the lovely, smooth, flutey musical laugh that Mademoiselle Objet had heard first yesterday, and which had already started to carry in her heart the sweet faint joy of a small familiarity.

"Can I come right now?" asked the enthusiastic Mademoiselle Objet.

At the other end of the phone, Madame Métier distinctly paused. She was suddenly wary. There would be plenty of time to "make order" as her mother had always called it. There would be days and weeks and years of tidying up, she could feel it. Thinking of this she felt suddenly sad, as if somewhere inside she knew that an era was ending, that soon she would have to become more focused on her work. She wanted one more high-noon picnic on the beach.

"Not now. Not just yet," she bargained. "I have an important appointment at noon. Come tomorrow at nine."

"No, not tomorrow!" said Mademoiselle Objet. "Today! Let's start today. I'm already ready. Besides, I've seen your room. I want to get going!"

"Well, then, if you must come today," said Madame Métier, conceding, "come at three."

"At three," said the suddenly overly effervescent Mademoiselle Objet. "I can't wait!" she said, and happily hung up the phone.

∼

CHAPTER 15

Madame Métier Contemplates Her New Situation

Knowing that help was on the way, Madame Métier felt immensely relieved. A spirit of lightness overcame her. It was happiness beyond happy that she should not, in the end, have to "pick up after herself." For she had known all along that, in spite of her multitude of efforts, this was the one thing in life she would never be able to accomplish.

Once at the beach she felt very contemplative indeed as, sipping her soda, she sat with her back against the rock. The clouds, as usual, were magical, moving Isadora Duncan-ish against the high *ciel* of blue, and as she gazed at them again, she was gradually taken over by the sense that somehow things were changing, that from this day forward, everything in her life would be different. She didn't know how exactly, but she could feel it. This Mademoiselle Objet would give her the kind of assistance that would allow her to thoroughly work on her cremes.

She realized, too, that in some ways she had never taken her cremes to heart, that is to say, had never taken her cremes work seriously. She had enjoyed concocting them and talking about them once or twice on the local TeleVisions station. She had liked, a few days ago, getting some from-the-public orders for her cremes. But when she thought about it really, she had liked even more sitting beside that silent young man in his hospital bed a few days ago—by the way, she must go back and see him again. Still, overall she had a great uncertainty about the value of her cremes, almost as if in some far small corner of her mind, like her husband the doctor, she, too, pooh-poohed them.

But getting help, having your life's work become so big that somebody else was working for you, was, in one's life, a serious step. Thus, as she sat there, munching the last of her rose-potato crisps, along with being excited, she was also feeling a pang of regret. Now she would *have* to make cremes. Now they would *have* to be good. Now she would *have* to succeed. Now she could no longer sit at the hospital bed of whomever she pleased for as long as she liked, daydreaming about her father and contemplating the mysteries of life and death.

She would have responsibilities now. And more work. And work was hard work, an undertaking to be sure, of very checkered attributes, some of which, as she thought of them now, seemed quite intimidating. Work, even a chosen work, was a structure. It shaped your days and told you who you were in certain ways. It gave you an identity. It was a freedom and a cage.

These all were weighty thoughts for Madame Métier. Thinking them, her eyelids became very heavy, and leaning back against her rock, she fell asleep.

∾

CHAPTER 16

Madame Métier Is Observed

"*You are very beautiful when you* sleep," said a voice melodic and deep, which, vaguely, Madame Métier recognized. She looked up and sitting beside her very still as, indeed, he had been for quite some time, was the young man with the round blue eyes who only a few days ago had given her the shell.

She saw him now more closely. He was young, much younger than she, although she could not guess his age. His hair, a slightly darker blonde than her own, was threaded minutely with white, but the whole of him, his strong limbs, his long hands, his smile so open and clear, and his spirit, the way it seemed not to have been too much dragged down by life, seemed young.

"You are very beautiful when you sleep," he said once again. "I've been here quite a while, just watching you, the way your eyes beneath their lids move gracefully, back and forth, back and forth, as if watching the long graceful movements of an elegant ancient dance."

How interesting, she thought. He was describing, precisely, the way she had perceived his movements the first time she saw him walking toward her on the beach.

"How interesting," she said. "*You* move like that. I must have been watching you in my sleep."

"I don't notice my movements," he said, "I notice you."

He had changed his position, and now pulling himself up closer beside her, looked into her eyes. "I see things are changing," he said. "The other day you were upset. Today you're different—concerned. You made the ad and now big changes are coming. New things are beginning. In your work. You fear for yourself." He looked off down the beach in the direction of the sun. Finally he said, "May I put my arm around you?"

Because she could feel that she trusted him—there was something about him so familiar—Madame Métier sat forward a little from her rock, and he very knowingly wrapped his arm around her shoulder. "You fear for yourself as a woman," he said. "Don't worry over this. There will be many miracles."

For the teeniest moment she allowed herself to lean into him, to rest her shoulder against his strong governing arm. She felt safe there, protected and soft, and this, to her, was a very good feeling. In fact, she wanted it never to end, but just as she was having this thought, he withdrew his arm and looked into her eyes. "Thank you for letting me watch you sleep," he said. "You look so beautiful when you sleep."

Then he stood up, and with long, elegant, dancer-like movements, he walked off slowly down the beach.

∼

CHAPTER 17

Madame Métier Goes Once Again to the Hospital

Feeling strangely moved by her encounter with the young man at the beach—*he is an angel,* she thought, *not a person; he carries such light in his eyes*—Madame Métier, seeing that there was still time, felt suddenly inspired to stop on her way home to see the young man in the hospital.

She put on the crumpled blue dress she kept in the bottom of her picnic basket for just such unexpected occasions, and when she arrived at the hospital, made her way directly to his room.

He was still there, and asleep. She pulled up a chair and sat down beside him, and taking his hands into hers, she looked very deeply at him. There was an unearthly tranquility about him. Cut off as he was from the troubles of the mind, he lay there placid and unmoving. How different he was from the young man she had just seen on the beach, the Angel One, who wore his life so easily. How strange it all was. How truly odd and utterly mysterious—life and death and the place beyond life, and how thin the line between them. That line seemed to melt, to have been dissolved in the being of this young man, whose soul still hovered in his body, which, according to medical definitions, was really no longer alive. How strange. She didn't know what to make of it, but it pleased her, nevertheless, to be sitting here beside him again, quietly holding his hands.

Without thinking, she started humming a wordless song. It climbed up softly out of her, and as she hummed, she felt what seemed to be a tremor in his hands, a quickening pulse of energy that vibrated into her own. It was strange to have movement come from where no movement was expected, unnerving to have things not be the way she imagined they should have been. He was, for all intents, dead. That's what the nurse had told her; but now he showed signs of life. It was unsettling, but just as she completed this thought his hands relaxed and once again lay limp on her own.

She looked at her watch. It was already 2:30. Mademoiselle Objet was coming at 3:00, was probably already on her way. Despite the actual time—in this room it seemed that there was no time—Madame Métier felt a sudden strange urge to sing him a song. *Who knows how long he'll be here*, she thought. *Maybe they'll pull the plugs out tomorrow, and I'll never see him again.* And so she started singing a song her father had taught her when she was young.

Her father had often sung the song as they walked together among the roses, but she had never noticed the words. She had just walked along beside him, holding his hand and being so happy to be there with him. But now as she sang, the words came back to her one by one, and she herself also heard them.

> *Oh, rose divine, whose fragrance sweet*
> *Our hearts embrace, our souls secure*
> *Surround us with your breath so pure*
> *And when we die our spirits greet;*

She sang the verse and as she came to the end of it, she felt once again—and she could scarcely believe this—a certain movement in the young man's hands. This time it was more than a tremor. She could feel him distinctly, almost with pleading, squeezing her hand.

This quite unnerved her. This young man who was supposed to be dead had made distinctly a gesture of living. Had he heard her or felt her, she wondered, or were these simply the last involuntary twitches of dying? She finished the rest of the verses:

> *And when the rose*
> *Envelopes us, our selves*
> *Dissolve, our souls arise*
> *We move into that essence*

> *Bright that lies within*
> *Our living eyes.*
>
> *And so we drop the*
> *Clothes of life, this body*
> *So miraculous, to*
> *Find a body made of*
> *Light—the jewel escapes*
> *What turns to dust.*
>
> *Oh sacred rose, whose fragrance*
> *Sweet, our hearts embrace*
> *Our souls secure,*
> *Give us the grace to die*
> *In peace, so we may*
> *Wake to live in joy.*

When she had finished, she laid his hands out beside him on either side of the bed, and quietly tiptoed out of the room.

〜

CHAPTER 18

Mademoiselle Objet Is Distraught

When Madame Métier arrived home, Mademoiselle Objet, standing at her front door and twirling in anxious circles, was distraught.

"Where have you been?" she asked, almost reprimandingly. "I was beginning to think—although I know it isn't possible—that I had come to the wrong house. It's twenty-two minutes after three," she went on, again reprimandingly. "You said we would meet here at three."

"I'm early then," said Madame Métier. "And I'm sorry. I forgot to tell you that as a rule I'm always seven minutes late. Unless, of course, it's a special occasion—in which case I'm even later." She smiled and unlocked the door, and Mademoiselle Objet, still slightly disgruntled, followed her in.

"So now that we understand about the timing," said Madame Métier, "let's go upstairs."

Mademoiselle Objet, who was thoroughly prepared—she had come with an attaché case filled with cards, notebooks, notebook dividers, pencils, and pens with which to diagnose the situation—was also (to say the least) a little put out by her new employer's appearance. Through the open neck of the indigo dress that Madame Métier was wearing, Mademoiselle Objet could detect, she was sure, the criss-crossing straps of a red bathing suit. How careless and odd, she thought to herself, to be out beach-bathing on a day committed to office organization.

When they got to the workroom, Mademoiselle Objet could further see that Madame Métier had done exactly nothing to prepare. The room was in the same obstreperous ghastly array that it had been in yesterday.

This also unnerved the fragile Mademoiselle. She could feel her already precarious balance slightly beginning to fray.

"I know you wish I'd done more," said Madam Métier, "by way of preparing, but you see, organizational efforts of whatever kind, preparatory or terminal, are precisely what I cannot do. So here," she said, taking Mademoiselle Objet's attaché case decisively from her hands and setting it down in the middle of the workroom floor, "let's have a few quiet minutes together before we begin, and then I can give you my undivided attention."

Taking her by the hand, she sat the fractured Mademoiselle once again on the couch where she had sat just yesterday. When she was settled, Madame Métier took both of her hands, like two shivering birds into her own hands, and quietly, for the longest time, held them. When at last they had stopped shaking, she passed her own hands very softly across them, then laid them on Mademoiselle Objet's lap.

"There," she said. "Now we can begin."

Mademoiselle Objet, who, unbeknownst to herself, had closed her eyes, now opened them and looked about the room. She felt remarkably serene and composed, and the workroom, which before had seemed totally out of control, an absolute ruin, now seemed like a wonderful playground. Even the straps of the red bathing suit peeking out from the neck of Madame Métier's indigo dress seemed delightful and amusing.

Once settled, Mademoiselle Objet went right away to work. Retrieving her attaché case from the middle of the floor, she pulled out various organizational devices. The first was a series of file cards on which she had written some questions. With these in hand, in an uncharacteristically authoritative manner, she took over. "What are you trying to do here?" she asked. "What are your most important projects? And what do you do in the morning?"

"In answer to the first question," Madame Métier responded, "I am trying to develop various medicinal cremes by harnessing the healing properties of living or once-living things. I don't know how healing occurs, but I don't believe it happens through chemical medicines. I am exploring the process of healing."

Listening, Mademoiselle Objet, was, in her very fine hand, taking notes on each card on which she had written a question.

"What are your most important projects?" she asked next.

"The development of my cremes," said Madame Métier. "And perhaps some research. To discover if, after all, they do have benefit."

"What do you do in the morning?"

To this question, Madame Métier, slightly, took umbrage. What business was it of hers what she did in the morning, and what did her morning routine have to do with the disastrous condition of her room? Thinking about it, she felt a nasty little clamp-like pinch in her brain, which was a clue, she surmised, that something of note would be revealed if, truthfully, she answered the question.

"I wake up when I wake up," she said. "I never *make* myself wake up. With an alarm device or anything else. I lie in my bed and look out the window at the leaves of the apricot tree—they're very beautiful, you know, heart-shaped," she said dreamily. "I look at the leaves until I see some things. Then, when I have seen enough, I get up. I do my morning oblations. I make some cucumber juice. I eat my cereals. I sit in my white wicker chair and have tea. I think strong blessing thoughts in my heart for my friends—and for all the suffering ones. And then, when it is given to me, I turn to my work."

"When it is given to you . . . ?" said Mademoiselle Objet.

"The sense, the message about which recipe to make, or some new recipe to try. When it is given to me, then I start working here, in the workroom."

"For what hours have you scheduled your clean-up?

"I haven't. There are none. Cleaning up holds no interest for me. It progresses nothing. It moves nothing forward. It simply returns you again and again to the self same place you have come from. This, of course, can explain . . ." she laughed her melodic tinkling laugh once again, "how my room has attained its present condition."

"I understand," said Mademoiselle Objet, trying, and succeeding very well indeed for her, to suppress the considerable degree to which she was appalled. "No clean-up time," she said. "You can't run a business—or a life, for that matter—without any clean-up time."

"I suppose that's true," said Madame Métier, "but I think it a pity that the essence of most lives is clean-up time—cleaning up the house and the desk, cleaning the car, cleaning the cupboards, the yard, the clothes, one's hair. It's endless, the permutations of cleaning-upness required by a single life.

"Making cremes is what holds interest for me. Change. Possibilities. Creation. The mysteries of healing. Unfortunately, or fortunately"—she laughed at her own somewhat bizarre predicament—"I have never been able to locate in myself any talent whatsoever for cleaning up."

"Then analyzing the problem won't help us, will it?" said Mademoiselle Objet.

"That's correct."

"So how can I possibly help you?"

"I don't know exactly. But not by analysis and not by scheduling."

Having thus been relieved of her two prime assistance techniques, something crumpled inside Mademoiselle Objet. Her plan, it was clear, could not be applied in this circumstance. It was upsetting, losing her bearings like this, but there was also, she noticed, a strange kind of happy freedom to it. "Well then," she said, "let's just clean up your table."

"What a wonderful idea," said Madame Métier. "I'd love to. How do we do it?"

Once again, Mademoiselle Objet was agog. This very unusual woman was really quite remarkable. She didn't know how to clean up her own table.

"It's simple," said Mademoiselle Objet. "You just look at each thing on your table and then put it where it belongs."

"That's actually very complicated," said Madame Métier. "It is that, precisely, which I cannot do. I wouldn't know how to begin."

Thus it was that, very patiently, really—for her three-pronged interview had revealed that here, in Madame Métier, Mademoiselle Objet had encountered a specimen of stellar-grade incompetence, domestic-wise, and that she herself would have to take the situation in hand—Mademoiselle Objet assisted Madame Métier to look at, sort, decide about, toss out, or catalog and organize the entire contents of her table.

As the day wore on, she picked up every leaf, twig, petal, and frond, ascertained what purpose it served, devised a container for it and a place to stow the container, and if neither existed, added it, with a description of its peculiar properties to the Requirements List of storage items and/or preservative solutions to be eventually obtained.

All in all, it was a pleasant undertaking. Madame Métier was encouraged as, gradually, the ancient wooden surface of her work table top emerged, and Mademoiselle Objet once again felt useful. In fact, she felt useful in a way she never quite had before. For, straightening her parents' house, endlessly throwing her father's wine bottles away, even organizing her own little house with Monsieur Sorbonne had never quite connected her to anything.

Here she felt connected to something, although she wasn't sure just what. But there was something about this Madame Métier and her cremes which she found deeply satisfying, and helping her get "set up" so she could develop more cremes had meaning for Mademoiselle Objet. For although she herself had no understanding whatsoever of either botany or medicine, she sensed that something important was happening here. Her own hands were the testament.

"There, I think that's enough for today," said Mademoiselle Objet, who had now put everything back on the table in orderly rows. "Except for this shell. Which doesn't quite seem to belong. Shall we throw it away?"

"Oh, no! Not the shell." said Madame Métier, whose demeanor seemed suddenly to be verging on panic. "It's very important. It definitely has to stay."

"But what for? It doesn't belong to any of the other categories of things. It's not a botanical item. It's not a good storage container either. Look," she said, "the petals in it have all gotten dusty. They're ruined."

"It was a gift," said Madame Métier. "It's the only thing, as a matter of fact, which I am certain belongs. And its placement is at the very center of the table."

It was strange, Madame Métier's being here at the end, so emphatic and clear about the placement of something. To Mademoiselle Objet the shell was a totally irrelevant item, but after Madame Métier had placed it at the center of her work things, she had to agree that it stood there like a sentinel presence which lent the work table a lovely kind of symmetry.

The workroom looked completely different. Mademoiselle Objet felt a deep sense of satisfaction, and within herself a certain unusual calm.

"You have done a magnificent thing here," said Madame Métier. "You have created a brand new room with your energy and your imagination."

"I just cleaned up," said Mademoiselle Objet.

"No, you have invented. With a heart. Tomorrow, because of you, my work will be different. Each thing will begin from a quite different place because of how you've arranged things, and so it shall also arrive in time at quite a different destination. Thank you," she said. "I'll call you soon to come again."

∼

CHAPTER 19

Monsieur Sorbonne and Mademoiselle Objet Have a Happy Reunion

When Mademoiselle Objet got home, the little house was filled with a wonderful fragrance. Having contemplated the meaning of his work—that it was meaningless—having picked up the photographs of Mademoiselle Objet he'd dropped off, and feeling relieved by the possibility of Mademoiselle Objet's employment, Monsieur Sorbonne had gone to the gourmand's food store, collected a fine selection of items, and was now preparing a sumptuous dinner.

So happy was Mademoiselle Objet about her afternoon's work that although it was late when she finally walked in the door, she changed from her work clothes and put on the seal-gray wool dress she had worn the first night they went out to dinner.

Monsieur Sorbonne lit candles and put on some music, piano gavottes, on their Victrola instrument, and Mademoiselle Objet very graciously served up the items of food which he had so cleverly prepared.

"You seem different, calm, almost peaceful tonight," said Monsieur Sorbonne as she sat down across the table from him. "It's nice to see you this way."

"It's quite simple, really," said Mademoiselle Objet. "I'm beginning to understand. When I have things to arrange, I'm happy. My hands stop itching and I can keep my temper in place. And if I don't, well, you know what can happen. It's strange, but spending the day with this Madame Métier and her mess seemed to change things. I feel different."

This was all most odd, thought Monsieur Sorbonne. Mademoiselle Objet seemed to be in some other state, not quite herself, so quiet and composed she was.

"But did you do any work?" he asked her finally. "And did you get a job?"

"Yes, we did do some work, but I don't really know if I did get a job," said Mademoiselle Objet. "The time just went by, and then it was past eight o'clock. And then I came home. All I know is that now I feel peaceful. I had a nice time."

"I'm happy," said Monsieur Sorbonne, 'that something has changed."

"So am I," said Mademoiselle Objet. "I wish this could be a real job, that just once, for a long time, like a profession, I could have things to arrange. Consistency. That's what I need. A routine. Day after day with the same things the same." She got up then, and cleared the dishes away.

When they had finished their special desserts—strawberry crêpes Suzette and Viennese coffee—he opened the white floss envelope containing the photographs. There, inside it, as if she had never once crabbed or screamed or squawked or scared him half to death, captured in all her loveliness, was Mademoiselle Objet.

Her pretty hands were touching her face; she was smiling ever so slightly. She looked peaceful, and although they were black-and-white photographs, there was a distinctly bluish cast to the crystal heart locket, which hung around her neck.

⌇

CHAPTER 20

Madame Métier Goes to the Hospital Again

So heartened was she by the ordering of her room, that the following morning after her usual ceremonies, Madame Métier decided to once again visit the young man in the hospital.

As usual, she pulled up a chair, sat down beside him, and took his hands into hers. His hands were motionless today, unrepentingly still, and as she held them she felt unbearably sad. It was strange, holy, to be in his midst. She was witnessing a mystery and she knew it. His body still partook of life, but his spirit—who knew where it was? Was it like a kite on a string, already somewhere far out in the clouds, already beautifully dancing? In the absolute simplicity of his present stripped condition, he embodied life as only itself, life as just being, pure being.

She knew that soon they would pull off his wires and he would be gone—no more the mysterious silent young man, no longer a man, no longer even a human being. Being overtaken by this thought—that any day now his whole humanness would vanish—she suddenly wanted—as if he as himself were still somehow inside his body, somehow still a person—to say goodbye to him. Closing her eyes and still holding his hands, she began very softly to speak to him.

"I don't know you," she said, "who you are or what your name is, how you came to this condition . . ." She said these words and the young man lay there motionless, immobile on the bed, not a flicker from his closed eyes, not a twitch of his hands. "But I have come here to thank you, because you have touched me very deeply."

"I came here in need, when I was discouraged. My father died in this room; I came here hoping that somehow he would give me a message.

Instead, I found you. You lay here silent and still and allowed me to be in your presence, to sing to you, to touch your head with my hands. This touching and singing was good for my soul. And so I have wanted to thank you." She paused. "Thank you," she whispered. "Thank you very much."

She had just finished these words when his hands seemed ever so slightly to start to wake up. They moved a little, and then as she watched, they moved once again. She could feel the tiny electric impulse she had felt in them just yesterday, starting to spread once again, like the faintest river of energy throughout them.

She was amazed, but went on. "I came here in need. I came to receive. But instead you allowed me to give. And my heart has been filled by this giving. It's a wonderful thing—a gift in itself—when someone receives what you have to give, and you have done that very beautifully. Received my gift . . . and so, very deeply, I thank you. My soul also thanks you," she whispered.

Once again—amazing, but it was true—his hand squeezed back in a kind of distinct acknowledgment.

"I don't know where you're going," she went on quietly, "when you are going, or if the journey will be easy, but I did want you to know . . . that my love will go with you. Thank you for staying as long as you did. And thank you for receiving my gift."

She felt overtaken by an immense and tender sadness as she said this. Great round tears rolled down her cheeks and dropped in small luminous puddles on his pale, still hands. No more words were given to her, and yet she still felt unready to leave. And so she stayed on as the dark light shifted throughout the room, making faint patterns on the walls, the sheets, the tubes, his hands.

And then—and she could scarcely believe this—from somewhere, inexplicably, though clearly from inside the room, she heard a small sound of crying, and then in a gurgling whisper, as if rising up through earth or through water, the words: "Thank you. I have waited so long to be loved."

She opened her eyes and looked up at the young man in the bed, at his still, expressionless face. His hands in her hands were warm now, and seemed, distinctly, to be holding on dearly to hers; and when she looked at his face once again—and she could absolutely not believe this—he seemed to be smiling.

So startled was she by these curious, untoward happenings, that she sat there awhile in silence. But no other sounds came, and although she sat there for many more minutes, he continued to lie there motionless. Finally, she felt ready to go. She slipped her hands free from his. "To where you are going, great love goes with you," she said once again. Then she passed her hands in a windward motion one last time across his face.

"Thank you," said the voice rising through earth, rising through water, "I can feel it."

Madame Métier was stunned. She stood up then, and quietly turned away and then very slowly walked out of the room.

∾

PART III

Chapter I

Madame Métier and Mademoiselle Objet

Three months had passed, and having been so heartened by the initial reorganization of her room, Madame Métier decided to employ Mademoiselle Objet half-time. Thus it was that daily, having done her ordering of the little house she shared with Monsieur Sorbonne, Mademoiselle Objet would go to Madame Métier's, assist her this way and that, organizing botanical items, transcribing recipes, packing and mailing out cremes, and answering the phone.

Because of her help, Madame Métier had stepped up her work. She had developed several new cremes. Word of her work was beginning to spread. More people were calling to try out her cremes. The television station, having heard once again of her work, called to schedule some interviews and asked if she would make a weekly TV program.

This was very gratifying indeed. Mademoiselle Objet was happy because, given this flutter of activity, she felt assured of her job, which she so very much enjoyed. Working for Madame Métier, she observed, had considerably improved her hands. In fact, in contemplating them somewhat mindlessly one night, she realized that her rash was entirely gone. This seemed quite remarkable because, to her recollection, it had only very infrequently that she had applied the medicinal cremes.

She was content. Joy of joys, she had endless items to catalogue, surfaces to tidy, objects to arrange. And it just went on and on. She never finished her work because there were endless interruptions in the workroom. Having heard the TeleVisions broadcasts, people would simply show up at the door, uninvited, with aching arms and pains across their heart, a blind spot in one eye or fogginess in both, a life-long stiff neck or fingers that wouldn't unbend. And with infinite patience—far too infinite, Mademoiselle Objet once opined—Madame Métier would shepherd them in, lead them up the stairs, and then bring them into the Seeing Room.

"The Seeing Room?" Mademoiselle Objet had asked her once, her eyebrows raised and a little turned sideways.

"Yes, the room where I see them," said Madame Métier, as if all this were actually quite self-evident. The workroom was now so crowded, what with Mademoiselle Objet and all the new cremes that Madame Métier had precipitously opened a bedroom across the hall and turned it into a room where she could, in private, see them. She would take them into the Seeing Room, set them down on a couch or a chair, and let them discuss their ailments. She would make her acquaintance with their complaint by waving a hand like a wing across its painful location, and, once having done this, would barge back into the workroom, rummage through Mademoiselle Objet's tidily stacked and half-packed boxes, toppling jars, dislocating orders and from time to time disrupting even her own botanical piles. Then, having found the appropriate creme, she would make off with it and disappear across the hall into the Seeing Room.

Mademoiselle Objet was both happy and unhappy about these trains of events. It was wonderful, she thought, the way that all the people showed up, because rarely, if ever, did anyone return who had once been administered a creme. On the other hand, these interruptions were . . . well . . . interruptions. They made it difficult for her to keep her objects in place, to mail out all the packages and answer the phone.

It was always the same. The To-Be-Seens would arrive. They would walk up the stairs and then into the Seeing Room. After a while, Mademoiselle Objet would hear things getting very quiet. Sometimes she could faintly detect the familiar sound of the opening of a cremes jar, then a silence (during which she supposed Madame Métier was applying the creme), then afterwards, as if from some strange ancient well, the melodic speaking of words:

"Applying the creme will not be sufficient; you must also open your heart. Someone has wounded you, whom now you need to forgive.

"Here, look at these troubled, folded-up fingers. You must use your hands for giving as well as for taking.

"Relax. A neck is to bend, to be willowy and swanlike, to move with the magic of living.

"Your eyes, my dear—a blind spot—you can't see yourself with compassion." Or, "That fog in your eyes—there's something you don't want to see—the sorrow, too, in other people's lives."

These little meetings would go on and Mademoiselle Objet, across the hall, would feel always a mixture of peace and irritation. She was irritated by the endless interruptions and untoward upheaval of her objects, and yet at times she herself felt strangely mesmerized, as if the cells in her body had taken on a slightly different attitude, been ever so minutely rearranged.

One day, after a great many To-Be-Seens, she was especially fretful and impatient. Why were there always so many of them? Why did it all take so long? Why did Madame Métier never have any time to help her in the workroom? She could organize it by herself, but with all her in-and-out bargings, Madame Métier continually disarranged things. Sometimes she wanted to scream. Thinking this, she could feel, oncoming, the telltale itch of her hands. She started to scratch and in no time at all she had scratched her hands raw once again.

"What a busy, over-exhausting day," said Madame Métier, coming in for the final time to the workroom. "Come, let's have tea. We need a few minutes together before you go home"

"So tell me, are you happy with your work?" she asked, as they sat together half an hour later at the kitchen table, sipping rose petal tea and looking out through the small paned windows, beyond which the apricot tree was in bloom.

"I am," said Mademoiselle Objet, a little tentatively. "I do like my work. I like arranging things." She was about to launch into the list of her complaints, but before she could even get started, Madame Métier dived in.

"I'm so glad then," she said, "because without you I couldn't go on with my cremes. You are a magician, a wizard of helpfulness. Because of your genius . . ." And here she looked out the window where in the palest pink the apricot blossoms daintily festooned the naked elegant branches of the little tree. ". . . I can go on to develop more cremes, to address the manifold hurts and ailings in the world, and to finally discover, in all their miraculous magic, the remedial healing properties that reside in all these beautiful plants.

"Isn't that wonderful," she said, so happily concluding, her voice like a beautiful musical bell.

Mademoiselle Objet wasn't sure. She'd had a terrible day. She'd scratched her hands to shreds and endured the upending of several small boxes of petals and twigs when Madame Métier had come fluttering in to pick out some cremes. She was desperate to complain, but, once again, before she could start, Madame Métier continued.

"And you, my dear, you are the one who makes it all possible," she said. "With your magician's hands." And here she reached across the table and ever so softly took Mademoiselle Objet's really very scratched up hands into her own.

"I do like my job," said Mademoiselle Objet, finally getting a word in edgewise, "but I'm upset! In fact, I see that I'm jealous. I thought it was all the chaos, all the spilled and disarranged things, but now I see it's the non-stop, endless parade of all the To-Be-Seens. They just show up whenever they want and you just let them in. I can't stand it! They're getting soothed. They're getting healed with your cremes, and I'm all alone in the workroom, scratching my hands to ribbons!"

"I'm sorry," said Madame Métier. "I know that must be difficult— doing all the tasks of the day by yourself. I can understand why you might be jealous. But, unfortunately, they are here with their needs, and that's the nature of human suffering. It doesn't happen on schedule, and it doesn't lend itself well to organization and control."

As she spoke, Madame Métier seemed not exactly to be speaking directly to Mademoiselle Objet. Rather, with her white-blonde hair spilling off to one side, she had turned away and was staring out the kitchen window, as if apprehending petal by petal, each individual apricot blossom.

When she had finished speaking and turned her face back into the room, there was a cloud of what appeared to be millions of smaller than pinpoint fragments of light suspended around her. Her whole body, its edges, the seams of her clothes, the memorable angles of her cheekbones, her hair, indeed all her physical dimensions, seemed, as Mademoiselle Objet observed them, to have melted out of focus and all she could see, suspended in the formless luminous haze, were the huge blue circles of Madame Métier's eyes.

"So I want to thank you, ever so much and so dearly," Madame Métier said finally, patting Mademoiselle Objet's hands one final time and then releasing them, "for all you do for me." She laughed a little, tinklingly. "And the plants thank you, too. For so long, I believe, they have wanted to be recognized for their mysterious healing properties."

Mademoiselle Objet was scarcely able to hear this. Her hands now felt strangely alive and tinglingly warm. In fact, when she looked down at them, they were no longer scratched up and raw, but perfectly smooth, and she herself felt mysteriously calm. She wondered what had just happened; but when she looked at Madame Métier once again, she was just sitting there across from her at the kitchen table, her white-blonde hair nicely framing her face, her hand on the loop of the teacup looking exactly, precisely and only, like herself.

Mademoiselle Objet was confused. Had the light cloud not happened? Had her hands not only moments ago been in ruins? Had she not felt the mysterious tingling in her hands, and were her scratched-up hands now not once again restored to perfection? In uncharacteristic silence, she finished her tea. Then, looking across at Madame Métier, she found herself wondering for a moment if perhaps it wasn't the plants, but Madame Métier herself who had the mysterious healing properties.

∼

CHAPTER 2

Madame Métier Is Encouraged

As time went on, Madame Métier felt an overflowing sense of joy about her work, and feeling her own good fortune reminded her, in contrast, of the wired-up young man in her father's hospital room. It had been weeks now since she had seen him. She had been so engrossed in her work, with the training and acclimatization of Mademoiselle Objet, that she had all but forgotten about him. Or, feeling the hopelessness of his situation, had she quite intentionally put him out of her mind?

Thinking of him suddenly and sadly one early morning when she was buying calla lilies at the Flower Vendor's Stand, she decided to stop by and see him—if indeed he was still there.

Walking down the hospital halls toward room 5244 and carrying the stately calla lilies, Madame Métier felt suddenly bereft, sensing that she had arrived too late to say a final farewell and instead, had come here to mourn him. When she approached she saw that the door to his room stood open, but when she looked inside, the room itself was empty. The green shades were drawn half-down and, in the empty room, on the empty bed, pillowless, but freshly made, the white sheets had been stretched so tight that for a moment the bed looked like a catafalque.

Tears streamed down her cheeks. As if it were his grave, she laid the calla lilies down across the foot of the bed. Then, shaken, she left the room and started down the hall.

"Can I help you, Madam?" asked the nurse who was standing at the door.

"No, thank you," said Madame Métier.

"Were you looking for someone?" the nurse persisted.

"Not exactly. Although there was someone . . . she turned backward, pointing to the empty room.

"Ah yes, 5244. Now I remember you," said the nurse. "You did look familiar. The young man . . . you used to visit him. He's gone. His parents came and took him away."

The minute she heard the words, Madame Métier could see that for several weeks now, she had been expecting the news—that they had finally pulled out the plugs. What a mercy it was in the end—such an ordeal. He'd been trapped in his body so long.

"Yes, most remarkable," said the nurse, interrupting. "They took him home two weeks ago. In fact, just a few days after you saw him, he started to open his eyes. And then he began to speak again. It was quite miraculous, really. The doctors were amazed."

"So now he's at home?" Madame Métier was incredulous.

"Yes, and doing quite well, so we hear. Up and even starting to walk. It really is a miracle."

"Thank you," said Madame Métier, and feeling an eclectic mixture of joy, uneasiness, and sorrow, she walked back into the room. Then, retrieving the calla lilies from the bed, she closed the door and started for home.

～

CHAPTER 3

Madame Métier Goes Home

When she got back to her workroom, calla lilies in hand, the morning was more than half over. Mademoiselle Objet, who had been there alone, had everything perfectly organized—the table, the jars on the table, the fronds, the pink phone call memos, to say nothing of a tidy stack of orders and miscellaneous items to be attended to.

"Look at the beautiful flowers! Those are incredible!" said Mademoiselle Objet, getting up from her chair, walking across the room and, with her pretty fingers, examining the edges of the stately calla lilies, which, like a scepter, Madame Métier was holding. "What are they? They're gorgeous. What do they cure? Do you have a recipe for them? Are you going to make a new creme? If you are, they'd be perfect for the TeleVisions show."

"They are calla lilies," said Madame Métier, slightly overwhelmed by this barrage. "As to their healing properties, I'm not quite sure yet what they're meant to cure. But I do know this—that they are the symbol of resurrection."

"Well, forget resurrection," said Mademoiselle Objet. "Put them in water. We've got a lot of work to do, answering all this fan mail. And isn't it wonderful," she said, "we have fourteen fan letters today! Everyone loves the new cremes. There were four letters on the rosebud creme alone. I'm so excited! I just love it! I'm so happy to be working here. I feel like we're doing something important. Those people who came here last week, those five To-Be-Seens, every one of them has already written to say that all their symptoms are gone, that their pain has been relieved. Isn't it wonderful!?" she said, emphatically again.

Madame Métier was somewhat overcome by all this effusive expressiveness. There were times, she thought, when Mademoiselle Objet's excitable aspects far more than outweighed her orderliness talents. Her excessive enthusiasm seemed, at times, quite overbearing, and especially now, when she herself felt confused. "I'm going to put these flowers in water," she said, and walking across the hall to her bedroom, installed the lilies in a crystal vase which she set to one side of the mirror on the white chest of drawers. Then she sat down for a moment on the northeast corner of her bed.

She was still caught up with the strange scene at the hospital. Room 5244. She felt foolish. She had, in effect, gone to wish the young man a good death. And then he hadn't died. After she had given up hope, the doctors and all those machines had effected a most remarkable cure. He was, if not entirely well now, certainly improved. Medical science had cured him.

Madame Métier was distraught. What, after all, was the point of her cremes? No one and nothing, it seemed, could hold a candle to the metallic wonders of modern medicine. Could a calendula creme hold its own against a respiration machine? Could a blessed thistle tea pull rank on a plastic feeding tube? He'd been getting better all along! And she'd been too stupid, too fixated on her cremes to even recognize it.

What a fool she was, to have ever imagined that cremes, in themselves, could actually heal anyone. Only medical science could do that. Her cremes were a topical ointment at best, and she an old-fashioned eccentric, enthralled by her father's botanical legacy, making cremes for her own esoteric enjoyment.

Having train-wrecked her mind with these harsh disparaging thoughts, she returned to the workroom, reeling.

Never had Mademoiselle Objet seen Madame Métier in quite such a mentally disheveled state. For the first time ever her mind seemed to be in the same sort of terrible disarray that her worktable always was. "What's happened? What's the matter with you!?" she asked.

Madame Métier pulled up the blue embroidered hassock and told Mademoiselle Objet the story—how she had found the young man, how he had been supposed to die, how they were going to pull out the plugs, how several times she had sat there with him, how she had put her hands on his forehead, how she had taken his hands into hers and told him good-bye, how weeks had passed, and how today, when she went again to see him, he was already gone. Not dead, but whole, healed and alive. How medical science had cured him.

Mademoiselle Objet, somewhat transfixed by Madame Métier's long accounting, the mellifluous lovely sound of her voice, though still listening, was twirling a tiger lily petal on the table with her index finger.

"I'm having a crisis of faith," Madame Métier concluded. "I feel as if everything that I've done—that I'm doing—is a total waste of time."

"That's not true," said Mademoiselle Objet. "I'm sure you had some effect. In fact, you're probably the reason why he's still alive." Then, as if she herself had unwittingly stumbled on something, she added, "You did it. Don't you see! You did it. You healed him!"

"No, I do not see," said Madame Métier. "And I did not. How could I have possibly healed him? Why, I didn't even bring in my cremes. That's what I've been trying to tell you. I never even applied to him any cremes of any sort. I administered no healing. I just sat there beside him, and sang him a song."

"Well, I see I can't convince you," said Mademoiselle Objet, "so let's at least answer these letters." She picked up the pile of fan letters. But Madame Métier had not the slightest interest. She sat on her blue embroidered hassock with a sad look in her eyes, in her mind running over the story of the dying-now-alive young man.

Madamemoiselle Objet looked at Madame Métier, who sat motionless on her hassock, her face as still as a looking glass. Finally, she said, "Well, I see that it's hopeless trying to get you to do any work. You're lost in your crisis of faith. You're useless. Why don't you just go to the beach and have an adventure?" she said a little cattily. "I'm going home." And with that, she put the tiger lily petal back in the dried petal box and picked up her purse.

"By the way," she said, finally heading for the stairs, "it isn't your stupid cremes that heal. *It's you!* Haven't you figured that out yet? *It's you!*—your presence—that heals everyone."

～

CHAPTER 4

Madame Métier Goes to The Beach

Madame Métier was upset. She was upset that she hadn't been able to work. She was upset by Mademoiselle Objet's upsetness, and even more that she had been the instrument of it and had caused her to go home. She was upset by the disappearance of the young man—to whom, if he was going to live after all, she would have wished to say good-bye. She was upset because, in view of the undeniable powers of modern medicine, she had to rethink in detail what she was doing with her cremes. And she was upset because Mademoiselle Objet had had a fit, maligned her cremes, and then had the absurd audacity to suggest that she herself might have something to do with the process of healing.

She put on her red bathing suit, and with only a bottle of crystals water and the small notebook in which, when things were troubling her, she sorted her feelings out, she headed for the beach.

It was already past noon. The sun had passed through its middle arc, and as she settled herself at the rock, she felt a vague sense of defeat, that old "square-one feeling" as she called it, the sensation of having, in *medias res,* to review a situation in its whole entirety, and then, once having reviewed it, perhaps having to start over . . . at square one.

Acknowledging this in itself brought a certain measure of relief. She opened her notebook, drew a large square and labeled it Square One. Then she made a few notes. Having reviewed her crisis of faith, she felt oddly renewed, as if she could either go on—or not—with her cremes. "To begin again," she wrote, in conclusion, "is a process of expansion, an act of faith." Then she drew a cheerful, almost exuberant arrow and beneath it wrote the words: "Now Anything is Possible."

Having thus righted herself, she closed her notebook, and, putting it into her basket, which she then hid in a cave in the rocks, she went for a walk down the beach. It was amazing, wasn't it, how looking at something directly, facing it and writing it down, could have so salubrious an effect. She felt free. Life was generous and kind. It would give her whatever she needed—more work with her cremes, or something entirely different. The sky was a luminous radiant blue, billow-spattered with clouds of translucent white. The sun warmed her body like a promise as, now feeling peaceful, she walked along.

Strolling thus, she felt a hand on her shoulder. "You look very beautiful as you walk," said a voice that by now was somewhat familiar. "Do you mind if I walk a while with you?"

It was the angel young man who had come up beside her.

"Of course not," she said. "In fact, it would be nice to have your company. Where did you come from?"

"I've been walking behind you for about a mile, but you were so lost in thought, or in something, that you didn't notice."

His footfalls, barefoot and quiet in the sand, repeated exactly her own. With his left hand he took hold of her right, and for a while, wordlessly, they walked on.

"This crisis that you think you're in," he said finally, as a warm breeze enfolded them both, "you don't have to change things. It isn't a crisis that calls for revisions. It's just another picture, a side-view confirmation of what you're doing.

"Until now you haven't had to decide if you really believe in your work. This was the first, how shall I call it? *Opportunity to believe.* Someday there will be others. To make your work more deep and true."

She had no idea what he was talking about, yet there was a powerful sincerity to what he had expressed.

"Thank you," she said, "for telling me."

"Thank you," he said, "for listening so deeply."

He squeezed her hand tightly, then let it go, and, turning to face her—his back to the rock wall alongside the beach, her back to the sea, the sunlight a luminous shimmering curtain between them—he looked into her eyes. Then reaching his arms out toward her he gathered her into a strong, encompassing embrace, and softly, knowingly, kissed her.

"I need to go now," he whispered. Then he turned, and with long, loping, beautiful strides, he walked away down the beach.

∼

CHAPTER 5

Mademoiselle Objet Has a Crisis of Faith

When Monsieur Sorbonne came home, Mademoiselle Objet, who had made herself a cup of tea, was sitting on the couch and desperately scratching her hands where, once again, her vicious rash had started to appear.

He was shocked, he had to admit, for, so long as she had been in Madame Métier's employ, her rash had been nonexistent. But before he could even inquire as to what was going on, she started telling him all about Madame Métier, how she had come in late to the workroom, calla lilies in hand—"a symbol of resurrection," she said cattily—and then instead of working had had what amounted to a breakdown.

"She wants me to help her. Her workroom would be a total disaster without me, and now, just when things are starting to happen, she decides to have 'a crisis of faith.' There are millions of phone calls, a million fan letters, a million people who want to be seen, and she decides to have doubts about what she's doing. I just can't handle it!" she said, giving her hand a cat-like clawing for emphasis—or relief. "I count on her to be calm," she went on, now veritably almost tearing at her own flesh. "But she's eccentric! Distractable! And Difficult! And full of doubts! She's impossible to work for, and I never want to see her again!"

Here, thought Monsieur Sorbonne, Mademoiselle Objet had finally gone 'round the bend. Not only was he overwhelmed by her outburst, he was also, he had to admit, distinctly troubled to hear this news of Madame Métier, who, from even his secondhand proximal position, he counted on to be calm, and therefore to calm Mademoiselle Objet. He prepared her a fresh cup of chamomile tea, plumped up the pillows on the bed, insisted her into it, and, handing her one of her poems books, left her there to prepare himself some dinner. Not long after, although it was still early in the evening, she drifted off to sleep.

Having finished his dinner, Monsieur sat down to read an artifacts magazine; but he was distracted by Mademoiselle Objet's condition. One's work, as he knew all too well, could be a diabolical thing. One did it, he knew, in hopes of achieving some small sense of purpose. In working for Madame Métier, Mademoiselle Objet had magically done that; but today, when it hadn't gone well, she was left with a sense of hopelessness, futility, really; and that was scary. He understood for a minute how people could work at jobs that had no meaning. If there was no meaning to have, there was no meaning to lose.

He was concerned about Mademoiselle Objet's pretty hands. If Madame Métier couldn't heal them, who could? And if, in her presence, they started their plummeting descent to ruin, who knows what could happen? He was miffed, he had to admit, at this seemingly unstable, definitely eccentric Madame Métier. Taking matters into his own hands, he decided to go to her house and have some words with her.

~

CHAPTER 6

Madame Métier Contemplates The Kiss

Madame Métier herself felt very tingly and delicious when she got home from the beach. It was amazing how, in the course of a day, so many things could occur, how she could have a crisis of faith, offend her employee, accomplish no work, come to terms with herself, be told some mysterious things by a stranger and, quite unexpectedly . . . get kissed.

Contemplating all this as she pulled on her spattered-with-red-roses white silk dressing gown, a soft little smile began to tango its way across her lips. He had actually kissed her, this angel young man with the round, blue, beautiful eyes, and his kiss had called back to her certain things about her womanly self, which, while she had been so occupied with her cremes, she had all but forgotten.

The kiss had seemed like a blessing, a seal on the words he had spoken; yet it had also had a romantically delicious and quite titillating quality.

Smilingly, she remembered it now, as in the quiet early evening, the fragrance of roses ascending through the high-paned windows of her bedroom, she sat on the bench at her small dressing table brushing her hair. She looked at herself in the mirror, trying to get a sense of herself. Her surface self, that is to say her appearance, appeared like a film almost in the mirror, but the inside things, that is to say her feelings, what she felt, imagined, and dreamed, she could see quite clearly. She could see, unmistakably, that she was happy, that she was delighted that she had been kissed.

Feeling thus magically a-tingle, Madame Métier was quite surprised a few minutes later to hear the sound of a knock at the door.

Hesitating a moment, she sashed up her red rose-dappled dressing gown and headed down the stairs, where she stood in front of the door until once again the knocking repeated itself. It had an inviting, almost lyrical quality about it and she wondered—she wished, in fact, momentarily that—possibility of all impossibilities—it was the knocking of the angel young man.

Thinking and, impossibly, hoping this, she opened the door.

～

CHAPTER 7

Monsieur Sorbonne Is Surprised

Monsieur Sorbonne was startled by the white-blonde apparition in rose-dappled silk who stood before him at the door. In fact, this woman so little resembled the woman whom months ago he had witnessed on the TeleVisions screen—she looked happier, prettier, softer, younger—to say nothing of being utterly unlike the two-horned, distractable, difficult woman whom Mademoiselle Objet had just described, and whom only moments ago he himself had been castigating on his couch at home, that for a moment he thought he had shown himself to the wrong door.

"I don't ordinarily take To-Be-Seens in the evening," said the apparition. But if you're having a special problem . . ." She paused, studying him for a moment, then immediately perceiving that not only his problem, but also he himself, was indeed quite special and unique, she said at once, "Please, come in."

She stood aside, and following a delicate but nonetheless insistent intuition, instead of shepherding him to the upstairs Seeing Room, allowed him to pass in front of her into the downstairs sitting room where, momentarily, she turned on a light.

Monsieur Sorbonne was surprised. He had expected a chilly reception.

"Sit down," said Madame Métier, before he could so much as introduce himself, "I'll bring us some tea."

~

Wearing his fine blue blazer and red silk handkerchief, Monsieur Sorbonne felt quite at home in this room of high white ceilings and beautiful multi-paned windows. Aside from the couch on which he was sitting and the low, glass-topped table which stood directly in front of it, it was entirely empty, creating a cathedral-like feeling. It was strange, he thought, how comfortable it felt, for ordinarily he should have wanted immediately, with art and artifacts, to fill up such a room, to civilize it with things. But for some reason in this particular instance, he was not so inclined.

"In emptiness," said Madame Métier, returning with a huge tea tray from the kitchen and setting it down on the marble-topped table, "there is room for so much." She smiled and sat down. "You must be Monsieur Sorbonne, my Mademoiselle Objet's life counterpart. I was just feeling that in the kitchen. I could feel your great equanimity," she said, pouring out from the blue-flowered porcelain pot two cups of chamomile tea. "I feel always the calm of your presence around her, the blessing of your steadfast love. She's as lucky to have you as I am lucky to have her." She passed him a cache pot of trumpet vine honey. "We are all so terribly lucky to have one another," she said.

She looked at him. What a splendid handsome man he was. His dark hair and green eyes seemed precisely the color of Mademoiselle Objet's, his stature and elegant manner of dress the perfect male counterpart to her exquisite loveliness. "It's delightful," she went on, "to think of you two together. You're perfect for her. I'm so happy to meet you at last. What a unique and sacred pleasure."

Monsieur Sorbonne, who, on the way over, had been preparing a speech, indeed an attack, was now totally disarmed. Perhaps, though, this woman, like Mademoiselle Objet herself, would now go on endlessly talking. But just as he entertained this thought, she crossed her long legs and, drawing her white, dappled-with-roses silk dressing gown a little more tightly around her, sat quietly sipping her tea. From time to time, she lifted her eyes to the night-shrouded window and stared out at the faintly etched limbs of the tall chestnut trees as if there were messages in them.

"I'm worried about her," said Monsieur Sorbonne finally. Of all the words and paragraphs and epithets he had prepared, this single sentence was the only one he could muster.

Madame Métier did not respond, but allowing a space in the air to encircle his words, waited for him to go on.

He told her then about Mademoiselle Objet's upsetness, her frustration with Madame Métier's "rather unconventional ways," as he diplomatically called them, his fear that, should she continue to be so upset, her hands would once again be scratched to ribbons.

"I'm so very sorry," said Madame Métier, setting her teacup down on the table. "I know this, and yet today, because of a crisis of my own, I became unable to know. Her help," and here she paused for a moment, breathing deeply as if to embrace with her whole heart and mind the full magnitude of the benediction of Mademoiselle Objet's energetic and organizing presence in her life, "is beyond what I could have ever imagined. Her very being here gives me the sense that what I am doing is right; and yet there are times—today, unfortunately, was one of them—when, for reasons of my own, I doubt."

"When one is *tout seule*—all alone—on a path," she went on, "for which there is no precedent, no map, one can be easily driven to doubt—as I was only this morning; and each testing by doubt must be somehow encountered and transformed, alchemized, as it were, so that in place of the doubt there comes an even clearer vision of one's calling." She paused, looking off at the stars, which, in a multitude had pierced the night sky and were dotting the blue rectangles of the sitting room windows.

"I'm so sorry," she said now, turning to him once again and feeling at the corners of her eyes the slightly astringent sting of oncoming tears. "I am so very, very sorry that my crisis of faith should have constituted such a hardship for her. And for you."

So touched was he by her expressions in the matter that instantly, with his red silk handkerchief (precisely the red of the roses on her dressing gown, he noted), he dabbed away her tears.

"I'm amazed myself, at times," she went on, "how upended I can become in the presence of my own questions, until I go through them. Or," she laughed not quite tinkingly, "until I allow them to go through me."

Beside her, Monsieur Sorbonne was transfixed. A great tranquility had settled in him. He put down his tea. He felt actually strange, as if all the wind of his intended assault had been knocked out of his sails, and yet he felt strangely whole, almost elevated for the moment. He could feel why being in Madame Métier's presence was an absolute necessity for Mademoiselle Objet.

"Your powers are from beyond the stars," he said. "And you must never doubt them."

"Thank you," she said. "I thank you most greatly. My soul also thanks you most greatly."

It was clear to them both that their conversation had ended. Together, as if it had been choreographed in advance, they both stood up, and with the moon ascending like a shimmering coin in the window, Madame Métier showed Monsieur Sorbonne to the door.

"By the way," she said as she opened it for him to leave, "be sure to hold Mademoiselle Objet's pretty hands tonight while you sleep."

～

CHAPTER 8

Monsieur Sorbonne Has a Crisis of Faith

Upon arriving at work the next morning, Monsieur Sorbonne felt strangely deprived. Having spent such a remarkable time with Madame Métier, everything he was doing seemed useless. What difference did it make if he sorted out and cataloged pot shards? Who cared if he could definitively distinguish an Anglo-Saxon from a Gaelic razor blade? Would people, *en masse*, stop filling the sky with burned oil or learn to keep their trash off the road? Would anyone's spirit be lifted? Would anyone's broken heart be healed?

It seemed suddenly all so ridiculous, what he was doing—of no merit whatsoever. He felt utterly despairing. He had found a job that he thought would have meaning only to discover now its total meaninglessness.

He was having, he realized, as he stared at the thick gray walls of his cell in the basement of the Artifacts Museum (which, suddenly, looked like the walls of a prison), a crisis of faith of his own. What was it Madame Métier had said to him only last evening? That each doubt must be encountered, alchemized, and transformed so that in its place there would come an even clearer vision of one's calling.

Well, here, certainly, was his doubt, a doubt of existential proportions, a dilemma with gigantic horns. But how could he, as she suggested, encounter, transform, let alone "alchemize"—to use her mysterious word—his own doubt? He hadn't the slightest idea. Affected as he now was, he found himself completely unable to work. Therefore, although it was barely eleven o'clock in the morning, he closed up his room and went out on the streets for a walk.

～

Outside, remarkably, the sun was shining. Monsieur Sorbonne had been in the dungeon of the Artifacts Museum for so long that he had forgotten about the sun. Now, as he walked down the boulevard crunching dry chestnut leaves on the sidewalk, it penetrated the threads of his blue woolen blazer, deliciously warming him.

The sky was exquisitely blue. The clouds, their myriad shapes like a crowd of mysterious animals happily playing, were floating and rolling above him. He tried to encounter his doubt, but having escaped the confines of his cell, it now eluded him. He thought, too, of his darling, the ever-exquisite Mademoiselle Objet, of how sweet and childlike she was, of how innocently and completely she adored—on her good days—Madame Métier. He thought even of how delightfully explosive she was, of how her hands would always tell all, and her heart, therefore, was forever a wide-open book. Her vicissitudes affected him deeply. *She* had meaning to him.

So too, now, did Madame Métier. He thought of the way that last night she had moved from deep speaking to laughter to tears, the way she had poured out the tea like a woman, and then stared off at the trees like a seer, the way she had spoken—and listened. He had never, he thought, been listened to so deeply, nor had he come forward himself with such striking, unusual words. He felt slightly disarranged now, as if he had somehow misplaced the map of his life and no longer knew where he was heading. But he did know one thing at least, something which only yesterday he had not known, and that was that whatever his life was really about, it was not about pot shards and old razor blades.

Having rooted this new truth in himself (this, perhaps, was what Madame Métier had meant by "alchemizing" things), he felt remarkably calm. He walked back, acceptingly, to the Artifacts Museum, determined that somehow he would find a way to weave meaning into the fabric of his life.

～

CHAPTER 9

Mademoiselle Objet Is Happy to Return to Work

Mademoiselle Objet was more than happy the next day to find herself back at work. It was amazing, the way her hands had become almost all better in the night. *Monsieur Sorbonne really is so wonderful,* she thought, the way he had made her the chamomile tea and put her to bed. She did get all too excited, over almost everything, and he did have a wonderful way of leveling her down.

She was thinking all this as she sat, legs folded, pencil tap-tapping at the still-orderly table in the workroom when Madame Métier, looking refreshed and lovely herself, and bearing a tea tray, came in.

"I am so very sorry," she said, pouring two cups of lemon grass tea, "about yesterday. I have bad days, too. I had one yesterday—with my crisis of faith—but I do want you to know that your being here means the world to me. I couldn't go on without you, and I do believe,"—she said it with a crinkle of hesitancy—"in spite of the monsters of doubt yesterday, that this is what I am meant to be doing."

"I'm so happy, so very, very happy to hear that," said Mademoiselle Objet, "because I know it too! Your cremes are helping so many people—way more than you know. Why, I gave my landlord a jar of lily creme for his little girl last week. He always used to scare me with his ugly cut-off finger and his weird blue-mirrored glasses, but when I gave him the lily creme, he practically burst into tears. As long as I've known him, he's been worried sick about his daughter. I think he was scared she was dying. He'd taken her to dozens of doctors, and still she could hardly breathe; but when he put your creme on her chest, she started breathing right again for the first time in six months.

"Besides," she went on, "I couldn't stand it, not being here working with you."

～

Having finished their tea, they set to work. Madame Métier dictated while Mademoiselle Objet wrote out, in her delicate script, the answers to all the fan letters. She called, under Madame Métier's direction, the TeleVisions station and scheduled, as she called it, "a calla lily appearance," the first in a possible series about medicinal flowers. Together they organized the new tins, recorded several new recipes, and at the end of the day—where had all the hours gone?—they stopped for a final cup of raspberry tea and a plate of nasturtium leaf sandwiches.

"You know," said Mademoiselle Objet, refreshed and encouraged by having accomplished so much, "you really should have a plan for the future. We're doing all these things every day, keeping up with the mail and the phone calls, and all the new recipes; but more people than just the To-Be-Seens should know about your work. You ought to go out and make speeches, have a TeleVisions series or write a book with all your recipes and teachings."

Madame Métier, sipping her tea, looked doubtful, but Mademoiselle Objet went on. "You're a genius about inventing your cremes, but frankly, you live on a cloud. You don't have any idea, just sitting up here in your workroom, sorting out your petals and twigs, what a hard time everyone's having. People out there are desperate. People need soothing. Just look at me—my hands fall apart the minute I'm out of your presence!" She paused for a minute, gathering steam, but Madame Métier interrupted.

"You're talking about doing more," she said, "I was just thinking about doing less."

"You can't do less! You can't have a crisis of faith! This is your calling! Stop doubting yourself and get back to work! You're not just eccentric! You're selfish!"

Madame Métier was taken aback by this attack-like outpouring bordering on attack. But maybe Mademoiselle Objet *was* onto something.

Perhaps writing or speaking could be a sort of external alchemizing of her doubts, and Mademoiselle Objet's emotional outbursts the crucible in which her reluctance could finally be fired to gold.

"Thank you," she said, quietly. "I needed to hear these things."

∼

CHAPTER 10

Mademoiselle Objet Is Happy
and Monsieur Sorbonne Is Unhappy

Mademoiselle Objet was happy, but Monsieur Sorbonne was not happy that night when he headed home from work. In spite of his attempt at "alchemizing," he had, in fact, had to return to the Artifacts Museum, where, as on all days before, all things remained the same. It was fine, he thought, to contemplate a change, to want it, hope for it, and even to expect it. But when, pray tell, did the alchemical results occur? Meanwhile, one went on mindlessly working.

The lovely mademoiselle was poaching a *poisson* and carving up *fleurets* of carrots when, a little later than usual, he finally walked through the door. First silent, then pacing and fretful, he put away all his things and started changing his clothes. "What's the point of it all?" she heard him mutter under his breath. "You work, you get paid, you buy suits, you pay your rent, you come home to the house you have rented, you get up and do it all over again. But what does it mean?"

He was fuming, still pacing like a lion when he sat down to partake of the lovely poached *poisson*. But instead of taking so much as a bite, he said, "This is a beautiful dinner, but I can't eat. I'm having a terrible day. What *does* it all mean?"

"What does *what* mean?" asked Mademiselle Objet.

"What does it mean that the work I do every day has no meaning? Nothing changes because I have done it. The world is no different. So what if the urns are all glued back together, if the razor blades are all organized and displayed," he was now practically shrieking, almost in the manner, he noticed, of Mademoiselle Objet.

"The things I once thought I loved—all the beautiful things, the artifacts and tools and equipments and esoteric machines—even they, when you really stop to think about it, even they don't have any meaning."

"What do you mean by *meaning*?" asked Mademoiselle Objet, feeling a somewhat out of her depth, but deeply distressed by his deep discontent.

"Meaning," he said, exasperated. "You know what I mean! Value. Purpose. Permanence. Effect. The capacity to change the way things are. You know what I mean! Something that changes the way you feel, the way that you see things, something that lifts you up out of the pit of the daily. Something that ties you to the eternal. Something that touches the human heart."

He paused, as if finally he had said it all. He seemed relieved to have delivered all his words. He heaved a great sigh. "You give me meaning," he said. "Just looking at you gives me joy. Discovering you at the Exposition of All Objects . . ." and here his voice became dreamy and distant, "was a miracle of meaning. When I found you I knew that my life would have purpose, but now, aside from looking at you"—and here he paused to look at her very deeply, to apprehend the sweet soul that lived behind her eyes—"I have no idea what that purpose might be."

They were both still for a moment. In the aftermath of his great outpouring there was a pool of silence, into which, presently, Mademoiselle Objet dropped a small stone. "Nor do I," she said, "but you yourself have said a clue—if it has to do with looking at me, then it has to do with looking, with seeing. Why don't you get your camera out and see what you can see?"

And with that, she got up from the table and put on the kettle for tea.

～

CHAPTER II

Monsieur Sorbonne Takes His Camera Out for a Walk

The next morning Monsieur Sorbonne retrieved the View Camera, which had been buried deep in his closet. How could he have left it there for long, when it was his search for meaning that had caused him to buy it in the first place?

How—and why—had it ended up in the closet? He had fallen in love. They had moved into their little house. He had lost his Oblong Credit Card. He had gone to work, and the camera—that treasure, the key perhaps to his sense of meaning—had languished in the closet, gathering fleas, as it were. Fleas—he laughed to contemplate it. Fleas! Perhaps this was in fact, how the Flea Fair got its name. Considering this, he laughed once again. He was happy that a little flicker of humor should have so crossed his mind. And feeling thus minutely cheered, he loaded it with the single roll of film, which, remarkably, still remained at the bottom of the small maroon velvet pouch.

Out on the boulevard the chestnut trees were in bloom, their towering blossoms a festival of pink. He photographed them and the clouds, the endlessly poetic sky, then a beautiful wrought iron gate. He *snap-snapped* a doorway of stately proportions, then another and another, its multiple layers of paint decomposing, and windows, light shadowing them, obscuring whatever mysteries the rooms behind them contained.

He was amazed, arriving at his office, to discover that he had already exploited the whole roll of film. So distracted was he by the possibility of seeing, that the morning raced by and at noon he went out to drop off the film at the Films Development Store, after which he ate a small sandwich lunch in the park.

The afternoon dragged. No more could he attend intently to his artifacts. It was fortunate, therefore, that starting out he had been so zealously committed, for even now, today, doing almost nothing, he was still far ahead with his work. When five o'clock came, eyes itching, he raced out like a schoolboy to the Films Store to pick up his photographs.

∼

CHAPTER 12

Monsieur Sorbonne Receives a Disappointment

"I'm so sorry," said the man at the Films Development Store, who looked a little like a monkey, "but none of the pictures have come out." He handed Monsieur Sorbonne a small gray envelope. "We've checked the film, Sir, and the film was fine. So there must be some problem with your camera."

"That's impossible," said Monsieur Sorbonne. "There can't be a problem with the camera. Why, just six months ago I took some photographs of my sweetheart and they turned out perfectly. I haven't touched the camera since. It has to be the film."

"It's not, Sir, I'm sorry. We can always tell. We have a special test to test film viability. Films, Sir, that is our specialty. So I repeat, Sir; it must be your camera."

When Monsieur Sorbonne continued to look incredulous, the monkey man went on. "Should you desire, sir, we can recommend an agent who can check it. But I do definitely advise that you should have your camera repaired."

Hearing this, Monsieur Sorbonne was downhearted, and, speaking of his camera, he realized he had left it at the Artifacts Museum. He therefore returned to his cubicle to retrieve it. There was going to be more to this search for meaning than he had expected. Film failures. Camera breakdowns. And now God-only-knew-how-expensive repairs.

∿

CHAPTER 13

Madamoiselle Objet Comforts Monsieur Sorbonne About His Camera

Monsieur Sorbonne was late getting home and Mademoiselle Objet was irritated until she saw how dejected he was. He set the camera down like a dead goose on the kitchen counter. "It doesn't work," he moaned. "None of the pictures came out. The film was fine, but there's something wrong with the camera! At least that's what the man at the Films Store told me."

It was interesting, thought Mademoiselle Objet, how like her Monsieur Sorbonne had momentarily become, now that one of his objects was dysfunctional. And it was even sranger that this week everyone around her—Madame Métier and Monsieur Sorbonne—seemed to be having a crisis of faith, when to her, for once, life was fine.

It was quite remarkable, too, she thought, how when people lost control over things they could start, a little, to lose their minds. It was interesting, seeing this now, with Monsieur Sorbonne and his camera, Madame Metier and her cremes. She herself had known all her life how problems with objects could warp out your mind and how setting them straight could give you, at once, a whole new sense of well-being.

Mademoiselle Objet felt sad now for the poor distraught Monsieur Sorbonne, whose broken camera had all but reduced him to hysteria. "Don't worry," she said, "it's just a camera, an object, and it can be fixed. Here, give it to me. Tomorrow I'll take it to the Camera Repairs."

⤳

CHAPTER 14

Madame Métier Contemplates a New Creme

As willing as she was to take Monsieur Sorbonne's camera to be fixed, Mademoiselle Objet, the next day, found it quite impossible to do. When she got to work there were twenty phone calls waiting on the recording machine, cremes to be mailed out, the stack of fan letters still waiting to be answered. Most pressing was the request—made by now three times—from the TeleVisions station, regarding the series on medicinal flowers, and insisting it be the occasion for the launching of a new creme.

"They only want you if you have a new creme," she said to Madame Métier. "They want to promote you—and you them. They've had hundreds of calls because of your last appearance and they want to make you a featured guest. They think you could improve their watchings ratings, put their channel on top; but we'll have to move fast. You'll have to have a new creme proposal by next week."

"I'm not interested," said Madame Métier, "in promoting a TeleVisions station's ratings, nor am I interested, haphazardly, in originating some new creme." She sat down on her blue embroidered hassock, and as if there were no hurry whatsoever, handed Mademoiselle Objet a cup of warm fig bark tea. "I just can't be pressured," she said. "The process is organic. I can't just willy-nilly—just because somebody wants it—whip up a new creme. Besides, the creme I am currently contemplating—a calla lily creme—I want it to be the cure for great loss, for the heartbreak caused by death—and I can already tell that its concoction will be most complex and difficult." She looked out the window as if searching for the mysterious components of its recipe, then mindlessly ran her hands back and forth across the smooth varnished surface of the View Camera's box, which, in anticipation of her taking it to be repaired, was now languishing on a corner of Mademoiselle Objet's desk.

"Why is that?" asked Mademoiselle Objet.

"Because calla lilies are white and when their cornucopias are broken down, reduced to the proper components for a creme, they will be inclined to turn brown. No one would want a brown creme. Brown is the color of earth, of heaviness, of solidity, and I would want the calla lily creme"—and here she stroked the camera again as if it were a magic box from which, eventually, a genie might emerge—"to be white, a symbol of resurrection, of the triumph of light over death."

Madame Métier stood up then, and excusing herself for a moment, retrieved the two calla lilies from the crystal vase on the dresser in her bedroom. "Here, I have an idea," she said excitedly, lurching forward and spilling some water from the calla lily vase onto the table (which Mademoiselle Objet immediately mopped up). She filled up the level of water in the calla lily vase with the rest of her brown fig bark tea. "Perhaps brown is the antidote for brown," she said, "and this tea will neutralize the oncoming brown and re-energize their whiteness." She watched anxiously while beside her Mademoiselle Objet observed, as gradually the slightly bronzed margins of the calla lilies began to whiten once again.

"There, I think I've got it," said Madame Métier. "I need to do some more thinking, but you can call the TeleVisions station." With that, she got up and with uncharacteristic tidiness, returned the vase of lilies to her bedroom.

To Mademoiselle Objet's surprise, however, when she returned to the workroom a few minutes later, Madame Métier was dressed to go out. "I'm going to the library," she said. "I'm sorry to leave you with all these letters, all this . . . everything, but I need to do some research.

"And by the way," she added, drawing a red silk scarf beneath the collar of her long black coat, "that camera does not need to be repaired. Tell its owner he will find that the camera will work when, once again, he photographs human beings."

"And why is that?" asked Mademoiselle Objet.

"Because human beings, in spite of their imperfections, of all creatures have the highest spirits. They can think, they can move, they can suffer, and they can feel; and they have—like no other living beings—the capacity for conscious love.

"Tell him that in photographing people, he will find the meaning that he seeks."

～

CHAPTER 15

Madame Métier Goes to the Library

Madame Métier felt somewhat uncomfortable as she proceeded to the library. She hated the library. She hated how ordered it was, how everything had a number, a card, and a place it belonged. She hated it because never, in all her impressionistic life, had she learned how to use the card file or the numbers system for locating books, nor really, aside from pure instinct (when roaming the stacks and her fingers had stumbled on something), had she ever learned how to locate what she needed in it.

She hated it further because of her father. Her father had loved it, and in an ongoing attempt to escape himself from the orderliness of his wife, had often walked the three miles from his house to its doors and planted himself in the outside courtyard where hour after hour, he would lose himself, reading esoteric plant magazines.

Having finished with the plant magazines, he would often go back inside and, in one of those wooden closet-like listening cubicles, listen in solitude to piano classical masterpieces. And if all that hadn't escaped him enough from his orderly house, he would go to the Reading Room and investigate all the new books or read, rolled up on one of those long bamboo poles, an odd newspaper or two.

It had been in one of these three locations that the young Madame Métier, having been dispatched as a posse of one by her mother, would eventually discover him. She had been sent to the library in search of him so often, in fact, and her father had always been so reluctant to go home—"I'll come in an hour," he'd always say, or "I need another two hours"—that in time, she had come to detest the library itself. For it represented, in concrete, the cross-purposes between her parents and her cross-purposes with them.

She realized, approaching it now, that she hadn't so much as walked past it since her father had died. Once inside, there was still that dingy sepulchral feeling, that thick mental silence she so abhorred. Old men were still sitting on chairs, still reading those newspapers rolled up on broomsticks. For a minute, from a distance one of them looked like her father. A few tears crossed her eyes, and as she walked through the huge reading room, she half expected that at any moment, passing from the courtyard to the Reading Room or one of the listening cubicles—but of course this was impossible—she would stumble across her father.

Being thus distracted and allowing more tears to fall—how appropriate, she thought, that she should have come here to work on a creme for mourning—she turned a corner to the reference room and ran smack forward into the from-the-beach angel young man.

"You look so beautiful in the library, here among the books," he said.

"What are you doing here?!" she asked. Indeed it seemed odd, totally inappropriate really, to come upon him here, he who seemed to be so much of nature, who appeared and disappeared in a haze.

"I was sitting out in the courtyard," he said, holding up a big book, "learning about the brain. About how the mind affects physical healing. But I got bored, outside, with reading; so I decided to come back in and listen to some music, in one of those listening booths.

"And you?" he asked. Then, noticing the shimmering pathways the tears had etched along her cheeks, he raised one of his great, smooth hands and wiped her cheek with his fingertips.

"I'm doing, or I'm about to do . . . " she said softly—but the touch of his fingers, a gesture so intricate and kind, had momentarily disarmed her, distracted her from her scholarly intention—"some botanical research."

"Come sit with me when you're finished," he said. "I'll be out in the courtyard waiting for some sun."

～

CHAPTER 16

Madame Métier Is Encouraged

Madame Métier was encouraged by the unexpected presence of Monsieur L'Ange, as she had now started to call this angelic young man to herself. Was he actually an angel, she wondered? He had a face of such innocence and purity and yet he always expressed such sayings of deep knowing that she couldn't tell. But she was relieved today—she was almost ashamed to admit—to have noticed that his hair was laced somewhat with white. He was older, it seemed, than she had first imagined. He was both old and young. But why was she even thinking about that? She was here to study plants, after all, to, in particular, unlock the chemical composition of the calla lily, whose chemistry she imagined would be most difficult.

Distracted, but also encouraged by even his distant presence, she studied intently; and after several hours, when she believed she had attained the necessary information, she came back to her senses only to realize that soon the library would be closing. She was distressed, in a panic almost, thinking that Monsieur L'Ange had probably already gone.

Gathering her notes and returning the reference books so far as she could remember back to their proper places on the shelves, she walked sadly through the library rooms. Through the tall French doors she could see that twilight had fallen, but—and she was astonished to see this—sitting on a chair in the center of the courtyard, his bare feet curled with prehensile dexterity over the lowermost rim of the fountain, sat Monsieur L'Ange. His eyes were closed, and on his lap, in great peace, were folded his two large, beautiful hands.

"So you're finished," he said, rising in a single elegant movement and speaking with a calm in his voice as if he had waited only ten minutes.

"I'm amazed you're still here," said Madame Métier.

"Of course," he said. "I would never have left without you. I could feel your work was difficult—that it would take you a long time to finish.

"And now," he said, picking up his big book and walking back toward the reading room, "would you like to join me for dinner?"

∼

CHAPTER 17

Mademoiselle Objet, Begrudgingly, Holds the Fort

In Madame Métier's absence Mademoiselle Objet was somewhat disconcerted. These long afternoons alone in the workroom when Madame
Métier was gone for one reason or another, were not, to say the least, her
cup of tea. Arranging things was one thing, but making decisions, talking
to the TeleVisions station, and composing thank you letters on her own
was quite a gigantic other. Furthermore, she realized that during the time
of her employ, something strange had occurred. She had changed. It was
no longer simply the joy of arranging objects and straightening things
out, but being in Madame Métier's strange but effulgent presence that
made her so like her job. When Madame Métier was gone, the whole
experience flattened.

Twisting her pencils wretchedly at her desk, she rang up Monsieur
Sorbonne at the Artifacts Museum.

"What's the matter?" he asked, hearing the distress in her voice.

"I'm upset," said Mademoiselle Objet. "I'm here all alone and I hate
it."

"Where's Madame Métier?" asked Monsieur Sorbonne.

"Gone again. She's always gone. She's always running off somewhere.
To the beach. To some stranger's hospital bed. To God-knows-where for
God-knows-what reason. Today she's gone to the library—supposedly to
do research."

"Well, she probably does need to do some research," said Monsieur
Sorbonne.

"Research! Bah humbug! Why need to does *she* need to do research?
She already knows everything about plants. You'd think that by now she'd

have figured it out. There isn't a thing that, instinctively, she doesn't know. She just doesn't feel like working. Well, neither do I. I hate it, working alone."

"Why don't you go home then?" said Monsieur Sorbonne, finally getting a word in edgewise. "And don't be so hard on Madame Métier. She probably does need to do some research. I know it's hard, but right now working alone is your job."

"Well, I can't do it," said Mademoiselle Objet. "I give up. I can't get anything done. I'm going to get your camera fixed." She hung up the phone, but then remembering Madame Métier's advice, instead of heading for the Camera Repairs Store, she picked up the View Camera box and tucking it under her arm, she headed for home.

～

CHAPTER 18

Monsieur Sorbonne Is Reunited with His Camera

By the time he got home, Monsieur Sorbonne was also disconcerted. He had had a terrible day, he said, at the Artifacts Museum, dealing again with dead artifacts. He desperately needed, he realized, his camera to be fixed, for having used it even the miniscule number of minutes he'd used it a few days ago, he saw how much he longed to capture the things in his vision.

"Well, don't worry, it's fixed," said Mademoiselle Objet, handing him the camera box. "Madame Métier fixed it. But she said that you have to take pictures of people. That it won't work otherwise."

"I can't believe it!" said Monsieur Sorbonne. "How did she fix it?"

"I don't know," said Mademoiselle Objet. "But why don't you try it? She does have her ways."

Monsieur Sorbonne picked up the camera and examined it. It looked exactly the way it had a few days ago, and he wasn't sure he could bear another disappointment; but then remembering the quite remarkable feeling he'd had a few nights ago in Madame Métier's presence, he called out to Mademoiselle Objet, "You're probably right. It's probably fixed. I'm going out to get some film." Then, pulling on his blue overcoat, he walked down the boulevard to the All-Night Films Development Store.

When he got home, he loaded the film in the camera and, stealing into the bedroom, he photographed Mademoiselle Objet, whose exquisite hands, like two lilies, lay gracefully across the pillow as she slept.

~

CHAPTER 19

Madame Métier Has a Date

The restaurant Monsieur L'Ange had chosen for their dinner was one she hadn't known existed. It was small and, except for the candles on the tables, dark; and, as she could see from the wall-posted menu, had the sort of odd foods that she liked to eat—crêpes, dandelions salad, sunflower walnut *pâté*—but which she had never imagined could be obtained in a public restaurant.

He seemed to have come here often. A waiter brought them at once two glasses of lemon-iced water.

Sitting across from him now, having removed her black coat and red scarf, and making visible the white lace blouse beneath it, Madame Métier felt suddenly school-girlish, soft, and unbearably shy. She was out on a date, it occurred to her now, or if not a date, then something quite more like a date than anything she'd been out on for years. She was nervous, and at the same time quite calm. For there was something at once so patient and strong about this young man—how old could he actually be, she wondered anxiously again—that allowed her, differently and deeply, to be herself with him.

She ordered her food—a salad with eggplant *pâté*—and he ordered his, and then in the candlelight, shifting, mysterious, subdued, he started talking about himself.

He had had a difficult life, an unspeakable father who beat him. At sixteen he had left home. He had lived in a box on the streets—"a refrigerator crate," he said, "it was actually quite roomy"—until eventually he had built up a profession—he was a furniture restorer—and obtained enough money to buy a small cabin. He lived, still, in this cabin, he told her. Over time, he had grown tired of furnitures restoring, and, in recent years, because of the dexterity his hands had acquired in working so finely with curves and woods, he had become interested in the use of his hands for the purpose of physical healing.

"And you?" he asked, when he had finished.

Madame Métier told him about her work, about the development, now, of the calla lily creme. "That's why I was in the library," she said. "I was looking up calla lilies, acquainting myself with their properties, for the invention of this creme. And isn't it lucky;" she said, smiling, "that's how I came to see you again."

She felt suddenly strange now, talking to him. Listening to herself, it appeared as if her whole life had been about her work.

"You have lost yourself in your work," said Monsieur L'Ange, as she started eating her salad. "You have disappeared from your life. You, the woman, the flower herself, has ceased, almost, to exist."

She felt oddly defensive, attacked almost, when he said this and yet, of course, he was right. She stopped eating and rested her fork on her plate. Necessity had led to . . . necessity. She had married the doctor, which necessitated that she become the doctor's public decoration. The doctor had died, necessitating that she begin again with her cremes. She had begun with her cremes, necessitating that she employ Mademoiselle Objet. Her work had succeeded so that now she was busier than ever. One necessity had led inexorably to another, and now here she was—inexorably entrenched.

And "the flower of herself," as Monsieur L'Ange had so charmingly called it, the woman in whose garden bloomed roses, the woman of the red silk flowered dressing gown—not the woman who created cremes, but the woman whose body might receive them—she, the flower, had disappeared.

Monsieur L'Ange sat across from her saying nothing. Vaguely she thought she saw him set his fork down on the table. When was it, she wondered—if ever—that she had last felt the flower of herself? When she was picking up scraps from the floor and washing the dishes and putting them up row by row for her mother? No, not then. When, as a young girl in school she had studied histories and maths and algebraic equations? No, certainly not then. When, with her father, she had walked in the garden watching him handle the petals and fern fronds? Yes, briefly then. Quite happily then. When, as still quite a young woman she had gone dancing? Yes, certainly then. When, one night after happily dancing, she had met her husband, the doctor? Yes, briefly, for a moment, then. But not after that. Not since the doctor. In fact, because of him precisely, her blossoming self had come to an end. She had wilted herself. Her self, along with the fronds and petals and stamens she had put away in the green striped hatbox, had been vanished away to some closet. She was shocked as she paused to contemplate this.

Quietly, thoughtfully, she picked up her fork and continued to eat her dinner. She felt frozen in some corridor of her life, while this mysterious man sat across from her in silence, observing, eating his dinner himself. She felt strange, irritated almost, that he had brought up such a personal matter. How, out of nowhere had she, with him, a virtual stranger, arrived at such a disturbing juncture? Very simply, it seemed. He had talked to her about himself and then asked her a simple question. And now, remarkably, here they were.

"You're afraid that your life will be only all work," he said then. "That there will never be anything else—no romance, no dancing, no playing."

"Yes, perhaps," she said. She could feel again a slight irritation. Irritation, was it? Or sadness? Or fear? He was persistent, invasive almost, but strangely caring; she could feel it. Inside her a little wall crumbled down. A woman who had been guarding something—her heart, perhaps, or a certain way of seeing herself—surrendered, gave in.

"I hadn't thought so," she said, "but now I see that you're right. There *has* been only the work." She paused. "And I hadn't known that"—she smiled a little, poignantly, allowing herself to discover the truth in what he was saying— "until I sat here with you. Now suddenly my life seems terribly one-sided. I feel like I've disappeared."

"I know," he said tenderly. "But you haven't. That's why I'm here."

Feeling his words, she stared off for a moment through the windows of the restaurant and into the distant rose-colored evening, as if in its pink voluptuousness the sky could tell her something. Streaks of clouds hovered, voluminous, filmy, like a woman's gauzy skirt across the floor of the horizon, and feeling its luminous ethereal beauty, her eyes misted briefly, and a few little tears started slowly skidding their way down her cheeks.

"The tears?" he asked, reaching across the table and taking her hand into his.

She sighed. "Ah, yes, the tears . . ." Now she could feel them, the intricate subterranean rivulets starting to spill, and yet she felt strangely comfortable with the little outpouring, as if here, in his presence, softly, she might become a woman with tears. "Your kindness," she said, "the thought . . . that you might have come here for me . . . I'm not even sure what you mean. . . . It's surprising . . . unimaginable really." She paused for a moment, allowing the slow tears to fall, then wiped them from her cheeks with the edge of her white linen napkin.

"And the other tears?" he said then.

She looked at him quizzically.

"The library tears. The tears you were in the midst of when I found you earlier today."

"Ah, yes. Those tears . . ." She gathered herself. "They were about my father. I used to meet him often at the library. Sometimes I miss him," she said, and unexpectedly, again, the tears started flowing.

"You are so beautiful when you cry," said Monsieur L'Ange. Then, standing up from his side of the table, he stepped around it to sit beside her. He put his arm around her then, and cupping her head with his hand, he tilted it ever so slightly until she found a place on his shoulder, where, softly, she continued to weep.

"You've waited so long to mourn," he said, brushing away the sheets of her hair which shrouded her face like a curtain. "Thank you for mourning with me. You give me great honor to show me your tears."

In the distance across the restaurant, a single black-suited waiter had turned out most of the lights. Except for the two of them, the restaurant was deserted. "I'm sorry, Sir," said the waiter approaching their table and presenting the check, "but we're closing. If you don't mind, could you take care of this?"

"Yes, certainly," said Monsieur L'Ange, and releasing her head from its place on his shoulder, and retrieving his billfold with his free hand, he paid the check.

It was strange, what had just occurred, a flood of tears she hadn't even known was there, and across the table and then beside her, this man's receiving of them. She stood up to put on her coat and he stood up beside her, helping her into it, arm after arm. She said nothing, and together they walked out slowly through the silent restaurant.

"I'd feel better," he said, as they stepped out into the street, "if, after all this, you wouldn't go home alone."

∼

CHAPTER 20

Madame Métier and Monsieur L'Ange Have a Seance

It was very strange, thought Madame Métier, being followed at night into her house by somebody else, especially a man. In the downstairs sitting room she lit several candles, and leaving Monsieur L'Ange alone, she went to the kitchen to make them some tea.

When she returned he was sitting there, shoeless, in the half-light, legs folded on the floor. "You have a wonderful house here," he said finally. "It has a very sanctified feeling, though the feeling, I can tell, was achieved at a great price."

"You're right," she said. She took off her shoes, sat down on the floor next to him, and poured out the tea.

He sipped it a moment, then set his cup on the floor. "I'm sorry the man who once lived here abused your spirit so much," he said finally. "He had a small spirit, a very constricted—how shall I say it?—selfhood . . . personality." He paused, breathing deeply, as if waiting for something— more information, or words, to be given to him. "He concerned himself with . . . the unimportant things. He was afraid. Of living." He paused, again breathing deeply. "And of your power. You have so much and he had so little. That was very difficult for him. That's why he needed fast cars. He was desperate, trying to keep up with you."

Beside him, Madame Métier said nothing. She had put down her tea and in the shimmering light of the sitting room was now taking in all he had said. He seemed to give words to what she had only guessed in her bones. What would he say next?

"May I kiss you?" he said.

She didn't answer. Instead she allowed herself to be gathered into his arms like a sparrow. For a time they sat there together, entwined in the half-light, pale soft shadows of the candles flickering against the walls, the heat of the light, the sound of the air, and the slow, strong pull of the stars encircling them as he kissed her and tenderly kissed her, until in a place unoccupied and distant, a cathedral began to open inside her.

～

Later, upstairs in her bedroom, the moon, through the high-paned window, imprinted a huge rectangle of light on the wall, as if the light itself were a room that could be occupied. Monsieur L'Ange stood quietly in it, as if indeed it were a room, removing his socks one by one, then slowly unbuttoning his shirt.

She opened the bed, folding back the white down comforter, the pale blue blankets, exposing a field of white sheets. He lay down beside her. Across the room, on her dresser, the two white calla lilies hovered in their vase, stately, regal, open, each single-petalled cornucopia luminous and shining in the moonlight.

Wordless, he entered the cathedral of her body, holding her head like a chalice in his two hands. In the dark she could smell his fragrance— clary sage was it? or saxifrage?—and see his round eyes, their lashes like two awnings above them, his hair streaked ever so finely with white. And when they had worshipped together, and he had returned to a place at her side, she wrapped herself to him, laying her head on his heart, half closing her eyes.

In the half-light, half wakeful, she breathed. She could feel his breathing beneath her, and the beat of his heart, a melodic, strange, vivid, comforting music, a hammock in whose hum she dozed, then awakened, then dozed once again, until hours had passed in such half-sleep and half-wakefulness.

It was then, inexplicably, in the half-light of the early morning, eyes half closed, that she first saw it—the crown of thorns above his head. An ominous circular shadow, it rose, ascended in her vision slowly, then hovered above him in the gray light of the room. It was vague at first, a silhouette only, but then as she washed it started to take on an ever more explicit form until she could see all its twisted interwoven branches, each thorn elegant and deadly, and then all its thorns and all its branches, intricately intertwined. Then a few minutes later, when it had finally attained full focus, it just as quickly disappeared. It was replaced then in her vision, by a perfect circle of crystalline droplets, a coronet of tears that laced itself across his chest, then rose up high above his body and hung suspended in the air.

She paused, stilled, quivering, then breathed and looked around the room. Then, quivering still, she laid her head down on his chest.

With her head on his chest, in his half-sleep, he reached out his hand and smoothed and smoothed out her hair.

"You have seen something," he said.

"Yes. And I don't know why, but it makes me unbearably sad."

"Stay close to me then," he said. And holding her head in his hand for the rest of the night, angelically, they slept.

～

CHAPTER 21

Madame Métier and Monsieur L'Ange Greet the Day

"You are very beautiful when you sleep," whispered Monsieur L'Ange. Morning light streamed in through the windows, and Madame Métier was astonished to see him still there beside her. There was a great peacefulness about him which never before in her life had she known in a human being. For her, now, the world felt new. It felt almost unreal, as if it now contained things of the dimension of another world, things unfamiliar, luminous, beautiful, and strange.

Wordless, she looked at everything—at him, at the light, at his eyes, at the calla lilies on the dresser, the frames of the panes on the windows, the folds of the blankets on the bed, the shape of his feet beneath them, the pale yellow walls, the high ceiling.

"Look," he said then, pointing to the dresser. "Calla lilies. I hadn't noticed them last night. How beautiful. The symbol of resurrection."

Incredulous, she looked at him. Resurrection—how did he know? She wanted to tell him in words the things beyond words—that for her, he was the resurrection, that with his body he had redeemed her, delivered her from the life of all work to the life of being a flower. But she felt shy. The words eluded her.

"It's alright," he said shussing her lips with his fingers. "No need for words. It's your turn now. It's your time." Then kissing her once again, he raised himself up from the bed. "I need to go now," he said, and started to put on his clothes.

"By the way," he added, pulling on his white trousers, fastening his white shirt, "the woman who works for you, she won't like me because I'll distract you from your work. But the man she loves—you have a very deep kinship with him; you can tell by the red handkerchief, the roses on your dressing gown—he'll help her come to her senses. They both love you more than you can imagine and they will be with you always, even until the end."

So saying, he embraced her once more. Then, in bare feet, he walked down the stairs and let himself out the front door.

∽

CHAPTER 22

Madame Métier and Mademoiselle Objet
Have a Salty Encounter

It was amazing, wasn't it, how everything could change. How at one moment you could be so entirely focused on one thing—your work—and then, with the touch of a hand or the strange rearrangement of your secret cells, you could be lifted up out of it all, be exquisitely refocused, suddenly redesigned. Truly, she had stumbled across some line. Madame Métier was thinking all this in the shower, streams of rain falling down like an endless array of small jewels, rhinestones and diamonds, moonstones and opals pelting her body.

It was true—now she could see it so clearly—that for years now, she had been breathing and sleeping and waking this strange botanical legacy of her father's, without so much as a moment's contemplation of what it had done to herself. It had been necessary, of course. She had needed a source of income, and the cremes had been her only choice; but it seemed sad now—wet ringlets of her hair fell languidly to her shoulder, and stepping out of the shower she gathered them up in a fluffy white towel and carefully tamped them dry—it seemed very sad indeed—she stepped on the small blue bath mat and applied some rose petal creme to her legs— how far she had gone from herself. It was strange, it was wrong, to have lived for so long a life of no life, a life of no words, of nobody and no body, of no whispering things in the dark. Of no touching, no hands, no making love.

Scarcely had she finished these thoughts and dried herself off than she heard the sound of Mademoiselle Objet's key in the door. Hurriedly, she straightened the bed, got herself dressed and presented herself in the workroom where Mademoiselle Objet, already planted, sullen, on her chair at the workroom table, had that particular countenance that threatened a slight or immense volcanic eruption.

"So how is everything?" asked Madame Métier, appalled by her own ridiculous trivialness. Distraction, indeed, passion, had reduced her to a temporary state of stupidity, and Mademoiselle Objet, as if insulted, refused to answer. I'll have to do better than that, thought Madame Métier; but before she could try, Mademoiselle Objet in her cattiest voice said, "So, have you finished your research, and are you an authority, now, on resurrection?"

It was shocking, how awesomely close to the truth, at times, Mademoiselle Objet's most seemingly offhanded and mean remarks could be.

"Yes, as a matter of fact, I suppose I have," said Madame Métier, being slightly catty herself. She was angry that already, at this early hour she should have to deal with Mademoiselle Objet and her verbal torpedoes. A red shaft of rage, uncharacteristic, startling, swept majestically across her eyes. Across from her, Mademoiselle Objet looked back with a steaming fury of her own.

Madame Métier absorbed its raw orange glow but said nothing, no word of defense, nor assault, nor explanation. But inside she could feel the forming of a deep resolve. This whatever it was—this dalliance, this resurrection, this summer calliope with Monsieur L'Ange—she would have it. And no matter how Mademoiselle Objet might react, no matter if she had tantrums out to the stars, Madame Métier would have it, this miracle, whatever its consequences for her work.

Having thus resolved her position, she softened. Feeling as loved as she did at the moment, she was moved to compassion for the vituperative Mademoiselle Objet. It *was* difficult, after all, for a person of such perfected organizational attributes, to put up with so eccentric a woman as herself.

"Let's have some tea," she suggested finally. "I'll bring some up."

"You always want tea," said Mademoiselle Objet, now petulant, frowning. "You always think tea can solve everything. Let's get some work done! It's always something with you. Every day's an exception, and you always have an excuse. I did as much as I could yesterday—all by myself—and now I can't do anymore. Besides, who knows where you were. At the library!? Doing botanical research!? I'll bet!" Her voice was a siren, a blowtorch, shrill, almost screaming. "For all I know you were having a secret romance at the beach!" There she was—almost exactly on target again. "The next thing I know you'll be running off in the sunset with some man half your age, and I'll never see you again."

Expended, she now started to cry, and Madame Métier, taking pity, sat down beside her. Then very gently laying Mademoiselle Objet's head on her shoulder, she patted andpatted her hair, and laid her hand very still on her forehead.

"I'm sorry," she said, herself still a little distracted. "I know I'm difficult. And I always get anxious when I'm about to do a new creme." Her voice trailed off. It was a half-truth, only a part of the equation, the part that had to do with her work, which now, in light of her night with Monsieur L'Ange, seemed totally irrelevant. But to speak of him, or of it, to Mademoiselle Objet, that was impossible. He was her treasure, a mystery unfolding, and Mademoiselle Objet with her scissors-sharp words would, she feared, stab at her secrets and cut them to ribbons as, in her uncanny intuition, she had already all but stumbled on them.

But Mademoiselle Objet had now settled down. Her sobs had diminished to a whimper. "It isn't even the work," she said finally, sighing. "We do enough work. We do have sort of a routine. It's just that I miss you when you're not here. When you're around, I feel light—as if everything is possible—and when you're not, I feel empty and scared. Working with you, just being here in your presence, gives me such peace. And peace— feeling peaceful—that's what I live for."

～

"I understand," said Madame Métier. "I do understand. And now that we've got all that figured out," she concluded, laughing a little, lifting up Mademoiselle Objet's head and wiping away the last tear, "let's get some ridiculous work done."

～

CHAPTER 23

Monsieur Sorbonne Begins to Photograph People

Having photographed Mademoiselle Objet as she slept, Monsieur Sorbonne had gone promptly to bed, but he had lain there for hours beside her thinkingly awake. There was something so true in the message from Madame Métier—that he should photograph only people—that once having heard it he had felt greatly relieved. Indeed, in capturing Mademoiselle Objet as she slept, he had learned some things. He saw that in taking her photograph, he looked at her with the eyes of his soul. Instead of seeing her anxiousness, her volcano-like aspects, he saw the loveliness within her; and although she would always remain his most favorite subject, he also felt moved from within now to also photograph other people.

Having at last gone to sleep, he arose the next morning in a state of confidence and great expectation, and, loading his camera with a new roll of film, he left early for work with the camera box tucked under his arm.

It was strange how, because of Madame Métier's instructions once-removed, all human beings now looked different to him. Although as he walked the long way to work he felt drawn again and again to the elaborate cornices of buildings, the elegant proportions of doors and windows (there was still, to his eye, great beauty in all the works of civilization); it was remarkable how suddenly it was human beings that captivated him.

A day-nurse holding the hand of a bawling child was crossing the street and he photographed them in motion. Then a taxi stopped at a school. Scarved, mittened, and squashed together in the back seat like a pile of marshmallows, a rosy-cheeked bundle of children from the Orphan's Home disembarked. He snapped and snapped as each one of them piled out. I'm in too much haste, he thought to himself; I'm wasting my film. But when he got to the Artifacts Museum and was greeted at the door by the tall, blue-uniformed guard, he was captivated once again and asked if, with the guard's permission, he might photograph him. The blue guard, with his thick leather gloves, stood back, and as he rested one hand on a curlicue of the huge wrought iron door, a look of great pride passed into his face. He smiled a wide smile, and for a moment he looked like a king.

As Monsieur Sorbonne passed through the halls, a hunch-backed chambermaid in a dark-green uniform scurried by, carrying a pile of fresh towels to the Ladies' Bathroom. As she approached, he asked her to pause; then he click-clicked and captured her look of surprise and delight.

He went to his cubicle in the basement, and leaving his camera out on his desk, decided that, spontaneously, he would photograph whoever entered his room. At eleven o'clock a young workman came to plaster a flaw in his ceiling. He had long, flowing Jesus-like hair and a ragged black pupil in one of his eyes. "Do you mind," asked Monsieur Sorbonne as the young man ascended his ladder, "if I take a photograph of you?"

"Not at all," he said, as trowel in hand, arms outstretched, he balanced himself high on the ladder not far from the ceiling.

At eleven-fifteen it was the lavender-haired secretary from upstairs. She had brought down a memo about a new shipment of wall stones from an ancient Egyptian temple. These were all to be counted and catalogued, and eventually reassembled to replicate the temple from which they had been retrieved. He photographed her as she stepped through his door, and as she laid the memo down on his desk, he photographed her plump hand.

So excited was Monsieur Sorbonne by his photographing adventure, that the so-called real work of his day—reviewing the memo, making a plan for the reassemblage of the temple—had utterly escaped him.

He looked at his watch. It was almost lunchtime, and in terms of his responsibilities at the Artifacts Museum, he had accomplished absolutely nothing.

Having so happily accomplished nothing, he went out at noon, and, in a spirit of anticipation mixed with a shadow of doubt—was his camera really fixed? he wondered—he wound up the film in its canister and dropped if off at the Films Development Store.

∽

CHAPTER 24

Mademoiselle Objet and Madame Métier Make Peace

"*I'm sorry,*" *said Mademoiselle Objet at* the end of the day, when they had finished their work and sat having tea, "that I was so cranky this morning. Thanks to you we finally did get a lot of work done. But frankly," she said, looking directly at Madame Métier, "even so, you have seemed a little distracted."

There she was again, thought Madame Métier, impeccably almost on-target again. She thought of responding, but just then the phone rang and Mademoiselle Objet jumped up to answer it. "It's the TeleVisions Station," she announced. "They want you next Tuesday, whether or not you're finished with the calla lily creme."

How could it be, Madame Métier wondered, that at precisely the moment she wanted to be nothing but a flower, she was overwhelmed by work and more work, and that, now, in addition to making her cremes, she was being caught up with TeleVisions deadlines.

"And, by the way, they won't do the show unless they have a photograph of you," said Mademoiselle Objet. "To put in the paper and advertise the series. And isn't it wonderful," she chirped, "I know just the person who can take it."

∾

CHAPTER 25

Madame Métier Is Alone

The workday was done. Evening had fallen, and Madame Métier prepared herself a pot of raspberry tea and retreated upstairs to her room. She took a warm bath with a lilac *bain mousse* and having thus refreshed herself, put on her red-rose-spattered dressing gown.

The bed, smelling faintly of clary sage, was it? or saxifrage?—she couldn't quite tell—was made, and pulling back the comforter and removing her dressing gown, she arranged herself amidst its avalanche of pillows. The bed felt suddenly huge, immense like the sea, and her body like a small paper boat, seemed lost and adrift within it.

The moon was a huge white eye at the window staring relentlessly in, and as she sat in the bed sipping her tea, she felt profoundly alone. How strange it was, to feel so alone. She had never, in fact, felt quite so alone.

She had not felt alone with the doctor—perhaps because then, when she was young, she hadn't known herself well enough to feel either alone or connected. She had certainly not felt connected. She had felt harassed and occupied and directed; but she hadn't, it occurred to her now, felt very much of anything with him. She hadn't, either, felt alone when he died. She had felt, if anything, relieved. And she had not felt alone with her work. Even before Mademoiselle Objet had arrived to deliver her from the chaos of all her objects, she had not felt alone. She had felt . . . occupied.

But now suddenly she felt alone. On the far side of the bed, there was a hollow, distinctly empty place where only a dozen hours ago Monsieur L'Ange had lain asleep.

Sipping the last of her tea, she felt suddenly angry at him. How cruel he was, to have treated her so well, to have entered her so deeply, to have opened her heart, and then disappeared. She had been fine, just fine before he arrived—all work and no play, but at peace with her one-dimensional life. Then he had appeared, insisting himself like a hummable, unforgettable tune into the folds of her life so that now, in his absence, she felt . . . alone.

Like an evening sky streaked with pink streamers of sunset, her spirit was streaked with a thin veil of sorrow. And smelling again the faint remembrance of his fragrance, the emptiness, the void, was poignant, palpable around her. Sadly, she turned out the light, and wondered if she would ever see him again.

~

CHAPTER 26

Mademoiselle Objet and Monsieur Sorbonne
Have a Happy Reunion at Home

When Mademoiselle Objet got home that night, Monsieur Sorbonne was happy as a lobster. He was sitting at the dining room table and studying, one by one, the contents of an envelope of photographs. There they all were, the people who had peopled his day: the day-nurse with the child, the orphan children with their mismatched coats and collars and leggings and foulards. Funny, he hadn't noticed before, the ancient sadness in all their eyes. And finally, the museum guard, his hat so crisp, his uniform so perfect and blue, his smile so strong and confident, as if he'd become much more than he'd ever expected in his life.

Monsieur Sorbonne went on through the pile: the Jesus plasterer, the secretary, the Ladies' Bathroom maid. Strange, he had never seen before that look of defeat, and simultaneously, of complete acceptance in her eyes. And the secretary—what character in her face, under the pile of lavender hair—the way all the lines in it were a journey from somewhere to somewhere, and how he could see she had taken the journey, bravely and sadly and gladly, and finally arrived at herself. And then, at last, at the bottom of the pile, the deeply sleeping Mademoiselle Objet, whose lovely face and exquisite hands were etched against the pillowcase in a look of such composure that his heart was overwhelmed with love. No matter her endless volatility. From time to time composure was its counterpart, and although at times it was difficult for her to achieve it, this composure was the essence of her soul.

It's amazing, he thought, what happens when you photograph people. You see *them*—not how they look, but who they are at the core.

∾

"Guess what," said Mademoiselle Objet, running into the room and throwing her arms about his neck.

But Monsieur Sorbonne, lost in a reverie of what he had seen in the photographs, just then did not want to guess.

"I don't want to guess. Not now," he said.

"But you have to!" said Mademoiselle Objet. She was bouncing up and down on her heels like an excited impatient child. "Come on," she said. "Guess!"

"I can't," he said, becoming irritated.

"All right, then, I'll tell you. Madame Métier needs you to photograph *her*! For the TeleVisions station. To advertise her new series in the paper."

Drawn back by her words to the room and to himself, Monsieur Sorbonne digested this news. "That's wonderful," he said. "That is very wonderful indeed."

∾

CHAPTER 27

Madame Métier Recovers Herself

Madame Métier was slightly more composed the next morning as she greeted Mademoiselle Objet in the workroom. She had made the bed and tidied her room. She had thrown the calla lilies, whose edges were finally irreparably edged with brown, into the workroom waste can. Trying gamely to ignore the vague strange feeling of loss that hovered around her, she started, uncharacteristically, to tidy up the workroom itself.

She was thinking of Monsieur L'Ange. Perhaps she would never see him again. Perhaps he was only the message that she should have more in her life than her work. In that, surely, if only for a minute, he had been a gift. But she "missed" him. She felt vulnerable, at a loss and askew, like a schoolgirl waiting for a phone call. She straightened some boxes and filed away a few recipes cards, and then she felt a small measure of peace. For a minute, she understood the power of arranging objects as a practice to quiet the mind.

"You look peaceful today, more like yourself," said Mademoiselle Objet, coming in a few minutes later. "I'm glad, because I've arranged for you to be photographed. Amazing!" she said, looking around the workroom, "you've tidied things up! You must have known. The photographer will be here any minute."

❧

Madame Métier was not entirely surprised to discover that the photographer, when he arrived, was Monsieur Sorbonne.

She at first shook his hand, then noticing that he seemed slightly hurt, a consequence, she imagined, of her forced formality, she took his hands into hers and held them both warmly.

From across the room, Mademoiselle Objet looked on. "You already know one another?!" she said, astonished.

"Yes, we do, as a matter of fact," said Monsieur Sorbonne. Then as if to defend against a possible oncoming explosion, he added, "Worried for you, I came here one night and talked to Madame Métier about some cremes for your hands."

"I'm so glad," said Mademoiselle Objet, her voice now light and cheery. "You're so much alike. Both so calm. Threads from the same peaceful cloth. I always knew that someday you'd meet. I just never knew when it would happen."

It never ceased to surprise him, the wild array of Mademoiselle Objet's reactions, the versatility of her moods, how at times she could be so upended, at others so completely accepting. But he was happy that she was happy, and thus relieved, he set up his camera on a tripod, and situating Madame Métier across from him in the light, he instructed her how to look this way and that way, and how to situate her hands in a variety of ways.

"That's perfect," he said, crawling out for a moment from behind the large View Camera box and removing a fleck of lint from her blouse. He was excited. These photographs, even more than the ones he had taken yesterday, would be wonderful, he could tell. This woman was so unusual, and she was dressed today like a spirit, in a white voile shirt with a soft wide collar that wrapped around her neck like a cloud.

"Smile," he said, and she smiled. "Don't smile," he said, and she held her face in repose. He arranged and arranged her in various positions, snapping and happily snapping. She was a worthy subject, an elegant human being; but there was something else, too, about taking her picture—what was it? He didn't quite know, but he felt, as he stood and talked and walked about, arranging her in pose after pose, as if ever so slightly within him all his molecules had changed. He felt suddenly gifted, as if almost without effort he could do his work, as if simply by being in her presence he could capture the perfect image. He felt light, almost beautiful himself, as if without thinking or trying, without metering the light or measuring the distance, the essence of her self would give itself to him.

Across the room, absorbed and content, Mademoiselle Objet observed the proceedings. She hadn't realized until this very minute how much she had wanted the two of them to meet—the two of them. Both whom she loved so very much.

Feeling as completely delighted as she did at the moment, she was almost startled awake when, a few minutes later, the workroom phone rang.

"She's busy. Occupied. She can't come to the phone," said Mademoiselle Objet to the caller. "Would you like to leave your name?" She paused briefly, listening, then repeated herself. "She's busy, I told you. She *cannot*, at the moment, be interrupted. Would you like to leave your name?"

The caller apparently did not want to, for Mademoiselle Objet, by now quite obviously irritated, had begun to tap-tap her pencil on the corner of the desk. "As I've already told you," she said, "you can't. No, not even later. You don't understand. She never speaks to anyone." She said it emphatically, with finality; then she semi-slammed down the phone.

"Who was that?" asked Madame Métier.

"I don't know," said Mademoiselle Objet. "A man. Some upstart. One of your fans. He wouldn't give me his name. But whoever he was, he has no idea how busy you are. He actually thought he could speak directly to you! But don't worry. He'll never bother you again."

"Smile," said Monsieur Sorbonne, across the room, but no longer could Madame Métier smile. A ribbon of sad contemplation had wrapped up the light in her eyes, and her sparkle had receded, irretrievable.

"Perhaps we're finished," said Monsieur Sorbonne. "Your mood seems to have changed. Perhaps it was the interruption."

"I'm sure you have enough photos," said Mademoiselle Objet, "and if you ask me, it's a good thing you got them before that nuisance called."

"Yes, certainly," said Madame Métier. Her voice was cloudy, distant, as if it had come from a cave, but Mademoiselle Objet didn't notice.

"So do you mind, then," she said cheerily, "if Monsieur Sorbonne and I go off together for the afternoon? He's taken the day off from the Artifacts Museum."

"I don't," said Madame Métier, insisting a smile through the veil of her disappointment. "Have a good time."

～

CHAPTER 28

Madame Métier Is Once Again Alone

It had been Monsieur L'Ange, she was sure, who had called, and Madame Métier felt almost desolate to have missed him. Who knew where he was or how she could possibly find him.

Work—in this case, having her photograph taken—had once again impeded her life as a flower. Had her work in itself ever made her feel happy, she wondered? Had it made her feel delicious or carefree? It hadn't. It had satisfied others, had healed and transformed them; but in the way that sitting by candlelight on the sitting room floor or lying with her head on Monsieur L'Ange's chest had made her heart happy, work hadn't made her happy at all. It had given her a deep sense of purpose, but it hadn't made her feel liquid or fluid. It hadn't made her feel like a woman.

She thought of Monsieur Sorbonne and Mademoiselle Objet, sitting right now as they must be, under a large umbrella somewhere, enjoying each other and the sun, and she felt pity, that most despicable of all feelings, for herself.

Perhaps it hadn't been Monsieur L'Ange on the phone after all. Yet the mere thought of his calling had somehow rearranged her. She had felt excitement. And sadness. One right after the other. She had *felt*—and that, after all, was the point. She had felt with him, after so many years of not feeling, and she had imagined that because of feeling again, life might now also contain some other new things: soft moments of stillness, beautiful words, romantic happenings.

She hated the mood she was in, twinged at the heart like a schoolgirl, feeling a crooked admixture of desperation and longing. It was unnerving. She needed to gather herself, somehow to collect the dispersed components of her fretted psyche so that whether or not she should ever see him again she would be able, in spite of herself, to go on with her work.

Desperate, she put on her red bathing suit and headed for the beach.

～

CHAPTER 29

Madame Métier and Monsieur L'Ange
Have a Reunion

"Having a work that you love is a gift. No matter how sorrowful your heart," Madame Métier had just written in her notebook, "you have had, always, the great privilege of your work."

"You look so beautiful, sitting there and writing in your notebook," said Monsieur L'Ange, who had just arrived through the mists at the beach.

He sat down beside her, and wrapping his arms about his knees, which he had drawn up pincer-like in front of him, he turned sideways, looking at her. "I called you this morning, but I was told you were busy. The woman who works for you was extremely focused on something. She was rude to me, in fact. I didn't want to further upset her."

"Thank you," said Madame Métier.

"But you're sorry you missed me."

"Yes. And . . ."

"You were afraid you might never see me again."

"I had been."

"I knew you were. I wasn't worried. I knew I would see you later. Here."

"How did you know?"

"I knew that after being sad you would come here, to try to make yourself feel better."

"You know everything, don't you?"

"Some things. Yes."

There was an immemorial quality about the moment. Silken. Blessed. Magic. A soft breeze, like the presence of clouds, blew over them. Fine strands of Madame Métier's hair unwound like long white ribbons striping her field of vision, and as she looked across the long *plage* of white sand, she felt suspended in time and she could find no voice, no language with which to speak of all the things she was feeling—where, only a few nights ago, together, they had been, where they were now, and where, in time, they might be going.

Beside her, mysteriously, he could feel all this. He unwrapped an arm from around his knees and wrapped it around her shoulders.

"I know it's hard to talk," he said. "Sometimes there are no words. But we don't need to talk. Let's walk. I need to walk." He got up, and pulling her up with his hands, helped her put her things in her basket. Then with long elegant strides, they walked together down the beach.

~

CHAPTER 30

Mademoiselle Objet and Monsieur Sorbonne Have a Tête-à-Tête

Monsieur Sorbonne and Mademoiselle Objet were, indeed, sitting under a white umbrella at an Outdoor Lunches Restaurant.

"I'm happy," said Mademoiselle Objet, as if this were a remarkable state of affairs.

"I'm happy, too," said Monsieur Sorbonne. "Why are you happy?"

"I'm happy because my rash is gone. I'm happy because you love me. I'm happy because we're sitting here in the sun. I'm happy because I like my work, and I'm happy because it seems like things have finally settled down. Why are you happy?"

The sun blasted down on the white umbrella, sheltering Monsieur Sorbonne from the harsh noonday brightness.

"I'm happy because I've had a good lunch—fumed salmon and pink lentil soup. I'm happy because you love me. I'm happy because I'm here instead of at work. I'm happy because today, again, I was able to take some photographs."

"Do you think you got some good photographs? Do you think you got *the* photograph for the TeleVisions station?"

"I think so, probably," said Monsieur Sorbonne, though slightly without conviction. He was thinking of Madame Métier's little breakdown— or so, at the moment it had seemed to him, the way her mood, like a sunny day broken by clouds, had suddenly changed.

Mademoiselle Objet tap-tapped her long silver lemonade spoon mindlessly on the table. "What is it about this day?" she said, finally. "Everything was wonderful this morning, and now everything's fallen apart. Something happened when that caller called. That man. Madam

Métier went out the window. And now you. What's the matter? Are you unhappy with the photographs?"

"No," said Monsieur Sorbonne pensively. "I'm sure the photographs are fine."

"Then what's the matter? Are your salmons over-fumed? What's going on?"

"Something. I'm not sure. Maybe *I* was upset by the phone call this morning."

"Oh, yes. The Pest. That nuisance. Wasn't it great, how quickly I got rid of him?"

"No, actually, it wasn't," said Monsieur Sorbonne. "You shouldn't have, I don't think. I don't know why, but I have, distinctly, feeling that Madame Métier really needed to talk to that person."

"But you were right in the middle of photographing her."

"I know, but there was something . . . necessary . . . I don't know."

"That's right, you don't." said Mademoiselle Objet. "These people call all the time, just to carry on about the cremes. If we let them all through, there wouldn't be any cremes. We'd never get anything done." By then her voice had ascended to the higher registers. "I'm sorry," she said, catching herself. "This is ridiculous. I'm sorry. I don't know why I'm so upset."

"And I don't know either—why I am," said Monsieur Sorbonne. "But there was something about that phone call, because afterward . . . Madame Métier could no longer smile. She had been so poised and radiant all morning . . . and then. . . .

With her long silver spoon, Mademoiselle Objet stirred her pink lemonade. "You're right," she said, thoughtfully, "I was being so efficient that I hardly noticed."

"Something, though," said Monsieur Sorbonne dreamily. "Perhaps we'll never know. Come. Let's take the film to be developed. I can't wait to see the portrait of our beautiful Madame Métier."

～

CHAPTER 31

Monsieur Sorbonne Returns to Work

When he returned to work the next day, Monsieur Sorbonne felt a slight disgust upon entering the Artifacts Museum. It seemed dusty. The marble halls seemed high and cold. The crypt in the basement, where he was still cataloging the wall stones from the ancient Egyptian temple, seemed sepulchral and grim. Where was the Ladies' Room maid he'd photographed two days ago? He sensed that, vaguely, he missed her. And where was Madame Métier? Distinctly he felt that he missed the radiance of her presence in which, for several hours yesterday, before the distracting phone call, he had been able to bask.

There was a memo on his desk from the Chief Curator of Artifacts. Where was—and when would the new collection of Pre-Columbian sculptures and toe rings be organized for display? It was soon to be overdue and Monsieur Sorbonne, the Chief Cuurator noted, had prepared it neither with his former promptness nor enthusiasm, and it was far behind schedule.

In fact—and here the curator seemed to be becoming long-winded, extending his memo over onto the second side of the insipid blue-lined yellow memo paper—Monsieur Sorbonne's performance in general, wasn't quite up to snuff.

"If it doesn't come back up to par soon"—vaguely, between the lines, Monsieur Sorbonne could feel the slight threat of removal—"We shall have to seek other means of accomplishing our exhibits," it concluded.

This threat, unnerving as it was, did not untowardly affect Monsieur Sorbonne; for by now he had been so deeply affected by something else—the sense, quite distinct, of the utter inappropriateness of his employment at the Artifacts Museum—that he simply could not be bothered by it.

He was thinking, too, of Madame Métier, and, more specifically, of how he had felt in her presence, of how arranging and rearranging her face, her hands, and her hair in the light, he had felt for the first time, a real sense of meaning. To capture the human consciousness, to reveal the mystery of a single human being, to deliver the picture of a soul—and, in particular, of her extraordinary spirit. Ah, yes, all this at last and finally and only, seemed to Monsieur Sorbonne to have meaning.

He studied the memo. He should, he knew, get to work. He unwrapped the boxes of Pre-Columbian figures. As usual, there was an infinity of fragments. Bored by them all, dejected by their endless minute incompleteness, the shattered ancient ridiculousness of every one of them, he laid them all out on the gray felt-covered surface of his long work table.

First it had been Iron Age razor blades. Then it had been Etruscan pot shards. It had been shattered Peruvian pillars and weighty Egyptian wall stones. Now it was Pre-Columbian crumbs. Where would it end—in what disorganized piles and elaborate reconstructions?

Feeling as if not ever again, not once, not even for a minute could he contemplate, let alone scintillate about cataloguing or rearranging anything, he put on his coat and closed up his crypt and, deciding to have a premature lunch, stole out of the Artifacts Museum and went to the Films Development Store to pick up the portraits of Madame Métier.

∾

CHAPTER 32

Madame Métier and Monsieur L'Ange Have a Dinner

"*I know very little about you,*" said Monsieur L'Ange a few hours later as, once again, they were sitting in the restaurant. In the background the faintest notes of piano music were playing and Madame Métier, entranced, had drifted off into them. "About your life, for example," he continued. "About who you really are."

She started again to talk about her work, the forthcoming TeleVisions show, the calla lily creme, the photographs yesterday morning.

"I know all that," said Monsieur L'Ange. "It's the rest, the everything else that I'm interested in—your hopes and dreams, what sparkles your heart, what you think about when you lie awake in the night."

"How kind of you to ask," said Madame Métier, "to want to know." The piano tinkled in the background, elegant and fine, a chain of notes that hung suspended, jewel-like in the air. "What sparkles my heart—how delightful!" she said and smiled. "The beach. My red bathing suit. My workroom. My silk dressing gown. Giving my love through my work. Feeling the love of the earth for the stones, of the air for the sun, of the wind for each petal and frond. Making things. Inventing my cremes—the magic of that, the incomparable joy of being a part of—how shall I say it?—the work of creation. Serving. Being a part, though only the tiniest part, of the healing. The mystery of all that. The privilege . . ." She paused.

Across from her, Monsieur L'Ange was deeply listening. "You walk such a beautiful path," he said. "Your love is so deep." He reached his huge hands across the small restaurant table and stroked her hands lovingly, gently. "Your work is your love, and I'm so happy it's been there for you, that it has sustained you . . . through all the losses."

She looked at him questioningly.

"There have been many losses." He said it matter of factly.

"Yes. I suppose there have been some losses." Once again, she could hear the piano in the background, delicate, haunting, and sweet, a counterpoint to her words, a cradle, a hammock to receive them. "Some dear ones have died. My husband. A beautiful child. My father. But there have been gifts always, also, that came along with them."

"The river of life," he said. "Shining. Flowing. Returning." He waved his hand in a sort of whispering figure-eight in the air. "You know the deep things—the losses and the gifts that come with them, and how in the end they grow your soul large. But I'm sorry you've had to go through them alone, that there's never been someone to hold you, no arms around you, no shoulder to lean on." Once again, magically, like a maestro, he waved his hands beautifully, hypnotically through the air. As if in so doing he had somehow mesmerized her, she quietly, dreamily smiled.

"So what *do* you dream of at night?" he asked.

She smiled once again. "Beautiful flowers. Flowers I've never heard of or seen. Plants with unimaginable healing powers. And love," she said. "Love so strong it could heal the whole world."

"You are that love," he said, tracing with one of his fingers, each of her fingers, and then her lips, then the lids of her eyes. "That's why you're so beautiful inside and out. That's why wherever you go, a sort of light follows you. But you also need your own experience of love. Come," he said. "Let's go home." So saying, he laid some money down on the table, and taking her hand into his, invited her to stand up. Arm after arm, he helped her into her long black coat, then wrapping his arm about her shoulder, he escorted her out of the restaurant.

~

Her body disappeared when he made love to her. It was as if she was no longer bound to it, contained by the configuration of her legs, her arms, the shape of her skin, but broken out of its cage, released into the seamless infinite whole, let go of and made free, so that when she came back—to the bed, to the pale blue blankets and white sheets, to the room with the high white moon staring in like a witness at the window, and even to his arms—she felt a small inexpressible sorrow as if the world, his body and her own, and even life itself, were somehow strangely an insult, a very small container for the huge, the magnificent thing.

"It's hard to come back sometimes, isn't it?" he said.

"Yes."

In the light of the moon she lay still next to him, adrift in the lapping tide of his breath, the sound of his steadily beating heart, waiting for sleep to overtake her. But she was strangely awake and he was, too, beside her. As she played with his hair and stared into his beautiful eyes in the moonlight, she felt a strange mixture of contentment and sorrow; but she was unable to speak it. The joy was the joy of being here now, beside him; and the sorrow—she couldn't quite name it.

"You're still awake?" he said, finally.

"Yes," she said. "And I don't know why, but I'm sad."

"Don't be sad," he said. "We're going to have a wonderful time." So saying, he clasped her close to his heart, and, wrapped to him like moss to a stone, she finally slept.

~

Morning light spilled in through the windows, radiant, golden. Madame Métier opened her eyes, surprised once again that Monsieur L'Ange was there beside her, his breath, his form, his beautiful eyes. She looked all around the room, which now felt different, inhabited, alive.

"Look!" she said suddenly, and he looked up. There, as if etched in color on the wall hung a huge pale orange butterfly, its wings spread out so flat and still that it looked as if it had been painted, *tromp l'oeil*, on the wall.

Then, even as she stared, its colorful, still configuration quivered, started to melt, to shift and change, until she could no longer see its elegant wings and speckled markings, but flames, orange flames, a great raging fire, and inexplicably again, she felt unbearably sad.

"You have seen something again," he said, holding her very near.

"Yes," she said "Fire. Flames. Fire."

Beside her, he was silent. Holding her. Taking one breath, then another. And another. She looked in his eyes, and she could see that he was weighing something.

"You have just seen the fire," he said.

She was shaking a little, her cells strangely dancing. "Tell me," she said. "What do you mean?"

"There was a very bad fire in our house when I was seven," said Monsieur L'Ange.

"I'm sorry to hear that," said Madame Métier.

"My mother died in it," he said.

Beside him, Madame Métier let out a little gasp.

He paused, breathing again; then he went on. "She had a disease . . ." He whispered its name but all she could hear was "Huntington's," then he went on. "It dims the powers of the muscles and the brain. She was at home alone one day—I was at school—she lit the stove and it exploded. Because she was already so weak, she was unable to put out the fire. The house burned down and she . . ." He paused, beneath the covers holding her hand very tightly, as if to provide punctuation, a semi-colon or a period—"and she . . . burned up in it."

He paused again, and she could feel him deciding something, perhaps whether or not to go on. He took a few breaths. Then he said, "My father blamed me because I was so late coming home. I was the oldest, and I had stayed late after school, playing ball."

"And the others?"

"The *other*. There was only one. My brother. He was younger and not yet in school. My mother, because of her illness, already could not take care of him. He was always cared for by a woman down the street."

"I see," said Madame Métier. "And now? Where is he now?"

Once again, beneath the sheets, Monsieur L'Ange squeezed her hand, breathing out, breathing in, with long empty pauses between. This time, clearly, he did not want to go on. Finally he said. "He also died."

"I see," said Madame Métier, quietly. She imagined his brother also being trapped in the fire, but then she remembered that he was being cared for by the woman down the street.

Beside her, Monsieur L'Ange waited again. Then opening both his eyes wide, very wide to the oncoming golden morning, he looked directly at her, as if to say that her eyes would be the blackboard, that in them he would read, as if written out in white chalk, exactly what she needed to know, the truth, or the truth necessarily obscured; and that then he would either continue or not go on. He looked in her eyes then, and he could see that she needed to know. To hear the whole truth. In words.

"He also died of the disease," he said. "It's hereditary, It passes . . . from mothers to sons."

"To *all* sons?"

There was a very long pause. Then, finally, he said, "Yes. To *all* sons." He squeezed her hand again beneath the sheets, and for a long time, both of them were silent.

"So then you . . . also?"

There was another long pause. Then finally he said, "Yes. That's why I walk so much at the beach. Exercise is very important. It delays . . . the onset."

Madame Métier lay beside him in shock. Once again, though differently, her body disappeared. She felt numb. Hair streaming around her, she laid her head on his heart. Then quietly, ever so quietly, ever so deeply, she started to sob. He put his index finger and his middle finger to her lips. "Shhhh," he said. "It's alright. We have every minute that we have. And every minute is a miracle."

As she lay upon him, she could feel his great strength far within, a wellspring of peace, as if having always known his own end, he lived each day in the deep acceptance of it. Adrift on his body, she wept now piteously, like a child. She felt for the moment not at all like a woman, but so young, so small, like a sparrow, a tiny bird in a world so immense that she could never traverse it. It was all, oh, so much, and she knew then the crown of tears that she had seen.

212 ~~~ *Daphne Rose Kingma*

She wanted to ask him when, under what conditions, and how long, but she could not. Instead, again, quietly on his body, she wept.

"Don't be sad," he said finally, smoothing and smoothing her hair. "When the time comes, it will be easy. I'll go to The Blue, where you just went, and I know it will be beautiful. You have to stay longer, because you have more work to do. You are my life's work. My work is to be here, to love you. But your work . . . is only beginning.

"And afterward . . . later, there will be other things. When you are old, and the pleasures of your beauty have faded, recognition, love, honor. But even for you, when your time comes, it will be easy, I promise. You will be wonderful. You will be ready. You will be surrounded by love."

She lay on him very still, until once again opened the river of tears. It flowed. And he held her close until every tear had passed from her.

~

PART IV

CHAPTER I

Monsieur Sorbonne and Madame Metier's Portrait

Monsieur Sorbonne was very excited the next day to go to the Films Development Store, where the clerk who ordinarily looked slightly like a monkey, today looked somewhat more like a baboon.

"I'm sorry, Sir," said the baboon, handing Monsieur Sorbonne a large gray envelope. "But once again there is a problem with your photographs. The prints, Sir, all have errors which, in spite of a number of printings, we have been unable to correct. Perhaps your light measurer was off, or you were shooting from an incorrect angle. In any case, there's a problem. Once again, may I kindly suggest, Sir, that you have your camera checked."

So downhearted was Monsieur Sorbonne that, paying for the misfit pictures, he put the large gray envelope, without so much as a passing glance at the photographs, into his dog-eared briefcase. He hadn't realized until just now how much he was invested in these particular photographs, how much, without admitting it, he had secretly hoped that photographing Madame Métier could somehow lead him to work that had meaning, deposit him eventually, or sooner, into a new profession.

Whatever, he wondered, could be the problem? The first photographs—buildings, cornices, and balconies—had been ruined, no good. The second set—the maid, the guard, and the orphan children—had all been fine. As well as the ones of Madmoiselle Objet. The camera had been so-called "fixed," but now, once again, problems. He could feel a small squall rising in him, that horrible, roller-coaster, out-of-sync feeling, which, as a man, he so despised. He hated emotions gone out of control. He felt awful—hopeless, helpless, deranged—the way Mademoiselle

Objet must feel, it occurred to him now, when she got so upset that her feelings came out in her hands.

It was amazing, awful really, how various things about one's work could be so terribly upsetting. Except that this wasn't his work. This was his art, his form of expression. That's why he was so upset. Unlike his job, which he did merely for money, this was his life's work, his calling—a source of meaning, a reason for living. And all true life's works, he realized now, had certain things in common. The forms of them were varied, but no matter how simple or grand they were, each was the expression of a single human spirit; each was unique in what it had to offer; each somehow spoke to the human condition and served in some way to heal and transform. Madame Métier did that by being her radiant self. Mademoiselle Objet did that by serving, one step removed, but devotedly, in the mysterious chain of healing. And he—he had wanted to do it, too—by taking Madame Métier's photograph, by capturing on film the spirit of this rare human being.

But perhaps, it occurred to him now, as once again he contemplated the failure of his photographs, he had merely been self-serving. Perhaps he had just wanted to be delivered from his crypt—his little death trap of a cell in the basement of the Artifacts Museum. Or perhaps he had overlooked the meaning that already existed in his work. Artifacts, after all, were a tribute to the human spirit. Even Iron Age razor blades were statements of human ingenuity. Maybe the photographs had vanished in order to teach him a lesson.

It was all so confusing. Maybe nothing had any more meaning than anything else. Or, maybe everything had meaning. Art did. Artifacts did. People did. Service did. Healing did. Even his search for meaning, he realized, had a meaning in itself. But in spite of his contemplations, he was mortally confused. Perhaps it was just that he had wanted so much to be the person to photograph Madame Métier, because like Mademoiselle Objet, he had felt a sort of beautiful internal tingling in her presence.

He had been so around all the corners of the cosmos in his thinking that now nothingwas clear anymore except that he was, indeed, disappointed that the photographs had not turned out. And thinking a little sadly of the plain gray envelope, he returned, almost acceptingly, to his crypt at the Artifacts Museum.

When he finally got home, Mademoiselle Objet could feel his deep disappointment, the sense of meaninglessness that had obviously invaded him, as, despairing, he set his briefcase down on the table. "The photographs didn't turn out," he said. "I can't believe it. That camera's jinxed."

"Not any of them?" asked a hopeful Mademoiselle Objet.

"I don't know. I haven't looked, but the man at the Films Store told me they didn't."

Hearing this, Mademoiselle Objet, too, was distressed. Like Madame Métier when she was distressed, Mademoiselle Objet suggested that they have some tea and then look at the photographs. And so it was that, in her most profoundly exquisite, object-arranging way, on two yellow-striped placemats, she set out two green-rimmed cups and two carved silver teaspoons. For she knew no other way, except by arranging objects, of how to comfort Monsieur Sorbonne.

"I can't even look at them," he said. "The man at the Films Store said once again that something is wrong with the camera. I can't believe it!"

Having poured out the tea, Mademoiselle Objet retrieved from his briefcase the large gray envelope.

"Now, close your eyes," she said, teasing, and then she opened the envelope and riffled through its contents. Then, one by one, upside down, she laid out all the photographs on the clear center field of the table.

"Now open your eyes," she said, and at once they both opened their eyes. One by one, Mademoiselle Objet turned each of the photographs over until there on the table before them lay seven blank sheets of shining paper. They were all marked out by only the merest, faintest immaterial mist of an image of a woman, shadows of light upon light, in which floated two beautiful blue-gray eyes.

They had not turned out, and yet, as she contemplated them, Mademoiselle Objet suddenly realized that they referred not to the person of Madame Métier, but to that mysterious something she always felt when she was in Madame Métier's presence, a weird consuming peacefulness that always made it worthwhile, no matter how hopelessly disorganized she was, to work with Madame Métier. Far from *not* turning out, the photographs had more than turned out. For most remarkably, they had recorded not Madame Métier's visage, but her essence.

∽

CHAPTER 2

Madame Métier Fails to Come to Work

The following morning, Madame Métier did not come to work. Her heart was with tears. Today nothing mattered and everything mattered. Monsieur L'Ange had left, and in time he would leave even more. Although she could feel the pull of Mademoiselle Objet in the workroom, the sounds of all her morning preparings, she knew she couldn't possibly face her. Finally, at noon, she wrote a small note and slipped it under the workroom door.

She was shattered, remembering his words. It was unbearable, really, the way that life, this miracle, could be so endlessly punctuated by loss, the way that, so trustingly, like a flower, you could open your heart and your spirit and even your body to someone and then be so deeply invaded by loss. Loss, was it?—Or love? Yes, it was love. But there was loss attached to it, like a tail of ribbons attached to a kite.

Loss, loss, loss: the word repeated itself like a haunting, insouciant music that seemed now to have been the counterpoint to her entire life. Loss: the visitation of emptiness, of infinite absence. The death of her father when she was young, the death of her daughter, her husband, and now this one, this Monsieur L'Ange, whose true name it occurred to her now, she didn't even know.

She felt a sharp pain in her chest, as if her heart had been wound around by a thin steel wire that kept being pulled up tighter and tighter by some huge invisible hand. For a minute she wanted to scream, to howl at the gods. The other losses—they had all come out of nowhere, unexpected, each in its own time. But this one had been announced, foretold. She would have to live every day in the face of it, waiting, knowing, every minute. How could she bear such a loss, or ever stretch her soul large enough to contain it?

～

CHAPTER 3

Monsieur Sorbonne Discovers His True Vocation

The following day, Monsieur Sorbonne was greeted in his cellar crypt by the artifacts Curator-in-Chief, who, like a monolith from Stonehenge, was standing just inside the door.

"You're late," he said, definitively, when Monsieur Sorbonne walked in. "You left untimely, prematurely early yesterday. You have done nothing, I see, with the Pre-Columbian group, and frankly, your days are numbered."

Monsieur Sorbonne, undaunted, hung up his coat on the hat rack, while the curator, like a starving, zoo-caged lion was fretfully pacing. "You don't seem to comprehend the seriousness of all this," he went on. "Your position, Monsieur, is in jeopardy. I am threatening you," he said now, quite nakedly, "with almost imminent unemployment."

"I understand," said Monsieur Sorbonne. He was amazed at the quality of his composure, so still and strong, so clear and lucent did his own voice seem. He was slightly aware as he spoke, of being vaguely, innerly haunted by the photographs of Madame Métier. They hadn't failed, it occurred to him now. They had, in fact, most exceptionally succeeded. It had been given to him, for no reason and for every reason, to capture not the material but the interior essence—the spirit—of a most extraordinary human being. And this—this was far beyond artifacts, this was far, far, far beyond the mere reconstruction of things. This was the meaning beyond, within, outside of, and inherent in all living things. He had breathed it, felt it yesterday as he sat and stood and moved in Madame Métier's presence. And he had captured it, in his most remarkable photographs. He had a direct experience of meaning, and in having it had found his true vocation.

Contemplating all this in the midst of the Museum Curator's presence, Monsieur Sorbonne felt strongly at peace, impervious to the threatening huffings and puffings.

Indeed, a circle of silence seemed to have fallen around them. As if he had felt the power of Monsieur Sorbonne's discovery. The Curator-Chief himself seemed strangely suddenly still, excerpted from all motion, and his voice, when he spoke once again, seemed somehow to have had changed. "Perhaps," he said, now quite sympathetically, "you have been going through some exigencies of your own."

"I have, as a matter of fact," said Monsieur Sorbonne, "and I more than a little appreciate your noticing."

"Well, then, we shall be more than patient with you," the Museum Curator said. "So have a good day." And so saying, he rather quickly let himself out of the room.

~

CHAPTER 4

Monsieur Sorbonne Comforts Mademoiselle Objet

That night, when Monsieur Sorbonne got home, he was utterly composed. Without thinking, without effort, frustration, or regret, he had set about his work and done it. Being himself thus at peace, he was disheartened to discover that Mademoiselle Objet, who had been home all afternoon, was mortally distressed.

It was somewhat distressing also, to see how endlessly teeter-tottering life seemed to be. Moment by moment, nothing seemed to stay the same. He was down; she was up—and comforted him. And now vice versa—everything. And yet in the midst of it all he retained, extraordinarily, his composure. Something had happened to him. Something deep. He had found his vocation: capturing light, revealing the human—no, not just the human, but the divine-within-the-human—condition. And having finally discovered it, he had also encountered a strange new strength in himself from which he could now address the fuming Mademoiselle Objet.

"What's the matter?" he asked, noting the minute he did, that his own composure started to crumble. Her moods, the endless variability of the human condition as it expressed itself in her, unlike pot shards or pre-Columbian fragments, did, he noted, still have the capacity to disturb him. Holding on as much as he could to the anchor of his composure, he sat down beside her, and, patting her lovely dark hair, prepared himself to listen.

"It's my work," said Mademoiselle Objet. "It's that wretched, outlandish, uncontrollable Madame Métier! She never even showed up today! I'd been working all morning, mailing out her damn cremes and charming the people at the TeleVisions station, and then finally at noon she slipped a note under the door, saying she wasn't coming at all. It was an insult! As if I'm not working for her! As if she's not even doing this work! All I know is something's changed. She hasn't been herself lately, and I don't know what's happening!! I finally had everything under control, and now this!!"

As she started in on her usual rant, Monsieur Sorbonne found it impossible to contain himself. "That's right," he said, a little testily. "You *do not* know what's happening and it's none of your business! You think the whole world revolves around you, your objects and schedules—the way that *you* want everything. But it doesn't! Everybody has circumstances. Everybody's going through something. Don't be so self-centered. Don't be so controlling. You're mean and judgmental and selfish and spoiled! Things change. People change. Reality . . ." He could feel himself revving up, moving toward or standing up on a sort of invisible soap-box, and although he was slightly surprised at himself, he pressed on . . .

"I've changed. You've changed. Everything's changing for everyone. Nothing is what it used to be. I used to think life was all about things—artifacts and cornices and balconies. But it isn't. It's about people. It's about the inner things. I learned that myself yesterday, taking all those photographs—that vanished—of Madame Métier."

Beside him on the couch, Mademoiselle Objet had slightly calmed down, or perhaps he had subdued her with his speech. Never before had he been so outspoken to her about herself, and never before had she been so receptive to his words. "Stop trying to run the world. It's not your job!" he said, finally. "Your job is to think about somebody else! To be patient. To serve. You're working for Madame Métier and she's giving something to the world. Stop criticizing and get to work!"

He paused for a moment and gathered his breath. "Besides," he added, "you *do not* know what's happening. And maybe it's something wonderful for our dear Madame Métier."

~

CHAPTER 5

Madame Métier Is in Love

It was well after noon when, finally, Madame Métier got dressed and made up the bed. The fragrance of Monsiuer L'Ange still lingered ever so slightly in the sheets, and as she smoothed them out, in a distinctly non-utilitarian way, her hands received from their fine cotton threads a remembrance of the sorrow and the beauty which only last night she had experienced in their midst.

She was utterly unable to work. She wondered, in fact, if she would ever again be able to work. She had been upended by Monsieur L'Ange, by his quiet strength, his purity, his knowing, mysterious words, the sorrow wrapped like wings around him. He had opened her to the joy of herself. She had fallen in love with him.

She had never before been in love, but now, finally, she felt in love. She could feel the deep sweetness of something so endlessly longed-for having at last been given to her, a joy quite separate from achievement, from even the sacred satisfaction of her work. The slow, tight-folded petals of some ancient beautiful flower had started to blossom within her. She could think only of Monsieur L'Ange, how he had come to her, how he would leave, what they would do in the meantime.

As in the wake of the doctor's death, though now for different reasons, she decided to go shopping. She wanted to bloom, to be beautiful for him. As she walked through the streets, she walked right past the Flowers Stand. Nothing, especially the wilted flowers, seemed to be of interest to her. What before had tantalized and intrigued, reminded her of her father, caused her fingers to itch, her imagination to scheme, now seemed to hold no attraction. In fact, except for some long-stemmed red roses, it seemed that her passion for flowers had almost entirely vanished.

Madame Métier had finished her shopping. She had bought black and red and pale ivory-colored lingeries, three matching sets, each embroidered with flowers and cut-out fine lace. The red was for joy, the ivory for her pale skin, and the black—she didn't want to think about what the black was for. As she stood at the counter, paying for all her new lingeries, she noticed a pair of silk emerald-green stockings. When would she ever wear them, she wondered? She had no idea, but something about them enchanted her, and so, impulsively, she bought them.

"You look so beautiful, picking out lingerie," said a voice. Madame Medtier had just picked up her pacquets and was walking out of the store, when out on the sidewalk, Monsieur L'Ange accosted her. In his right hand, wrapped in green florist's paper, he carried a huge bouquet of long-stemmed red roses, which, kissing her tenderly on the lips, he handed to her.

"I thought you might like some fresh flowers," he said. "Flowers not to make cremes with, but just to enjoy."

~

CHAPTER 6

Madame Métier and Monsieur L'Ange
Have Another Encounter

She felt strange, later, when they were lying in bed. They had gone out to dinner and then had come home. They had had some tea in the living room and then they had walked up the stairs. In the half-light, in a crystal vase, she had arranged the red roses and placed them on the dresser.

Wordless, then, they slipped into the bed, the light of a half-moon shadowing the curtains, ever so faintly quicksilvering the room. In the shimmering stillness she stretched out beside him, laid her head on his chest while he wrapped his enfolding arms around her and lovingly clasped her to him.

It was there, lying ever so close to him—she could feel the poetry of his heartbeat through the bony cage of his ribs, iamb after iamb in the dark—it was there, as she lay still beside him, breathing out, breathing in, feeling the feel of his hair, inhaling the sweet sharp fragrance of his skin, that once again she began to see certain things:

On a desert, yellow sand, and sand clouds up-blowing in the wind. The forward charge of hundreds of horses, pale horses with red embroidered blankets, moody dark eyes. Hoofs pounding, stampeding, stamping three-quarter-round imprints in the sand. Now galloping toward them, and him riding on at her side, his face so close that for a minute she could see him, read his blue eyes beneath the burnoose. Then, out of nowhere, off to the right, a javelin hurled, steel glinting, inches from her, flying through air. But he had fallen already, pierced from behind, and then she fell too, and from where she had fallen and lay on the sand, hooves pounding above her, around her, on every side—on her chest, on her arms, on her eyes, bloody eyes—she looked up from the floor of the desert to see his body arch backward, receiving the charge, then watched him crumple, then fold, then fall forward, then backward again, then sideways, then down altogether, until he was lost in a forest of horses' legs pounding, galloping over him, trampling, crushing, until his body was nothing more than a carpet of blood on the sand.

She twitched, half-dozing, and let out a small little scream.

"You're dreaming," he said. "Don't worry. I'm here. I'm right here with you." With his great hand he smoothed and smoothed out her hair, until she slept once again. And dreamed once again.

A river by moonlight, arched over by still almost winter-bare trees, their branches atangle with buds of spring green, and she in a blue velvet dress, lace petticoats lifted, sitting there on the banks of the river, sitting there on her dapple-gray horse. The smell of wet woolen blankets, pressed leaves, crushed violets in the rain. She could see the white trillium, bent-over hats of striped jack-in-the-pulpits, tri-partite leaves of spring wintergreen, and the river so deep, so blue-black with huge rocks up-jutting. And him—he was there too, in a fine suit of armor, sword harsh-clattering, horse's hind end up-rearing against the fast-rushing current, as he kept crossing and trying to cross the wide river, rocks churning up against his horse's dark legs, battering them, battering him. Then in the sky, thunder and lightening. Then, against the white-foaming current, him trying again to cross the wild river, to come to her there, where she waited for him, there on the banks, far down on the opposite side of the river. And minute by minute, him becoming more distant, the current more raging, dragging him farther and farther downriver, until in the black night welter of water, chain mail dragging, armor loud-clanking, she watched as he fell down and into and under the surging black water, the great brown mound of his horse's hind end rising up like a brown huge stone in the roiling black water. Then the horse's loud whinny and moan. Then more lightening and her scream.

She screamed then. In her sleep, she started again.

"I'm here, I'm still here," he whispered, holding her now, again, more closely, her head on his chest, her folded-up hand gathered into his folded-up hand until she slept once again.

She was in a hospital—or was it a cathedral?—so high were the walls, so high to high heaven, and the windows jewel-like. And there was a vaulted high ceiling of blue, painted over with little gold stars, and a long walking aisle from the front to the doors. There were people beside her, a man all in black—a doctor perhaps, or a priest, with a cross—or was it a stethoscope?—around his neck, and a plain white tablet on which were written no words. And he, Monsieur L'Ange, in the front of the church, was laid out on a catafalque—or was it a bed?—she couldn't tell. But there was a woman, older, with white-blonde hair who stood beside the man all in black—the priest? the doctor?—and she was weeping. A younger woman, holding a white lace handkerchief, and a younger man were standing there also, next to the woman with white-blonde hair, who was quietly weeping, who was wearing green stockings and a red dress.

Then, with the beautiful woman behind him, the doctor? the priest? stepped over to—the catafalque?—the bed?—and placing the—stethoscope?—the cross?—on the heart of the man laid out, he listened, then removed it. Then, gesturing to the woman, who stepped up beside him, he set two coins on the dead man's eyes and pulled the sheet up over his face. Then, as if they had all enacted this before, as if it were all just a play in which, for the hundredth time they were starring, he lifted a pen and wrote some words on the plain white tablet. Then he turned to the empty long walking aisle and pronounced the words: "The King is Dead."

In her sleep now, quietly, tears, a small rivulet of sobbing. "I have watched you . . ." she said, extricating herself from his arms, sitting up a little on the pillows, and touching his living face beside her, which, in the moonlight now was waxen, immemorially familiar, "I have watched you . . ." she said it through a soft well of tears, ". . . I have watched you die so many times before."

"I know," he said. "And you are so beautiful, always, when you watch me die." He laughed a little and, unexpectedly, she laughed, too. Then she fell back on the pillows and into his gathering strong embrace, until dreamless, in his arms, she slept.

～

CHAPTER 7

Mademoiselle Objet Has An Awakening

Penitent the next morning, Mademoiselle Objet arrived on time for work. She had been set straight, as it were, by Monsieur Sorbonne, and she was determined to squelch whatever outbursts might try to rise up within her. He was right—things had, and must—change, and her need to control everything, to always have things be her way, that also needed to change.

Monsieur L'Ange had already left. He had risen early, and kissing Madame Métier on the cheeks and lips, had quietly stolen out of the room. Having slept a strange sorrowful sleep, Madame Métier had awakened surpringingly refreshed. It was as if through the strange tableau of her dreams she had been given to see everything—Monsieur L'Ange and the many times she had already lost him. And seeing that she had lived through the loss and that he was still here—was here once again—she felt strangely at peace.

So affected though was she by what she had dreamt, that now everything and nothing mattered. She no longer cared about what Mademoiselle Objet would think, how she might react or even if, in a fit, she would leave. In her body, now, she felt a strange new energy. Inspired, though just beneath the surface, sad, she moved through her room with a studied peacefulness, picking things up, quietly making the bed.

"I'm sorry," she said to Mademoiselle Objet a few minutes later when, dressed in blue silk, her hair nicely combed, her face suffused with radiance, she entered the workroom. "I'm very sorry about not coming to work yesterday. I know I'm difficult. I know that every day everything's different—and I know all that's the worst for you—someone like you who likes everything perfect—it's just that . . ."

But Mademoiselle Objet interrupted her. "It's just that you have your own circumstances, and something wonderful's happened for you. I already know! That's why you're acting so strange. And it's none of my business. I know that, too."

Hearing this, Madame Métier was amazed. "Yes, yes, actually it has," she said. She wondered whether, in detail, she should explain, but when she looked at Mademoiselle Objet, she saw in her eyes a quite unfamiliar composure, and she knew that explaining was unnecessary. The actual facts were unimportant, because clearly, Mademoiselle Objet had changed.

Madame Métier was amazed. For a minute she didn't know whether or not to believe what she had just seen, but when she looked once again she could see it was true. Indeed, it was as if every cell in Mademoiselle Objet's body had taken on a slightly different coloration. Her entire being now gave off an air of acceptance—of willingness and openness and thoughtfulness and calm.

Taking in the miracle of Mademoiselle Objet's quite obvious transformation, Madame Métier was quietly overjoyed. There were moments in life—and this she knew was one of them—of infinite grace, when suddenly, for no apparent reason, a conflict is resolved, when, from the back room or the basement of another person's consciousness, a new awareness arises, so that all the pains of the past can be laid down, and a whole new chapter can begin.

"I'm sorry, too," said Mademoiselle Objet, confirming Madame Métier's perception."I'm sorry I've always been so impatient."

"It's true," said Madame Métier. "You haven't always been patient with me, but you have always been most unbelievably helpful; and for that I am infinitely grateful."

"Well, I'm glad that at least I could help, even though I'm so willful and selfish."

Madame Métier was stunned, and was about to disagree, but Mademoiselle Objet barreled on, "And impatient and controlling and self-centered and judgmental and mean! That's what Monsieur Sorbonne told me last night. I want things my way and no other way. I'm spoiled!"

"You have been," said Madame Métier quietly, "but you've changed. Today, just now, in saying these things, you have gone past your old self. Last night you listened with your heart and recognized the truth, and today, already, the light of compassion has started to come in." She smiled at Mademoiselle Objet, and embraced her, and for a moment Mademoiselle Objet could feel in her brain a tingling molecular effervescence, the derangement, it seemed, of the last of her discontents.

~

"I *am* sorry," she said, a few minutes later, joining Madame Métier at the workroom table, "truly sorry for the way I've been, but now that I've changed,"—she laughed a little, then became suddenly almost parental—"I have a few things to say. You *do* need to work. I know you don't want to. I know that you're tired. I know you just want to be a free spirit, but you can't be. You have a great work—a great *métier*,"—and here she laughed a little again—"and you have no idea how many people are going to be transformed by it. You need to listen! You need to hear me once and for all! You think it's your cremes, all this calla lily and saxifrage nonsense that heals everyone. But it isn't. It's your presence, your essence. It's *you!*"

~

CHAPTER 8

Monsieur Sorbonne Is Content

Having claimed the new strength in himself because of how he had spoken to Mademoiselle Objet, feeling the residue of light in his body from having photographed Madame Métier, and having received the onslaught from the Curator Chief in a state of composure, Monsieur Sorbonne was also changed.

No longer did anything matter. Or rather, it all now mattered differently. What no longer mattered was his work, his gainful employment, the endless demanding and boring particulars of it. He had no passion for it anymore, no overweening concern. Instead he saw it simply as a job, and he did it. No longer enslaved by Etruscan crumbs or Peruvian pot shards, now when his eight hours were done, he quietly locked up his crypt and went out walking with his camera, his third intelligent eye, until he could see—that is to say, be moved so deeply by something—that he felt compelled to record it.

He found a great satisfaction in this, and each time his photographs were developed—a beautiful face, a body elegantly in motion, the encounter of two lovers, children imagining things—he made a large portfolio of them. In time, he showed them all to Mademoiselle Objet, who was quietly astonished by them. And when he saw the pride in her eyes as she admired his work, he felt moved once again, to photograph her. So it was that often, on a Saturday or Sunday, in the pale gray light that fell in through the high curved windows of their little house, with music playing in the background, her eyes to the sky, her hands to her cheeks, sitting, knees folded, arms wrapped around her legs, he would once again capture the soul of the lovely Mademoiselle Objet.

Such joy did he feel in all this, such a quiet refined contentment that Mademoiselle Objet in his presence also always could feel it.

"You're happy now, aren't you?" she asked him one night before they went to sleep.

"Yes," he said.

"Why are you happy?" she asked.

"Because you love me. Because you have found peace. Because from time to time I can photograph Madame Métier and sit in her presence. Because at last I have found a life's work with meaning." So saying, he reached out beneath the soft blankets and sheets and took hold of her hand. Then, blissfully, holding her pretty hand, he fell asleep.

～

CHAPTER 9

Madame Métier Confesses

Basking in Mademoiselle Objet's new peacefulness, Madame Métier became more organized. Now every morning she came in on time to the workroom. Each day she had sort of a plan, an overview of what needed to be done. Rather than always running off, disappearing at noon in her red bathing suit, she attended to her work. She could attend to her work, she knew, because in the background hours after work, she was enjoying Monsieur L'Ange—walking and talking, waking and sleeping, making love with him.

In the midst of this, her newly acquired ability to focus, she was able, with Mademoiselle Objet's assistance, to lay out an entire plan for the TeleVisions station, a series on the magical properties of plants. "We shouldn't perhaps call it 'magical,'" she said. "Someone might misunderstand. We should call it simply the 'healing properties of plants.'" And so, not long after her program introducing the calla lily creme, she started filming a ten-part series on medicinal flowers.

Meanwhile, orders for all the original cremes kept flooding in. From time to time she still made visits to the Orphans' Hospital. She had also started making speeches, to a variety of groups, about the healing power of plants and their electric energy and how to extract the power of light from living botanical foods.

In all she did, she now seemed more quietly, insistently radiant at the center. Day by day she had become surprisingly efficient; and Mademoiselle Objet, in her presence, had become remarkably calm. It was less interesting, less dramatic to be sure, the way they now passed the days, but to Mademoiselle Objet, it was heaven. She could now endlessly bathe in Madame Métier's luminous presence, and she sensed that for Madame Métier, too, these days held a special magic.

"You're happy, too, aren't you?" she asked Madame Métier one afternoon, when as usual, after work they were sitting together and drinking tea.

"Yes. I am," said Madame Métier dreamily, looking out the window. "I have always been happy by virtue of the miracle of having been chosen to be alive. And I have always been grateful for my work, for this exquisite relationship with the spirits of plants. I've been happy—in spite of our sometimes misfits of the past—that you've been here to help me so long. But I'm happy now because now I also have love."

She stumbled a little as she said this, was aware of the tiniest clattering of her pale-blue teacup against its pale-blue saucer. Uncharacteristically, Mademoiselle Objet said nothing. In the pale-violet light of the late afternoon she waited, leaving a space in the air should Madame Métier choose once again to occupy it with words.

"I'm so fortunate," Madame Métier went on, "to now finally, also, be loved as a woman." She wasn't sure whether, once having made this disclosure, she wanted to say more or if she preferred simply to let it stand as it was, a fact that was also a mystery, without elaboration.

"I'm in love," she said finally, setting her teacup down like a period at the end of a sentence.

Once again, Mademoiselle Objet said nothing; then finally she couldn't resist. She knew that Madame Métier had once been married to a handsome doctor, and her curiosity got the best of her. "You weren't in love when you were married?" she asked.

"No," said Madame Métier. She looked out the window, drifting. "I was young," she said, "very young. I married for the wrong reasons. As you perhaps know, marriage just in itself isn't always a guarantee of love. It's a habit of the human condition, a way we have to go about living—and sometimes, for the fortunate few, it is also about love."

She paused. She felt revealed in saying all this, like an open sardine tin with all its silvery contents exposed. She wondered, in fact, just why she was saying all this. Was she saying it for herself or of Mademoiselle

Objet? She didn't know. And yet she felt open, willing to speak for some reason, like a person, merely, a woman with a woman's life, not as a maker of cremes; and it was from this new, this unfamiliar and vulnerable place, that she was choosing to say all these things.

"Personal love . . . that's what I've never had," she said, finally. "Love in the body. The love of a man for a woman."

She listened to what she was saying. Each sentence seemed like a statement from a billboard, so bold, so huge was its message. She could feel the great silent complexities that each of her sentences contained, and yet she felt utterly unable to elaborate. Her skin sang. Her heart was full. That was all she knew at the moment. Finally, she said simply, "Thank you for asking. Yes, I am very happy."

～

CHAPTER 10

Madame Métier and Monsieur L'Ange Are Surprised

They spent many days and nights together, Madame Métier and Monsieur L'Ange. Days walking, late afternoons in twilight, strolling along the white beach where first they had met, stopping sometimes at sunset to have a small picnic or go out to dinner. And it was one afternoon at the beach, her broad-brimmed straw hat protecting her from the sun, the two of them sitting against a rock (the very rock she realized, against which she had been sitting when Monsieur L'Ange had first appeared through the silver mists in the distance), that once again in the distance, through mist, Madame Métier could see a figure approaching.

It seemed, as she watched, almost as if Monsieur L'Ange had doubled himself, so reminiscent was it of their first meeting, almost as if, while sitting here at her side, he was also simultaneously approaching. But the person who now approached, though familiar, was not, of course, him.

"You look so beautiful sitting there together," said Monsieur Sorbonne. "I hope you don't mind if I should take your photograph. Actually," he confessed, "I already have. But now I'm asking permission—to take another, or several more, if you don't mind."

"Thank you. That would be lovely. Please do," said Monsieur L'Ange. "Your timing couldn't be better." Beside her now, he stood up, and when he held out his hand, she stood up beside him. As she did, her beautiful hat brushed his shoulder, going suddenly askew and revealing her face.

Seeing it was Madame Métier whom he had just photographed and seeing the young man beside her, Monsieur Sorbonne felt a red prickle of embarrassment start climbing up his neck, as if untimely, he had discovered her secret.

Seeing her now in this young man's presence, he felt not only embarrassed, but, he had to admit—could it be?—a tiny bit jealous. As he observed her, wrapped in another man's arms, he realized how deeply he was connected to her, not only through Mademoiselle Objet, nor even through all the changes that had come over him when he photographed her. As he saw her here, being so tenderly embraced, he realized that he, too, though differently, so deeply loved Madame Métier.

Allowing himself to feel his great love, his jealousy dissipated, and he allowed himself to appreciate them, man and woman together as the embodied image of love. As in the past when he had been so singularly transfixed by Madame Métier, he was now transfixed by the pair, the duo, the double, the blue-eyed almost angelic lightness that resided in both of them, how each was so perfectly the complement of the other. "If you don't mind, then," he said, "I'll take a few more photographs."

"That would be lovely," said Madame Métier.

Pausing, breath-taken, in front of them now, he invited them, majestically and deeply, to invade the wisdom of his film. Holding the camera box, snap-snapping, he could feel their spirits imprinting themselves, like the shape of two ghosts in a darkened hallway, on the retina of his camera's eye.

"Thank you," he said, when he finished. "And now I will leave you to your evening." Behind him, orange, violet, and pink, the sun fell magnificently down, and turning to leave the lovers behind, Monsieur Sorbonne walked quietly on.

∼

CHAPTER II

Madame Métier and Monsieur L'Ange Return Home

Having been thus photographed, and having packed up the crumbs of their picnic, Madame Métier and Monsieur L'Ange walked down the beach in the early dark of the summer evening. Madame Métier had always liked it, walking with him. For although he was much taller than she, their legs were of exactly the same length, and as they walked, their hip joints matched up joint to joint, in a way that made her feel protected and connected, very similar to him. This gave her a feeling of ease, of grace, as if even in his stride, she had found her perfect reflection.

When they came into the house, she made them some tea and brought it up to the bedroom. It was a soft, very warm summer evening and in the bedroom, already, Monsieur L'Ange had opened the windows. Somewhere, not far in the distance, someone was having a garden party, a wedding reception, perhaps, and Madame Métier could hear the faint sounds of the music, the traces, ever so elegantly, on the evening air, of a song, the words of which she faintly remembered.

It was a song about angels and heaven and remembering forever, and she started singing it out in a whisper, and presently he joined her.

"You know that song?" she asked him finally.

"Yes," he said, "I've always loved it. And I *will* remember you."

Madame Métier was slightly taken aback when he said that. The summer had been so long and sweet, so peaceful and graceful, and she had grown so accustomed to waking with him in the morning, sleeping beside him at night, that she had forgotten that he was under a sentence.

"Do we have to think about that?" she said sharply.

"We don't have to," he said, brushing his fingers across her lips and kissing her. Then, with the notes of the music floating in on the warm evening air, he unveiled her, layer by layer, until she lay there, her whole pale, petalled self before him.

And when he made love to her then, she could see—not his face in the room, but his form in light, and around him many beings of light. She could see, too, that he spoke to them, almost without words. Then, vaguely, she saw that he introduced them to someone—a woman? herself?—and she saw that they were glad when he did. It was beautiful there, the peace of it beyond anything she had ever seen or felt or imagined; and when she returned to the room, to the bed, and Monsieur L'Ange, he was already asleep beside her.

But she could not sleep. She knew she had seen where he would go, where she herself would one day go. She felt deeply blessed that she had been given to see it, but she lay fitfully awake all night, receiving again its unimaginable beauty, and falling only at sunrise, finally, to sleep.

～

CHAPTER 12

Mademoiselle Objet, Having Changed, Has a Relapse

Mademoiselle Objet was once again in a huff and Madame Métier was once again late, very late, coming in to the workroom. Sometimes it seemed like nothing did, after all, really change. Madame Métier had had little epochs of organized-ness—it had actually been almost two months now, *sans* relapse, that she had worked. But then she would start disappearing again in her red bathing suit, or showing up late to the workroom after staying up way too late with that man—whoever he was.

Given all that, Mademoiselle Objet, herself, was capable of a relapse. Here she was once again, self-focused, self-centered, judgmental, the whole nineteen yards, tap-tapping her pencil on the table, feeling her rash, her demeanor beginning to verge on hysterical. It was amazing, wasn't it, she was thinking, how you could come so far, only to discover, in an odd moment or two, that in fact you had traveled no distance at all. It made her angry, furious, really, that her own condition seemed still to be so contingent on this eccentric teenaged middle-aged woman.

Desperate, she opened a jar of sunflower creme and applied it to her hands with exactly no result. She tried another, wisteria salve, and as she was wildly, madly applying it, Madame Métier, fully dressed, eyes red and exhausted, walked into the room.

"What's the matter?" she asked. "You look awful! You look like you've seen a ghost! Something terrible's happened! I don't like this man, whoever he is. He's scaring you and wearing you out and taking you away from your work. And, frankly, I wish he were dead!"

～

So saying, she slammed down a huge pot of creme whose white glass jar shattered, leaving a jagged, gooey mess all over the workroom table. She had just started for the door, when, with a sudden uncharacteristic forcefulness, Madame Métier spun her around and seized her by the shoulders.

"You can leave," she said, "but leaving won't help, because what you hate, what you resist, what you are trying to escape from is exactly what you need to face."

"What do you mean?" asked Mademoiselle Objet.

"That what you want is control. And that life cannot be controlled. It has a mind and a heart of its own, and it will have its way with us. And that as long as you try to control it, you'll miss the point."

"And what *is* the point?" said Mademoiselle Objet, with her former usual cattiness.

"To surrender," said Madame Métier. "To receive what is trying to be given."

"And when you do, then what?" snapped Mademoiselle Objet.

"Then life will offer up its miracles."

Across from her, Mademoiselle Objet was silent. She had no idea what Madame Métier was talking about, yet she could feel a dizzying, almost electric current passing through her entire body, and she suddenly knew the truth of it. Finally, Madame Métier said, "You may go now. In fact, I think you should go. But please, I do hope you'll come back tomorrow."

"I will," said Mademoiselle Objet, amazed at herself, and feeling disoriented still by the tingling, strong, strange energy that had just passed through her body, she added, "I certainly will, and I hope that until then you will be all right."

∿

CHAPTER 13

Monsieur Sorbonne and Mademoiselle Objet
Have an Afternoon Tête-à-Tête

Shaken by this latest difficult upset with Madame Métier, Mademoiselle Objet was relieved, when she got home, to see that although it was just after noon, Monsieur Sorbonne was already there. He had taken the afternoon off, he told her, because he couldn't wait.

"Couldn't wait for what?" asked Mademoiselle Objet quietly.

"To see the photographs," he said.

As if she already knew they were special, she sat down at the table and waited for Monsieur Sorbonne to open the large gray envelope.

One by one, he pulled out the prints. In the first, at a distance, a beautiful couple, the woman wearing a broad-brimmed straw hat, in another, two lovers entwined and about to kiss, a picnic spread out before them on the beach.

Apprehending, vaguely, the form of Madame Métier, Mademoiselle Objet felt an immense and overwhelming regret for all the vicious terrible things she had just said. She was stunned, she had to admit, by the haunting similarity between Madame Métier and this angelic looking young man, by the fact that in spite of the really quite obvious difference in their two ages, there was a similarity in their elegance, a mysterious appropriateness to their connection.

"They match," she said, quietly. "They're a pair. They belong." And now, along with feeling ashamed about her most recent terrible unkindness, she felt a faint rush of excitement, a fine, bright happiness for Madame Métier, because clearly she had found someone so perfectly suited to her. She waited almost eagerly now, poised, suffused with a quiet delight, for the further revelations of the photographs.

Monsieur Sorbonne pulled out another. Here they were at close range. Madame Métier had removed her hat and the two of them were looking adoringly at each other, strands of her pale hair blowing out in the breeze and forming a sort of halo around them, although, remarkably, once again, in the black-and-white photograph, their eyes had printed out crystal blue.

Silently taking this in, Mademoiselle Objet said nothing. Hand quivering on the print, Monsieur Sorbonne also said nothing. He turned the print over face-down, exposing another image. Here too, Madame Métier and Monsieur L'Ange were both smiling, lips poised in a half-formed, soon-to-be delivered kiss. Her eyes were still blue, but his—and Monsieur Sorbonne and Mademoiselle Objet both observed this in silence—had faded, gone gray almost to black, and around his hair there had formed a pointillistic mist of light that hovered in a circular cloud above him. Silent, Monsieur Sorbonne turned the image over, then lifted up the final print, which now lay alone on the table.

In this photograph, Madame Métier was herself, as her beautiful self she remained. But to her left, where before Monsieur L'Ange had been, there was now only the faintest pale, shadowy apparition. He, as himself, was no longer there. In place of his face there were only two black holes for his eyes, and around him and above him, pixillated and radiant, was a shimmering circle of light that spread out beyond him, reaching to the farthest limits of the page.

～

CHAPTER 14

Madame Métier and Monsieur L'Ange Have Dinner

Wearing a red silk dress and her new emerald-green silk stockings, Madame Métier was sitting in shadow and looking across the table at Monsieur L'Ange where, interestingly, back and forth, light and dark—chiaroscuro—candlelight played across his face.

They had just finished dinner. Madame Métier was tired, and yet she felt happy because of the many events of the day—the debut of her new TeleVisions series, the launching of the new calla lily creme ("the antidote for deep heartbreak"), a peaceful sweet interlude afterward, with Mademoiselle Objet, the bouquet of long-stemmed white roses Monsieur L'Ange had just brought her, the sitting here with him now by candlelight—as if her life at that moment held all the joy it could ever contain.

"I have never been more happy," she said dreamily. "I will never, ever, be happier than I am at this very moment. I have always, as you know, been happy because of my work—I have seen it always as a gift. But you have given me—how can I say it?—the purest joy of being alive . . ."

She paused. Could she actually say them—all the beautiful heart-swelling words? "This being with you . . . in love. It has been so very beautiful—a resurrection of the body, and of all the elegant exquisite feelings in my heart . . . so tender and sweet and . . . real. I had never imagined or expected to experience . . . love I could actually feel."

She paused, stirring with a small silver spoon her after-dinner cup of tea. "All this beautiful love you have brought me, this feeling of bliss in the body, of just pure joy in the simple moments of being alive, this is why—I suddenly now understand it—this is why we all come to earth."

"You are so beautiful when you say such beautiful things," said Monsieur L'Ange. Across from her, angelically, he smiled, as if he had taken in with his soul each syllable she had spoken. The smile ascended his face, inhabited and recomposed it, and then above him and around him—was it true, or had she imagined it?—there appeared the faintest circle of light.

In the bedroom, in the half-light of the half-risen moon, she was removing her emerald silk stockings while Monsieur L'Ange, already ensconced in the bed, a faint rectangle of light from the window framing his face, was quietly watching her. "What a beautiful evening we've had," he said.

"Yes," she said, slipping into the bed beside him. "It was wonderful, extraordinary, once in a lifetime."

"So true," said Monsieur L'Ange. "One doesn't have often in life such perfect occasions, when everything—work, love, honor, a wonderful meal, celebration—all at once comes together." His voice had become soft and dreamy, as if perhaps he had eaten too much and momentarily would drift off to sleep.

With her fingers shadowed by moonlight, she was tracing the lines of his face. His forehead, the caves of his eyes, his cheeks, his lips, and as she did—as if the movements of her hands all bathed in moonlight, were conferring light on him—there seemed to bloom all around him, distinctly, a circle of light.

"You are surrounded by light," she said.

"I am becoming light," he said. "I am moving toward the light." His eyes fluttered closed. "Ah, yes," he said, as if on a distant screen he were watching a movie. "So beautiful. We are all moving toward the light. But you and I—we are the fortunate ones, the privileged ones, to have had so much, to have had it all together at once, love in the body, love from the heart, a life's work that is love, so many beautiful moments together, the sun . . ."

"Yes," she said. "So many beautiful afternoons . . ." Then suddenly she felt strange, uncomfortable with all this recounting, as if the events of the day, despite their special beauty, were unworthy of all this attention.

"And I want you to remember all this, to think of it often and always be glad when I am . . ." but he didn't finish the sentence. His voice had drifted into a whisper.

Madame Métier was startled. He must be already almost asleep, she was thinking. She raised herself up on her elbows, the more directly to see him, to look down more at his face. And when she did, he was smiling. His eyes, half-glazed and misty, were focused and not-focused both at once.

He continued to speak. "I'm going to go now. Soon. Tonight. Tonight, I'm going to step through my body. Tonight. I can feel it. It's time."

She looked at him disbelieving. A snake of pain ascended her spine. For a minute she wanted to scream, but when she looked down again at his face, it was a portrait of pure bliss, of absolute radiant calm. He reached across the pillows then, and drew her down into his arms, his huge beautiful hand beginning to open and fasten itself like an ivy stem along the curve of her shoulder.

"You have already seen this," he said, "with the eye between your eyes. Remember the green stockings? The catafalque? The white sheet?"

Yes. It was true. The red dress. The green stockings. The catafalque. You and the others. Remembering all this, seeing again what she had seen on the night she had seen his so many deaths, she laid her head on his heart, and piteously, she wept.

"But how can you . . . ?" she said finally, lifting her head up to look at him.

"I don't know. *How*—I don't know. But I will—I do know that. It has been given to me to see that. As it was given to you to see what you saw. And . . . I can feel it. I can feel already the door beginning to open, the door through which I will step through my body."

Believing yet disbelieving, knowing, yet hoping beyond hope, she lay on his chest, feeling each beat of his heart, each breath of his breathing. His utter peacefulness was strangely beautiful, was beautifully, strangely compelling. Could it be true that he was dying? Could a person be so alive, so filled with the essence of life—hands that touched, arms that embraced, eyes that beheld, lips that ever so tenderly, brushingly kissed you—and in the same breath or the next, cease to be?

"We are all always dying," he said. "Life is the practice of death, and death is the great re-birth, the great new beginning."

Vaguely, effortfully now, as if already for months he had been dying, he propped himself up on the pillows and, struggling, raised his head. A certain deep weakness and, she could see, had already come into his body.

"And so," he said, "there are some things I want to tell you now . . . before I go. And I must speak quickly; there isn't much time."

There was a depth of tenderness, a great encircling wreath of compassion, of immemorial knowing now in his voice, as if he spoke to her now no longer as himself, from inside his own heart or mind, but from some ancient well of wisdom.

"There will be . . . something untoward, something unbelievable around your work, a test," he said, "something so cruel you cannot imagine . . ." But here his voice drifted off, as if in watching a movie the film had suddenly snapped, leaving a jumble of sideways-printed white letters on the still, black screen . . . "the woman who works for you . . . and the man next to her—her husband? . . ." he strained, as if with his eyes to see in the distance more clearly the image of this man—"they will go through it with you. They love you more than you can imagine, and they will be with you always, even until the end."

He struggled, then, to sit up, and his whole body for a moment, was framed in a pale rectangle of light. "And finally . . ." he said, looking off through the window and into the distance, "I also will always be with you. Whenever you see a rectangle of light . . ." and once again his voice drifted off, ". . . that will be me holding you. That will be you, sheltered in my embrace."

He turned back then from the window, and looked directly at her. The huge blue irises of his eyes, she could see, had gone pale now. They were slightly blurred, soft-focused and ethereal, strangely infused, as if illumined from inside, with some far, mysterious light.

So steady and calm had he been in all this saying, so absolutely clear and strong, that for a moment she was dissuaded from her grief.

"Thank you," he said, and then, rearranging himself so that once again he could see her, his great hand once again enclosing the curve of her shoulder, he went on. "I came here to love you. Loving you has been my life's work. Loving you . . . is what gave my life meaning. Loving you . . . "—and here she could see a thin stream of tears starting to wind its way down his cheeks—"holding you, making love to you, watching you be beautiful every which way,"—softly, faintly, a little, he laughed—"has been the greatest joy of all my lives."

She had propped herself up on her elbows and now she was looking down at him. He took a single long breath. Then he heaved a great sigh, and then, as she watched, he opened his eyes—wide wide wide—as if to take in a whole other world; and then, as she continued to watch, unmoving and silent and still, all the light all at once went out of his eyes.

For some minutes she sat there, transfixed and silent beside him. Then her white tears fell and fell into his blue empty eyes. And when she had finished, she closed both his eyes and got up from the bed and pulled the white sheet up over him.

～

PART V

Chapter i

Madame Métier, Monsieur Sorbonne, and Mademoiselle Objet Have a Little Ceremony

"*I don't know how to grieve,* and I never quite did understand your relationship to him, but I can help you with all the objects, and I can arrange things."

So saying, Mademoiselle Objet had arranged for Monsieur L'Ange's body to be burned to ash, and his ashes gathered into the beautiful cedarwood box, which, with his exquisite taste, Monsieur Sorbonne had chosen.

It was almost winter, November, a stunning clear day, with luminous cumulo-nimbus above, when, with Monsieur Sorbonne to her left, wearing a gray morning coat with back lambskin lapels, and Mademoiselle Objet to her right, wearing her-seal-gray dress and the pale-blue heart locket (and crumpling nervously in her left hand a lace-edged handkerchief), Madame Métier, wearing a flowing simple black dress, and quietly weeping beneath a black tufted veil, scattered Monsieur L'Ange's ashes among the bare twig branches of the pruned rose bushes in her garden, where, for a moment, catching the sun, they blew up like motes of light in the wind.

∾

CHAPTER 2

Madame Métier Is Subdued

In the weeks that followed, Madame Métier was very subdued. Quietly, steadily, one day after another, she gave herself to her work, and tried to accept, in a way that she never had before, that her life was her work. Inside, she felt a deep peace and an infinite sorrow, for she could remember having been loved, and the love she had felt resided now within her like a blossom in her heart.

No more did she skip out of the workroom at odd hours and head for the beach in her red bathing suit. She had, in fact, thrown it out. "No time, anymore, for the beach," she said, point-blank to Mademoiselle Objet during one of their frequent cleaning-up fits.

"I understand," said Mademoiselle Objet, and she had lovingly folded it up and put it sadly into one of the brown paper throw-away bags, knowing it wasn't because there wasn't any time, but because of Monsieur L'Ange's death, that Madame Métier no longer wanted to go to the beach.

It was sad, she thought, this patina of quiet stability which had affixed itself to Madme Métier. As irritating as her eccentricities had always been in the past, this plain predictability was somehow even more upsetting.

Although she continued each day with her cremes, as Mademoiselle Objet had suggested, she had also started making speeches, and in them and on her TeleVisions program, she had become more deep, more philosophical, talking not so much anymore about each of her cremes and its particular attributes, as about the deeper meaning of things—which habits of the mind or losses of the heart created the conditions that necessitated cremes, and which revolutions of the spirit, in addition to her cremes, might be required to change them.

At night, though, alone in her room, from time to time, she wept, especially when at certain times the moon would shine in through the window, imprinting a huge rectangle of light on the bed. It was then that, leaning over and grasping the distant pillow—the one that still smelled faintly of clary sage, was it? or saxifrage?—she wept most piteously of all.

～

CHAPTER 3

An Untoward Thing Occurs

Mademoiselle Objet was very startled indeed, upon arriving at work one morning, to see Madame Métier standing handcuffed in the front hall, two policeman, a fat one to her right and a wizened one with a menacing beard to her left, restraining her forcibly, like a criminal, by the shoulders.

"And who's this?" snapped one of them, as Mademoiselle Objet, parcels in hand, stepped through the front door.

Madame Métier was about to explain, but Mademoiselle Objet interrupted. "What's going on?" she demanded.

"As if you don't know!" said one of the policemen, yanking Madame Métier by the arm like a dog on a leash. "You're probably part of this whole operation."

"I am. You're right," said Mademoiselle Objet, whereupon the policeman to Madame Métier's left took a threatening step in her direction.

"She's not," said Madame Métier. "Leave her alone!"

"What's going on!?" shrieked Mademoiselle Objet, unpacking a piece of her long-retired hysteria.

"This woman, as if you didn't know," said the fat policeman, scowling, "and I'm not sure you don't!—is a white drugs trafficker and has been for years. Someone just died from the drugs she sold him. You think you work for a saint. These cremes, this botanical nonsense—it's all a front. Apparently, you have no idea just who you're working for."

Mademiselle Objet was aghast. She felt crazed. Turned upside-down and sideways. Suddenly everything made no sense. Or could it be true? Had she been so caught up with herself, so self-involved and spoiled and controlling, that she'd never read the signs? Where *had* Madame Métier been all those afternoons? Had she really been at the beach? And what about Monsieur L'Ange? What *had* he died of after all? And why had he died so young? For a minute everything seemed to make some terrible diabolical sense. Madame Métier and her cremes? How *had* she made a living from her cremes? Maybe it *had* been a front. But even as she entertained all the unspeakable possibilities, she found herself, at the core, unable to believe them.

"You're wrong," she screamed at the policeman. "This is crazy. You're insane!"

The two policemen in tandem turned and wheeled on her. "Don't talk to the law like that," said the one to Madame Métier's left. "Or, with or without a warrant, we'll bring you in, too!"

Shaken, Mademoiselle Objet ran up the stairs to call Monsieur Sorbonne, and the last thing she saw, as she vanished, quivering, into the workroom, was the fat policeman hauling Madame Métier by the handcuffs, out the front door.

～

CHAPTER 4

Madame Métier Is Detained

"There will be something untoward, something unbelievable, around your work—a test . . ."

Madame Métier was thinking of that when, in the Holdings Room of the Police Station where she was being detained, a rectangle of pale-yellow light fell in through the window and surrounded her. Behind her a janitor had let up the dark-green shade, allowing the midmorning sunlight to enter the room.

Standing in its midst, several tears crossed her eyes, and as the rectangle of sunlight continued to embrace her, she remembered Monsieur L'Ange's words: *"Whenever you see a rectangle of light . . . that will be me holding you . . ."* and she quietly smiled.

"What's so funny?" barked the officer. "You don't seem to comprehend the seriousness of your situation. You drug scum are all alike."

"I'm sorry," said Madame Métier, "I was just thinking of something."

"You should be! Someone has died—a very prominent person! And four other people are getting their stomachs pumped out right this minute." The policeman rolled over some pages on a rusty masonite clipboard. "Is it, or is it not true," he growled, looking down at a scribbled report, then back at her, "that four years ago you sold a huge packet of white powder to a Monsieur Morte—who himself is now dead—for $5,000?"

Incredulous, Madame Métier shook her head.

"Is that a denial? Or an admission?" he barked.

Madame Métier was both reeling and infinitely calm. She was reeling because it was all so preposterous, and calm because she was standing in the light. For, as she followed the officer across the room and sat speaking to him now inside the dark-green grillwork of his cubicle, the rectangle of light in which she had been standing in the Holdings Room continued to surround her.

"Answer me!" said the policeman, pounding his fist on the scuffed leather top of an old wooden desk. "Or don't answer me! Don't bother to tell me your lies. We already know all about you—the deal with Morte, and who knows who else. It's just unbelievable, what you've been getting away with all these years. Or are you going to tell me that you really do make cremes!? Your fingerprints were all over the biggest packet in his stash. Only yours! And his! So just for the record, did you or did you not sell Morte a packet of white drugs powder—$60,000 worth—the biggest single stash this force has ever come across!? Did you?! Or did you not?!" He looked across at her, eyes glaring, teeth bared.

"I did," said Madame Métier, her voice subdued. "It's true." What else could she say? It *was* true. How amazing. How strange. It was, in fact, true. She *had* sold the packet of white drugs powder from her husband's Medicines Chest to the now extinct Monsieur Morte. "But . . . I was completely unaware . . . I had never even . . . there were extraordinary circumstances," she said haltingly.

"How could you!?" asked the officer, once again slamming his fist on the desk.

"I don't know," said Madame Métier, quietly. Vaguely, it was all coming back to her now. The white powder packet. The $5,000. Her husband, the doctor. It was incredible. Perhaps that was why—or how—he had scrambled himself all over the road.

She looked down at her hands, clamped in handcuffs, rigid, immobilized in front of her. This was impossible. Real. Impossible. Real. The truth waved in and out of her mind like a tattered flag in the breeze.

It seemed impossible, but clearly it was true. True and not true, both at once.

～

CHAPTER 5

Madame Métier Is Further Detained

Madame Métier passed the night in the jail cell disbelieving. In the morning when she awoke, disoriented and weary, she looked up, as through the high barred windows, morning sunlight fell in on her lap, shedding a small rectangle of light that framed her still, folded hands.

At dawn a guard had brought her some breakfast, sugared crackle flakes with imitation milk, which she left on the tray and refused to eat. Instead, she poured herself some water from the metal pitcher that stood on a small metal table beside her cot and sat down on the metal chair in the corner. She was going over things in her mind, wondering how she had come to all this.

She had married the doctor—that's how. But how could she have been so blind all those years? It was amazing—the things that were true about people—about yourself—that you could be right in the midst of and yet still not see.

She was just thinking all this when Mademoiselle Objet appeared in the hallway outside her cell, newspapers in hand. She, too, looked weary, yet remarkably composed as she held up the paper for Madame Métier to see. "Inventor of Cremes and Noted TeleVisions Personality Arrested on White Drug Charges," read the headline.

"The news," said Mademoiselle Objet. "Do you want to hear it?"

"Yes," said Madame Métier. "I must."

Mademoiselle Objet started to read, "Incarcerated last night on charges of trafficking drugs . . ." but here tears clogged her throat and she was unable to go on, "I just can't believe it," she said, "I just can't believe that this is really happening."

"I know," said Madame Métier. "It *is* . . . quite unbelievable."

"And already it's all over the place. The TeleVisions station has canceled your show. The stores are sending back all your cremes. People are calling, saying they always knew you were a fraud. She was so upset she was shaking, yet instead of careening, as she might have in the past, into a tidal wave of hysteria, she was a living portrait of calm.

"I know," said Madame Métier. "People are scared. And when they're afraid, they blame."

"But this is so unfair!" said Mademoiselle Object. "They're not even letting you tell your side of the story, and already this lie's all over the place. They're going to shut down your work and ruin your life! How can you just sit there and not even try to defend yourself?"

"I have no defense," said Madame Métier, "except the truth. And right now the truth is not available." For several minutes she sat in silence, digesting what Mademoiselle Objet had said. Perhaps there was some other meaning to this. She had worked for years. She was heartbroken and weary. What if they *did* shut down her work? Would it matter? Maybe this was the time to stop making her cremes, to quiet her life and grow old in peace.

She had just had this thought when across the cell a ribbon of light skated slowly down the opposite wall. Tears crowded her eyes and she thought sadly, with an almost unbearable longing of Monsierur L'Ange—of his fragrance, his touch, of their beautiful mysterious days; she had been given in him a rare and beautiful gift, but now, in his absence, why should she go on with her work? Without his love, what was the point?

Thinking of him, she thought sadly of all the people—great numbers of them—who went through their lives without even so much as a moment love. And thinking of them, she thought of all the suffering ones who came to her door. The needs of the world for love and healing were vast, heartbreaking and endless; and somehow it had been given to her to address them through her cremes. Sitting there alone in her jail cell she suddenly realized that no matter what was said or written about her, she must go on with her work. The making of cremes was not a choice, not something to do if, or when, or because she was happy and felt inspired—

but a responsibility. It was the reason, in fact, why she was alive, why she was still taking up space on the earth. She would be alive so long as she had the strength to make them, and when she no longer did, her life would be complete.

Perhaps this was what she had come here to see.

She looked out to the hallway where, patiently, Mademoiselle Objet stood waiting on the other side of the bars. "I know it's hard to imagine," she said now, with conviction, "but I *know* that all this will be resolved. The truth will come out. Because in the end, though not always in the middle or at the beginning, the truth will always prevail."

"I believe you," said Mademoiselle Objet, in her heart not quite believing. "I want to believe you, but today I can't.

"I know it's difficult, "said Madame Métier. "But the things we cannot quite believe, we must. Because only then can a miracle occur."

~

CHAPTER 6

Weeks Pass

But two weeks had passed, and a miracle had not occurred. In fact, quite the opposite had happened. Madame Métier's fingerprints found on the white drugs packet and enlarged ten times were published in the paper, as were scenes of the grieving widow and his children at Morte's funeral, for which his assistant, successor, and young protégé, Monsieur Presque Morte, had performed the high embalming honors.

Alone in her jail cell, Madame Métier looked older, worn, but deepened somehow, her face transfused with light. Her hair, it seemed, had turned all at once indelibly white, and Mademoiselle Objet was shocked each time she came to see her, that in spite of how thin she had grown, she remained very still and was always at peace in her cell.

"There has been," said Mademoiselle Objet, one day, as she stood in the hallway despairing, "no miracle. And I'm afraid there won't ever be one."

"Don't be afraid," said Madame Métier. "Fear is the antithesis of miracles. Faith is the only condition in which a miracle can occur. I don't know how, exactly, but I do have faith—I have the absolute, unshakable conviction—that, somehow, miraculously, all this will be resolved."

~

CHAPTER 7

Monsieur Sorbonne Pays Madame Métier a Visit

It was when Monsieur Sorbonne finally came to the jail to photograph her—"You really should take her photograph—strangely enough, she's more beautiful than ever," Mademoiselle Objet had said to him—that unexpectedly, following in his footsteps, a guard Madame Métier had never seen before unlocked her cell, and without so much as a single word of explanation, lifted her up by the hand, opened the door to her cell, and preceding her down the long hallway, showed her the way out.

In the main room of the jail, flanked on every side by dozens of photographers, Mademoiselle Objet was waiting as thin, incredulous, and regal, Madame Métier stepped into the room.

"Do you have a statement for the news?" asked someone.

"I do," said Madame Métier. "To forgive is to receive back into your heart those whom in error you have wrongly judged. Forgiveness is a life's work. It is the highest calling of love."

"What kind of a statement is that?" someone shouted. "Don't give us your botanical gobbledy-gook. What about the drugs?"

"I have no further statements," said Madame Métier, and leaning on Monsieur Sorbonne's arm, together with Mademoiselle Objet, she walked out.

∽

CHAPTER 8

Monsieur Sorbonne, Madame Métier, and Mademoiselle Objet Have a Reunion

"What happened?" asked Madame Métier.

"A miracle," said Monsieur Sorbonne.

The three of them were sitting together in the workroom, which, because of Madame Métier's long absence and Mademoiselle Objet's inordinate tidiness, seemed almost sepulchral in its perfectly ordered demeanor. Mademoiselle Objet had made some tea and Monsieur Sorbonne had brought Madame Métier her strewn-with-red-roses white silk dressing gown. She seemed overwhelmed by it almost, as she put it on, so large was it now on her thin frail frame, like a room instead of a dressing gown.

"We don't know, exactly," said Monsieur Sorbonne, but before he could say another word, they were startled by a knock at the door.

"I can't take it," said Mademoiselle Objet. "I just can't handle one more thing!!" She stood up and looked out the window to see if she could see anything, and as she did, a small passage of light formed around her feet on the floor.

"It's all right," said Madame Métier. "Whoever it is, I know it's all right. Let them in."

∿

CHAPTER 9

More Is Revealed

It was the blue-mirrored sunglasses-wearing landlord who now followed Monsieur Sorbonne up the stairs.

"It was me!" he said, shaking. "It was me! And now I'm terrified."

"It was you who what?" asked Madame Métier, standing up from her blue embroidered silk hassock and walking over toward him.

"It was me who informed the police. And now I'm terrified." Still shaking, he collapsed on the couch and Madame Métier sat down beside him.

"First of all," he said, collecting himself, "I'm so glad to be here. I've always wanted to to thank you for saving my little girl's life. A few years ago, she had a terrible breathing condition. None of the doctors could help, and I was sure she was dying. It was only when Mademoiselle Objet, here, gave me one of your cremes that she started coming back to life."

"But the drugs," Mademoiselle Objet interrupted. "What about the drugs?"

"Yes, well, anyway, the drugs," the landlord continued. "Well, I had a hunch," he said, taking his sunglasses off and revealing sunny brown eyes, "that something not-good was going on. I'm a carpenter, and over the years I've done a lot of work for Morte—wainscoting, cornices, French doors, once in a while a coffin stand for his laying-out rooms. Then one day he asked me to do a 'special project'—build false bottoms in a lot of children's coffins—for bodies that weren't big enough for the standard-sized children's caskets, he told me. At first, I refused—that's when my little girl was so sick, and the thought of children dying . . . But then . . ."

And then he told the whole story, how, in the end because he was desperate for money to pay the doctors to help his daughter, he had modified a dozen coffins, how all along he'd smelled something fishy, how, as a consequence, night after night he'd parked and watched outside of Morte's establishment, how finally he'd seen some men with dark glasses and hearses, loading them two or three at a time with the caskets that he'd just "adjusted," how he'd called the police with his hunch, how at first they hadn't believed him, how finally they had, how then they'd sent an officer in disguise who'd bought an "adjusted" coffin with a layer of white drugs packets stashed between the real and false bottoms, how then they'd arrested Presque Morte, apparently the ring leader, and how now, he was afraid they still hadn't arrested everyone.

"That's disgusting, horrible," said Mademoiselle Objet, when he finished. "Using poor children's coffins as a cover for drug trafficking!"

But the carpenter wasn't listening. "I'm terrified," he said, "that there are more of them. And that they'll come and get me."

"They won't," said Madame Métier, noticing the patch of light that remained, even now on the wall. "It's over. Finished. I know it. They've arrested everyone, but here, in case you're scared . . ."

But, across the room, Mademoiselle Objet had already understood, and, opening a drawer, she took out a white glass jar that she handed to Madame Métier.

"For panic," said Madame Métier. "Some tiger lily creme."

"Thank you," said the carpenter, "I owe you my life."

"And I owe you my freedom," said Madame Métier. "We all owe each other much more than we can ever repay." Then, standing up from the couch, she embraced him briefly before Monsieur Sorbonne showed him out of the workroom.

～

CHAPTER 10

Madame Métier Reflects

When they had all left, Madame Métier walked alone through the house, reclaiming it, remembering, going back over things, going back to the doctor. "How could she," as the policeman had asked, ever have "been so stupid?" Yes, how could she have trusted a doctor who had pooh-poohed her cremes, who had made her throw away all her lipsticks, who only believed in disease?

As she walked in the kitchen to make some tea, a small rectangle of light spilled out in front of her on the floor. *"To forgive, to receive back into your heart those you have wrongly judged, is the highest calling of love."* Ah yes, forgive herself, too. That, of all the forgivenesses, was always the most difficult. And now it was time.

Taking a cup of hibiscus tea, she padded upstairs and opened the door to the bedroom. There, on the far side of the bed where he had always slept was a huge rectangle of brilliant white light. She set her cup on the bedside table, and she lay down in it.

≈

Chapter ii

Madame Métier Experiences the Truth of Who She Is

Six months had passed, and although from time to time Mademoiselle Objet kept insisting that it was not her cremes but she herself that had such a salubrious effect, Madame Métier seemed now, more than ever, driven to keep on creating new cremes. It was almost as if she imagined that there was a creme, if only she could perfect it, that could cure every pain in the world. "Stop! Please stop! You've got to stop!" Mademoiselle Objet pleaded with her one day. We already have too many cremes. I'm tired of sorting them out and mailing them out and explaining their differences to everyone. I'm willing, but it's not needed. You already have enough cremes!"

But Madame Métier could not be convinced. In fact, since she had come home from the jail, she had seemed even more obsessed with her cremes, and yet she was also distressed to think that she might be overly taxing the steadfast Mademoiselle Objet. Trying to sort things out one day, she went to the beach with her notebook. She thought and wrote, but got nowhere. She was a maker of cremes, and if the making of cremes was no longer important, what would she do every day with her life? She wrote the question again and again but came up with nothing. How she wished that Monsieur L'Ange could appear out of nowhere to help her. Finally, when the air had grown chill, she packed up her things and decided, miserably, to go home.

"There's a monster child upstairs with his parents, waiting to see you," said Mademoiselle Objet when she stepped through the front door.

"What do you mean?" said Madame Métier.

"A child who will more than not-behave," said Mademoiselle Objet. "A child with demonic aspects. He spits and attacks and claws at people and screams. He's totally out of control—and his parents want you to heal him."

As she stood on the landing outside the living room, Madame Métier could hear loud sounds from upstairs, crashing and banging and screaming, the likes of which in all her life she had never heard before.

"Well, I can't heal him," she said. "His parents will have to take him away. I do not deal with such contorted aspects of the psyche. I have no cremes for such untoward behaviors."

No sooner had she said this than from upstairs in the Seeing Room, she heard another loud crash, as if a piece of furniture had fallen and broken into a million pieces.

"You'll have to tell them to leave," said Madame Métier, setting her things down in the hallway and preparing to go to the kitchen.

"I can't," said Mademoiselle Objet. "I've already told them you'll see him."

"Are you out of your mind?!" said Madame Métier. She—and Mademoiselle Objet, too—was shocked when she said this. She had never before said anything quite so rude or hopeless or seemingly mindless and mean to Mademoiselle Objet, nor, could she remember, to anyone else. As she spoke them, the words felt like bricks in her throat, heavy, untoward, and thick—as if they had been excavated from some far, dark, unknown place in herself. "Get them out!" she said, even more loudly in a voice almost not her own, as she circled like a dervish in the hallway. "I've already told you, I cannot and I will not see them!"

Once again, Mademoiselle Objet was shocked. Never before had she seen—or heard—Madame Métier in quite such an emotional tenor. Indeed, it was almost as if she was not herself, as if some other voice or force had taken over her body and was now using it to speak.

Madame Métier, too, felt more than strange as she said this. More than the words had started to affect her. Inside her body she felt a great upheaving convulsion, as if all its interior contents, its organs and fluids and cartilages and filmy connective tissues were somehow, beyond her control, all rearranging themselves, as if she were leaving her body, or it, with a mind of its own, was leaving her.

"Get them out!" she said once again. "I can't help them. This is not the work that I do!"

But, by then, with Mademoiselle Objet practically hauling her up the stairs, Madame Métier had ascended, almost, to the Seeing Room.

"It may not *have been* your work," said Mademoiselle Objet, in a clear strong voice, "but it is today. They have arrived. They are in need. And *you* have to help them." Then in a softer voice she added, "I know you can help. I know you can heal him."

Mademoiselle Objet then opened the door to the Seeing Room, which was in a total chaos. Books from the bookcase had fallen all over the floor, the couch, one leg broken, had been turned over. Shreds of cloth, rippings, apparently, from his parents' clothes, were strewn across the floor, and pots of cremes had been thrown, leaving splatters with splinters all over the walls. Cowering in the corner were a man and a woman, the parents, apparently, of the monstrous boy; and the boy himself, a boy of about seven years, was running wildly around the room, screaming and tearing at things, making loud howling noises, running up to his parents, slapping and biting and clawing at them.

Mademoiselle Objet walked into the room, and the minute she did, the boy threw a pot of creme at her. It shattered directly above her head, then fell at her feet on the floor. Then he ran maniacally across the room, and charging at her like a bull, bit her viciously on the arm. She pulled back in pain, and slapped him on the arm, and then, to her horror and amazement, also many times on the face. Finally, dragging Madame Métier behind her, she practically shoved her into the room.

The minute Madame Métier entered the room, the boy, who had now started howling, banging his head on the wall in a corner on the far side of the room, screaming and stamping his feet, turned suddenly around. Slowly he stopped banging his head; slowly he stopped screaming.

He looked at Madame Métier, and as if he'd been struck by a bolt from the blue, he paused and stood stock still, staring across the room at her.

Somewhat relieved, Madame Métier sat down on the blue embroidered hassock which, remarkably, was the only object in the room that had not been practically destroyed. As she did, she felt once again, a most remarkable sensation in every cell of her body, as if its very substances were being rearranged, as if it were no longer her, or hers, but infused with an energy outside of and beyond herself. She felt terrified for a moment, utterly out of control and then—and then in some far distant corner of her heart she heard the words—spoken in her own voice—*"And the point is to surrender. To receive what is trying to be given."*

She relaxed then, and let go. And far inside she felt some ancient exhaustion, the way she must have held herself always, inside her body, begin to fall away and dissolve. Indeed, she felt that she was no longer her body but something—she didn't know quite what—an essence, an ineffable energy that resided at once both within her and beyond her; and she relaxed into this energy, allowed it to overtake her, allowed herself to become it—allowed everythg that she knew of herself—as a person, trying to find her way; as a woman, heartbroken by loss; as a maker of cremes, a success, so to speak, in the world; as the employer and teacher of Mademoiselle Objet; as the personage of the TeleVisions series—to all fall away. She became suddenly and entirely not any of these things. She had become her essence—who she was beyond and within all of them; and she felt an immense and transforming peace as gradually her personality dissolved and slowly, strangely, she surrendered to becoming everything and nothing.

Across the room, the boy stopped suddenly mid-scream and turned around. He walked halfway across the room and planted himself like a tree in earth, in the middle of the floor. He looked at Madame Métier, and she looked back at him; and although she had no way of putting this sensation into words, she could feel great pale streams of light flowing out of her eyes and into his.

Quietly, steadily then, as if his body was now weighted with a depth of knowing far beyond the number of his years, he walked over to Madame Métier and stood before her, curious and silent, as she herself sat unmoving, silent and still on the blue silk hassock, inhabiting the strange huge energy that now inhabited her.

Then—and Mademoiselle Objet and his parents, too, from where they were standing, could scarcely believe this—he reached up, and, as if he were blind and she a statue whose surfaces he was carefully discovering with his hands, he touched Madame Métier's face, his fingers tracing the bones of her cheeks, her eyebrows, the orbits around both her eyes, the edges of her hair.

Madame Métier sat there, quiet, simply receiving his touch. Then, finally, when it seemed he had finished, she opened her arms and he climbed up into them and sat on her lap. She put her arms around him then, and he leaned his head on her shoulder, and as he did, she could feel herself—which seemed no longer to be herself—melt into him, and his small self begin to slowly melt into her.

There was what she could only call a flow of light between them, a wholeness that was neither one of theirs alone, but an essence seamless and continuous residing in the two of them. It was the essence of all things, and in her heart—or what she as a person she had always known to be her heart—she felt a vast undifferentiated bliss, the great joy, the incomparable privilege of being in this light with him.

She looked around the room then, and in it, too, it seemed that everything had changed. The chaoses, all the strewn and broken objects, the stains on the wall, the tipped-over couch and its shattered leg, his parents, and even Mademoiselle Objet, all seemed to have melted, luminous and shimmering, into a single vast, exquisite, and undifferentiated substance. The colors and outlines of each of the objects and persons remained, but the particularities of each had been subsumed in a shimmering, enveloping wholeness that undulated and moved, vibrated with a barely audible humming and scintillated with millions and millions of pixels of light.

Madame Métier could feel too, just then, that she and the boy in her arms, and his parents and Mademoiselle Objet and the room itself and even all the objects in it were part of this vast mysterious luminous effervescence, this infinite and exquisite, vibrating, pulsating energy. She could feel it now, magnificently and hugely, inhabiting her body, and she knew that although she might not remember it every day or be able to feel it always in exactly the way she felt it now, that this energy was her essence, that its name was Love, and that it was the author of all healing.

The boy on her lap now started to wiggle. He looked up at Madame Métier and smiled. Then, reaching up, he touched her face, and happily kissed her on the cheek. He jumped off her lap then, and running across the room to his parents, took hold of his father's and mother's hands, and then with the two of them, he started skipping, practically, across the room.

Mademoiselle Objet stood up, too, and started walking across the room to open the door. The boy's parents, with the boy in hand, walked over to Madame Métier, and weeping, bowed before her.

"We're speechless," said the father.

"We don't know how to thank you," said the mother.

"We have no idea how much to pay you," said the father.

"Yes," said the mother. "We've been everywhere and spent thousands and thousands of dollars."

"Paying—it is unnecessary," said Madame Métier. "You have brought me a great gift."

Across from her, the father and mother looked puzzled.

"She means," said Mademoiselle Objet, laughing a tinkling, light-hearted laugh, "that she always enjoys a challenge, and that she loves her work."

The parents looked at her once again, confused. "But what about the room?" they said, "and all the broken objects?"

"It's all right," said Madame Métier, nodding at Mademoiselle Objet, "I just happen to have someone here whose genius it is to solve exactly such problems."

"Well, thank you, then," said the father.

"Yes, thank you very much," said the mother.

Mademoiselle Objet opened the door, and with the boy now standing relaxed and peaceful between them, they exited the Seeing Room and started walking down the stairs.

When they had left, Mademoiselle Objet came back into the Seeing Room, where Madame Métier was still sitting on the blue silk hassock. Madame Métier stood up then, and the two of them embraced.

Madame Metier was silent for a moment, and took a step backward. Then, looking directly at Mademoiselle Objet, she said in a deep, quiet way: "Thank you. Thank you for seeing what I could not see, for knowing what I could not know—what for so long I have needed to know."

"You're welcome," said Mademoiselle Objet softly. "I don't know why it took you so long, why you had to be the last one to know. I've always told you, it's not your cremes, it's *you* that heals everyone."

"Now I see," said Madame Métier. "Now, finally, I know."

"Shall we have some tea then?" asked Mademoiselle Objet.

"Yes, that would be nice," said Madame Métier.

∼

Part VI

CHAPTER I

Much Time Had Passed

Much time had passed. The three of them were sitting at a table under a huge white umbrella on the sea-washed *plage* of a white sand island, where, for several years running now, they had come together on vacation.

Tanned, and in spite of her now all-white hair, looking young and immensely beautiful, Madame Métier, in a new red bathing suit, though not quite so daring as the old one, was sipping a pink lemonade, when, from a distance, a young man, walking along down the beach in long loping strides began gradually to approach them.

"You always had adventures at the beach," said Mademoiselle Objet, noticing him. "You never told me, but I know you did."

"You look very beautiful sitting there, drinking your lemonade," said the young man, who, having arrived at their table was now standing in front of Madame Métier. He was tall and strong and had blonde hair and blue eyes. He was wearing a square gold watch and its crystal, catching the sun, laid down a small rectangle of light on the blue tablecloth.

A tear, many tears, fell slowly out of Madame Métier's eyes, and, discreetly, she wiped them away.

"Would you like to go for a walk?" he asked her, raising his arm in a single long elegant gesture. "The light is so pure. The beach is so calm." He pointed into the distance, and as she watched, the rectangle of light was lifted up from the table and disappeared in the air.

"No, thank you," she said. "Though I do thank you for the lovely invitation. But we have so little time here together on the island, my dear friends and I, that I'd like to stay here and talk a while with them."

"I understand," said the young man, and, turning slowly away, he walked off with long loping beautiful strides until he was gone.

～

CHAPTER 2

As Time Went On, How They Changed

Monsieur Sorbonne had long since quit the Artifacts Museum. He had become a famous photographer. Because of his extraordinary portraits, especially those of Madame Métier, he had had many exhibitions of his work—"Images of the Soul," he called them—in many cities around the world.

And it wasn't—as he so often told Mademoiselle Objet when they were sitting at home having tea—the photographs in themselves that gave his life's work its meaning. It was—as he had learned so many years ago when he photographed cornices and buildings and all the images disappeared—because now he photographed with love.

Mademoiselle Objet had long since become peaceful. She had gone through so many things with Madame Métier, and so many things had passed through her, that she could no longer hystericize about anything. The peace of having been for so long in Madame Métier's presence, like a molecular change, had settled within her and become, at last, her own true possession. At night, at home with Monsieur Sorbonne, she returned to reading her poems books. Gradually, she started writing poems herself, and from time to time she retrieved the twisted tubes of watercolor paints from the small grey Belgian linen bag, and made little paintings to accompany her poems.

And Madame Métier also had changed. She had become more deeply herself, had become, as she said simply, "more big inside." And outside, where, as she always said, it really didn't matter, she had become famous. Indeed, wherever she went, she was recognized. People would call out her name and touch her clothes, and quietly bow in her direction.

"It's a nuisance, being famous," she said to Mademoiselle Objet, who finally bought her a red wig so that, incognito, she could pass through the streets.

She also got fan mail from all her fans, great bags and bags of it. In the beginning, Mademoiselle Objet had tried to sort them out and get them organized, but in the end she gave up. "They all say the same thing, anyway," she said. "They all say you saved their life." And so every day when the big canvas mail bags arrived, she brought all the letters to Madame Métier to bless them, and then she threw them away in the trash.

In her diamond jubilee year—*"and when you are old, and the pleasures of your beauty have faded—recognition, honor . . ."*—there was a festival, a public celebration in honor of Madame Métier. "I don't like public events. I don't want to go. These recognitions aren't what's important," she said to Mademoiselle Objet.

"Not to you," said Mademoiselle Objet. "But to them. To the others. To them it's a gift simply to be in your presence." And so, in the end, she agreed to go. In a green velvet dress, embroidered across its bodice with fine gold threads and little round mirrors ("so I can hold the reflection of all their faces over my heart"), escorted by Monsieur Sorbonne and Mademoiselle Objet, Madame Métier arrived at the party.

There were hundreds of guests of every generation, old people who said that her cremes had kept them young, middle-aged people who said that her cremes had helped them gain wisdom, young men and women who said her cremes had given them hope, lovers who said that her cremes had healed their estrangements, young couples with babies who asked her to hold them and bless them so they would have a good life.

There were vases of lilies and hundreds of candles, and huge silver trays with tiny T-fish and cucumber sandwiches. There were urns of tea of every flavor, bottles of flavored crystals waters, and, in the background, beautiful music—a piano player, note after note unwinding a beautiful song in the summer evening air. It was a song about angels and heaven and remembering forever, and Madame Métier was enchanted. With a beautiful sorrow in her heart, she thought of Monsieur L'Ange.

At last, after many people had spoken about her work, Madame Métier herself stood up. She walked up to the stage to the sound of a long and thunderous applause, and took her place at the podium.

"Thank you. Thank you so very much," she said, as the clapping quieted down. "I thank you all very deeply for being here tonight.

"It has been my great joy, my great privilege for so many years, to have done this beautiful work, to have offered to you through my cremes, the healing spirits of the plants. It has been my sacred honor to serve, and I am deeply grateful. But, in truth, my work, like any great work, could only have been accomplished through the miracle of relationship—collaboration with those whose gifts so perfectly complement mine that their fulfillment and my own have been for so many years now, exquisitely intertwined.

"And so I wish to thank first of all the dear ones who have assisted me most, who have done all the important, intricate, tedious, daily tasks to help me accomplish my work"—here she smiled out at Mademoiselle Objet and Monsieur Sorbonne—"the ones I have loved, who have loved me so well. Who have stood at my side . . . through everything. To them I owe a great debt." She paused for a moment, and nodding at Monsieur Sorbonne and Mademoiselle Objet, invited them to stand up. They rose for a minute, and, turning, smiled as the audience clapped and clapped for them. "From my deepest heart," said Madame Metier, folding her hands across her heart as they sat down again, "I thank both of you."

"I wish also, deeply, to thank all of you who have received my work, who have allowed me to touch your pain through the healing spirits of the plants. Each of you, with your hurts, with your needs, with your anguish, has shown me what I came here to do. In so doing, you have granted my life its meaning. And so I wish to thank you all very dearly." She paused for a moment, and then with her eyes traced a circle around the entire audience.

"I know it is my work, my so called 'achievements,' that we have gathered here to celebrate, and I am deeply grateful for this honor. But I have been given to learn, through the long and gracious span of my life, that it is not what we do, not our accomplishments in themselves that have meaning, but the love with which we undertake them. Indeed, with love, whatever our work, whether the simplest act of service—straightening a pencil, washing a dish, serving a tea—or the most complex achievement—building a temple, governing a nation, unravelling the strange equations of the universe—no matter how humble or grand it may be, whatever we undertake in love becomes a sacrament.

"So it is that each plant which gives its essence for a creme, each person who manufactures the jar or tin in which it is delivered, each person whose suffering need has called it into being, each artist who enchants our hearts with color or exquisite images, with beautiful words or breathtaking notes of music—insofar as his or her work has been undertaken with love, it comes alive with the power to heal, to move all our souls a bit closer to the dazzling brightness of our being.

"For, it is in fact, *only* Love that heals, and everything else—all our particular achievements—are really only the means we have each been given for delivering love in its many-splendored multitude of individual expressions.

"Each of us has love to give. We give it through our work. We give it through our waiting and our praying. We give it through our words and through our silence. We give it through our grieving and through our celebrations. We give it through the beautiful, complex, ever-flowing array of our emotions. We give it with our bodies, through touch and movement and passion. We give it with our hearts when they skip a beat for pure joy, and when they rest in the peace that passes all understanding.

"And that, my Dear Ones, is because Love is our one true work. It's who we are. It's why we're here. It's what we came for. And it's what we have to give."

Madame Métier paused for a moment. She looked around the room, with her eyes engaging for a moment the eyes of each person present. Then she laced her hands over her heart, and bowed softly to her audience.

"And so, once again, and ever so deeply, I thank you," she said. "I thank you all with all my heart. Thank you for being here. Thank you for the love you bring. And thank you for allowing me to give you my love these many years through the healing spirits of the plants."

When she had finished, everyone stood up and clapped. They raised their hands high in the air and some of them shouted, "Thank you," and, "Bravo!" Many faces were washed with tears, and a few people noticed with interest the large rectangle of light that seemed to contain and follow her as she stepped away from the podium, walked down the center aisle of the room, and then out the back doors, where under a starry sky, Monsieur Sorbonne and Mademoiselle Objet were waiting to take her home.

∼

CHAPTER 3

Madame Métier, Monsieur Sorbonne, and Mademoiselle Objet Have One More Reunion

It was not long after this that, one night, upon entering her bedroom, Madame Métier found every inch of it, from corner to corner, bathed in a huge rectangle of brilliant white light.

The pillow also, on the far side of the bed, seemed, more than usual, to smell distinctly of clary sage, was it? or saxifrage?—and clasping it to her heart and feeling finally free to weep for all the losses of her life, she cried in a way that she hadn't cried for years.

In the morning, she went to work as usual, but in the afternoon she told Mademoiselle Objet she was tired and she went to her room to lie down. She slept and dreamed that she had awakened in her bed and looked up at the ceiling to see a huge pale orange butterfly, its shimmering wings spread out so flat it seemed to have been painted, *tromp l'oeil*, against the wall. It fluttered a moment as she watched, then slowly it dissolved.

The following morning, she was unable to rise from her bed, and she called to Monsieur Sorbonne and Mademoiselle Objet to come in. "Sit down, my Dear Ones," she said when they arrived.

Monsieur Sorbonne would not sit down, but stood at the head of the bed beside her, and Mademoiselle Objet, on the blue embroidered hassock, sat near the foot of her bed.

"Thank you for coming," said Madame Métier. "Soon now, I will slip through my body, and I wanted you to know. I can feel it. And I wanted also, before I leave, to have a little time with you." At the foot of the bed, hands folded, Mademoiselle Objet began, a little, to cry; and for the first time ever, Madame Métier was unable to reach out and touch her hands.

"Don't cry," said Madame Métier. "It's just a change of address. We'll see one another again. But before I go, I have a few little gifts for you."

Mademoiselle Objet stood up and joined Monsieur Sorbonne at the head of the bed and, as they stood there together, Madame Métier handed them each a smallish square package, then watched as first Monsieur Sorbonne opened his. Inside its red paper wrapper was an elegant black box, and inside the box, in a cradle of gathered black velvet, was a crystal ball. Monsieur Sorbonne held it up to the light, which was pouring in through the bedroom window. "A new lens for you," said Madame Métier. "So you will see, always, the mystery and the wholeness of life."

"Thank you," said Monsieur Sorbonne, and as he did, a ribbon of tears threaded its way down his cheeks. Then Mademoiselle Objet opened her gift, which was wrapped in white paper and tied with a white satin ribbon. Inside it, beneath a golden lid embossed with its namesake flower, was a cachepot of calla lily creme. "In case you should ever have need of it," said Madame Métier. "And because you were so patient,"— she laughed a little, remembering—"while I was creating it."

Stilled by the elegant beauty of her gift, a stream of tears flooded Mademoiselle Objet's eyes. She turned to Madame Métier and whispered a "Thank You," and Madame Métier smiled. Then she looked across at the two of them. "I'm tired now," she said quietly. "And it's time. I want to say good-bye. Thank you for being such beautiful friends. We have had a most beautiful life here together. So many beautiful moments. So much love. Such a long and beautiful journey of healing and compassion."

So saying, she gathered her strewn-with-red-roses white silk dressing gown a little more closely about her, and lifting her arms to embrace each one of them one more time, slipped free of her cocoon.

∾

CHAPTER 4

Monsieur Sorbonne and Mademoiselle Objet Have a Ceremony

From her bed then, Monsieur Sorbonne and Mademoiselle Objet took the pillow that smelled faintly of clary sage, was it? Or saxifrage? Her casket they lined with rose petals of every color from her garden. With her exquisite hands, the way that in life Madame Métier had so often done for her, Mademoiselle Objet smoothed and smoothed out Madame Métier's white hair and finally, as if in heaven to protect her from the loss of both of them, applied some calla lily creme to Madame Métier's hands before folding them over her heart.

As she lay there in repose, beautiful, translucent, and more at peace than ever in life they had seen her, knowing in advance that it probably wouldn't turn out—"It'll just be a shimmering sheet of white light, but please try anyway," said Mademoiselle Objet—Monsieur Sorbonne at her insistence, one final time, took a photograph of the very unusual woman.

And afterward, whenever they came to her grave to lay flowers down upon it, they noticed that it was always marked off by a perfect rectangle of shining white light.

Fini

∽

Glossary

Métier (met-e-ay)
Métier A life's work for which one's talents are particularly suited, hence a life's work which is an expression of purpose.

Sorbonne (sore-bawn)
Sorbonne A place of great learning, where many of life's questions are answered and curiosities resolved, as for example, the Sorbonne, a university in Paris.

Objet (ob-jay)
Objet A material object, possession, or artifact of physical life, perceptible to vision or to touch.

avant garde	unusual, ahead of its time
bain mousse	bubble bath
beau	beautiful
café cremè	a coffee with a lot of cream
ceil	the sky
compliqué	complicated
crêpe	a thin, delicious pancake
en masse	in a group, all together
exactement	exactly
fumed	smoked
ici	here
la bas	over there

medias res	in the middle of things
melanges	mixtures of various things
mort	dead
pâté	ground up paste of a food
plage	beach
plus	more
poisson	fish
presque	almost, nearly
raison d'être	reason for being
sans	without
séance	a time of sitting together
soirée	a lovely evening event
soleil	the sun
sous chef	an assistant chef
trés	very
toujours	always
tête-à-tête	a little talk
toute seule	all alone
trompe l'oeil	something painted so accurately that what has been painted appears to be real
vetiver	plant with a lovely fragrance

Acknowledgments

Immense gratitude to the Mysterious Force which left the note with the words: "*Madame Métier* in a corner of the armoire of my Paris hotel room."

A fan-deck of thanks to my agent, Johanna Maaghoul, for her passionate conviction about this book, and to Olivia Maaghoul, one of its premier readers, for her unbridled and contagious excitement.

A deep bow of thanks to my deft, delightful (and elegantly patient) editor, Alexandra Hess at Skyhorse Publishing, for her vision and enthusiasm, and for shepherding this book into the world.

I am once again hugely and humbly grateful to MJ Ryan for an infinitude of assistance, hospitality, and deep companionship along the way (It is always a gift and a joy), and to Donald McIlraith for, once again, welcoming me into the family circle.

To the many people at my little hotel on the Left Bank who tolerated years of my "you-can't-change-the-bed-yet; I'm writing," a heartfelt *Merci*.

To my daughter, Molly, at whose many kitchen and dining room tables this manuscript was endlessly refined, a dear and ever-delighted Thank you. I. L. Y.

Finally, and always, I am grateful to the voice that quietly directs my hand. It is always a privilege to transcribe your words.